Praise for Hari Kunzru's

WHITE TEARS

Hari Kunzru

WHITE TEARS

Hari Kunzru is the author of four previous novels: *The Impressionist*, *Transmission*, *My Revolutions*, and *Gods Without Men*. His work has been translated into twenty-one languages, and his short stories and journalism have appeared in many publications, including *The New York Times*, *The Guardian*, and *The New Yorker*. He is the recipient of fellowships from the Guggenheim Foundation, the New York Public Library, and the American Academy in Berlin. He lives in Brooklyn, New York.

www.harikunzru.com

ALSO BY HARI KUNZRU

The Impressionist

Transmission

My Revolutions

Gods Without Men

WHITE TEARS

WHITE TEARS

HARI KUNZRU

VINTAGE CONTEMPORARIES
VINTAGE BOOKS
A Division of Penguin Random House LLC
New York

FIRST VINTAGE CONTEMPORARIES EDITION, FEBRUARY 2018

Copyright © 2017 by Hari Kunzru

The Library of Congress has cataloged the Knopf edition as follows:
Names: Kunzru, Hari, [date] author.
Title: White tears / Hari Kunzru.
Description: First edition. | New York: Alfred A. Knopf, 2017.
Identifiers: LCCN 2016011904 (print) | LCCN 2016018518 (ebook)
Subjects: LCSH: Sound recording executives and producers—Fiction. | Murder—Investigation—Fiction. | GSAFD: Mystery fiction.
Classification: LCC PR6111.U68 w48 2017 (print) | LCC PR6111.U68 (ebook) |
DDC 823/.92—dc23
LC record available at https://lccn.loc.gov/2016011904

Vintage Contemporaries Trade Paperback ISBN: 978-1-101-97321-9
eBook ISBN: 978-0-451-49370-5

Book design by Maggie Hinders

www.vintagebooks.com

Printed in the United States of America
10   9   8   7   6

For Katie

I rolled and I tumbled
Cried the whole night long
Woke up this morning
I didn't know right from wrong

WHITE TEARS

▼

THAT SUMMER I WOULD RIDE MY BIKE over the bridge, lock it up in front of one of the bars on Orchard Street and drift through the city on foot, recording. People and places. Sidewalk smokers, lovers' quarrels, drug deals. I wanted to store the world and play it back just as I'd found it, without change or addition. I collected audio of thunderstorms, music coming out of cars, the subway trains rumbling underfoot; it was all reality, a quality I had lately begun to crave, as if I were deficient in some necessary vitamin or mineral. I had a binaural setup, two little mics in my ears that looked like headphones, a portable recorder clipped to my belt under my shirt. It was discreet. No one ever noticed. I could roam where I liked and then ride home and listen back through Carter's thousand-dollar headphones at the studio. There were always phenomena I hadn't registered, pockets of sound I'd moved through without knowing.

Every sound wave has a physiological effect, every vibration. I once heard a field recording of a woman singing, sitting on a porch. You could hear her foot tapping, keeping time. You could hear the creak of her rocking chair, the crickets in the trees. You could tell it was evening because of the crickets. I felt I was slipping, that if I wasn't careful I'd lose my grip on the present and find myself back there, seventy or eighty years in the past. The rough board floor, the overhang of the roof, her voice traveling through the moist heavy air to the diaphragm of the microphone, its sound converted into electrical energy, frozen, then the whole process reversed, electricity moving a speaker cone, sound spilling into my ears and connecting me to that long-ago time and place. I could feel it flow, that voice, inhabiting the cavities of my body, displacing the present like water filling a cistern.

I heard Charlie Shaw on one of those recording walks. It was evening. I don't remember why I'd gone out. Perhaps I couldn't sleep—that happened. Perhaps I just needed to be outside or spend some time on my own. I often felt claustrophobic after long sessions; we could spend twelve hours in the studio without coming up for air. It was hot, the stifling New York heat that empties the city on July and August weekends. My shirt was clinging to my back. Passers-by were sheened in sweat, everyone desperate for the weather to break. I was recording by the chess tables in Washington Square. A guy called PJ, evidently the home favorite, was playing another man whose name I didn't catch. They'd drawn a little crowd. There was money on the table. A bottle was being passed around.

PJ was one of the hustlers who sit at those tables day in day out, playing all-comers for ten bucks a time. He was a flabby white man in his fifties or sixties with thick glasses and several plastic bags of nameless crap stashed under the bench. The other player was skinny and black, hard to say how old because his face was hidden under a baseball cap. He wore a clean white undershirt and baggy blue jeans. His bare arms were painfully thin, like two twists of fuse wire. This man was taking his time over his moves, enough for some of the onlookers to be muttering and telling him to make up his mind. He ignored them. Unlike PJ, who was chatting to his buddies, he kept his head down and seemed absorbed in the game. He was a good player and soon he forced PJ to give up a knight, then his queen. There goes my rent money, said PJ to anyone who'd listen. He was stuck on the phrase, repeating it until it became a tic. Each bad move: there goes my rent money, there it goes. Something about the stranger was making the spectators nervous too. He would reach over the table, settle his long fingers on a piece, move it, then suddenly bring his palm slapping down on the clock.

Each time he did it, an audible flinch traveled through the crowd. Coughing, keys fondled in pockets. He was killing PJ, showing no mercy. They didn't like it.

Mate in two, said the thin man, almost under his breath. Around the board, people fell silent. PJ nodded glumly and knocked down his king with a forefinger. Shoot, he said, now what am I going to do? As his friends gathered around to commiserate, the stranger counted his winnings, a wad of small bills. I was already turning away when I heard him sing. It was a blues, just a line. *Believe I buy a graveyard of my own,* he sang. Then he ran it again.

Believe I buy me a graveyard of my own

On the audio, I can hear the change in the position of my head, the mics over each ear picking up a slightly different range as I swing round to listen. I don't know how to explain what happens next. My memory is clear. There was a skater, a girl. You can hear the rumble of a deck, but it's in the background. I distinctly remember turning to watch her. I saw long black hair, tattooed sleeves, a nice ass in cutoffs, weaving between dog walkers. How would I know that if I hadn't turned? But the audio shows I didn't. The singer remains in the same spot. I remember that when I turned back, the game had broken up. It felt strange. It had only taken a few seconds for the girl to pass, but already the players and spectators were gone, the tables completely deserted. At the time, I didn't think too much about it. I was hungry, so I walked over to Sixth Avenue to get a slice.

▼

WE WERE ON THE VERGE OF BEING FAMOUS. Bands wanted the sound we could make. We were booked months into the future and I, for one, could not have been more surprised. One day I woke up and there I was, twenty-five years old, in New York City, and *cool*. I'd never been cool before, not at high school, not at the liberal arts college upstate where Carter and I met. *He* was cool. Blond dreadlocks, intricate tattoos, a trust fund he didn't hesitate to use to further the cause of maximum good times. He had the best collection of vinyl records, the best drugs. He'd traveled, and not just to high-tone places with his parents. He'd hiked in Nepal, driven a bus along the Skeleton Coast in Namibia looking for surf. I was a suburban kid, out of my depth even on our little campus in the middle of nowhere, with its toytown Main Street, its atmosphere of sheltered rehearsal for the real world.

My family didn't call it by a medical name, but in my teens I had some kind of break or event. After my mom died, my dad and I discovered we had nothing to say to each other. He taught high school physics and was preoccupied with the problems of my kid brother, who was rebelling in a conventional cry-for-help way, smoking weed and shoplifting. It was easier for him not to notice that I was sliding too. So what if I didn't want to talk to him? One less person taking up his time. I was allowed to get on with it, whatever it was.

Losing my mind. For six months, I didn't go to school, didn't even go outside. I only left my room on late-night missions to kitchen and bathroom, scuttling back and forth like a cockroach.

At the time it suited me. Four walls. I used to lie on the carpet with my laptop and a keyboard and a battered old mic, making loops of my breathing, of the sound of the floorboards creaking as my dad and my brother walked around outside the door. I'd record these small noises and fool around with them—making phases, pitching them up and down. I was trying to hear something in particular, a phenomenon I was sure existed: a hidden sound that lay underneath the everyday sounds I could hear without trying. Sure enough, after months of obsessive listening, a sound did make its presence known, but it wasn't the one I'd hoped for. No pure high Buddha tone, no aural white light. I began to hear the past, the ambience of the room as it had been ten years previously, then twenty years, then fifty. The footsteps in the hall didn't belong to my dad or my brother. They belonged to someone else.

Getting back from that took me a while.

By the time I went to college I was no more than averagely introverted, but I was still a weird kid, no doubt. It took Carter Wallace to pull me out of my cockroach hole. Everyone wanted to be his friend and no one much wanted to be mine, which was why I was alone one day on the lawn in front of the band shell, holding a directional mic mounted in a homemade parabolic reflector, a configuration that was allowing me to listen, with impressive clarity, to conversations taking place all the way at the other end of the lawn by the library. I was eavesdropping on a picnic, a bunch of drama students updating each other on the gossip, shrieking with attention-seeking laughter every thirty to forty-five seconds, loud enough to cause clipping. Clearly what I was doing was objectively creepy. I didn't much care. Fuck humanity, was my basic position at that point. The conversation was banal: my work your ex incredibly moving hooked up needs to check his privilege blah blah blah. For my purposes, the content was irrelevant. It was just a sound source, so I could test the equipment. It might as well have been birdsong. I was really happy that the reflector—which I'd made myself out of an old satellite dish—was working so well. I lowered the gain and the meter stopped peaking when the people laughed. Just then, I felt a touch on my shoulder and found Carter standing behind me with a stoned half-smile on his face.

I knew who he was, of course. Blond beard plaited into a sort of fashionable rope, no shirt and a tattoo of Mexican *calaveras* on his chest. I assumed, with a sinking feeling, that this hipster Jesus was something to do with the trendy crowd of picnickers and was about to kick my ass for spying on his girlfriend, something of that kind. Instead he asked me about the reflector and seemed to understand at least some of the technical language I used in my explanation. I found myself giving him the headphones so he could listen. He told me the reflector was "sick," and though this was hardly an incisive remark, it made me feel as if I'd won an award. Then, to my frank astonishment, he suggested we go back to his dorm room and listen to music.

At that time I had strict rules about the kind of music I would listen to. I wanted to avoid slippage. Old songs made me feel nervous. Also old recordings. I wanted to be one hundred percent forward-facing, moving into tomorrow at top speed. I'd grown up listening to a lot of seventies progressive rock, songs about space travel and chivalry with frequent changes of time-signature and bombastic effects. As a teenager it had seemed superior to me, evidence of my intelligence. I had begun to listen to sixties psych and garage, inching backwards through the years, but at a certain point, I'd decided there were certain echoes I couldn't afford to hear, so I made a run for it, away from human history and its dark places, into techno, the aural city on the hill. Here was a shiny sound-world made of pure electronic tones, in which I could float free of all context, cocooned in the reassurance that yesterday was long gone, or perhaps never existed at all.

When I went to Carter's room that afternoon, I hadn't voluntarily listened to the sound of a guitar for three years, but I was so in awe of him that I broke my rules. We sat on his bed and he played me records. Vinyl records, old and expensive, lovingly dusted with an antistatic cloth and placed on a deck positioned on a paving slab to isolate it from vibration. His setup was impressive. All his decisions had been technically sound and the equipment was peerless. The turntable was connected to twin valve amplifiers, fifty years old or more, engineered to specifications that would be considered excessive today. They in turn were connected to a pair of British studio monitors that, he boasted, had once hung in the control room at Abbey Road. Until then I had held a low opinion of the audiophile fetish for analog equipment. I considered it sentimental. Carter completely changed my mind.

At first I was solely preoccupied with audio quality. I appreciated the range and dynamics of the reproduction, without paying much attention to Carter's music taste. Gradually I noticed that everything he played was by black musicians. Many different styles, but always black music, most of it completely unfamiliar to me. I began to listen with increasing pleasure. Carter didn't so much play me his record collection as narrate it. He began with Jamaican dub. From there, he introduced ska and soca, soul and RnB, seventies Afrobeat and eighties electro. He spun early hip hop and Free Jazz and countless regional flavors of Bass and Juke music. Chicago, London, Lagos, Miami. I had not known there was such music.

Over the next weeks and months, Carter taught me to worship— it's not too strong a word—what he worshipped. He listened exclusively to black music because, he said, it was more intense and authentic than anything made by white people. He spoke as if "white people" were the name of an army or a gang, some organization to which he didn't belong. I paid no mind to his garbled explanation of the source of this black intensity. The sound was good, and I'd noticed something extraordinary that was occupying most of my attention. I was listening to songs that had been recorded twenty years before I was born, and they had no ill-effect on me. There was no backwards pull, no sensation of vertigo. I forgot what it was I'd been scared of. I let it all go. I could not remember the last time I had felt so happy and carefree.

In between marathon listening sessions, Carter initiated me into the campus party scene, which I'd previously found opaque and threatening. As a DJ, he had quasi-celebrity status, arriving in rooms through a thicket of daps and hugs and fist bumps. Soon I was helping him out, setting up, troubleshooting the sound system. I'd hang back behind the decks as he spun his vinyl-only set, watching girls making fuck-me eyes at him and their jealous boyfriends pretending they didn't care. There was such a need to connect with him, to receive the blessing of his attention. None of the cool kids could work out why I was the one to carry the conquering hero's record box. I was a loser, who dressed (as I was once told) like a "homeless computer scientist." They didn't understand Carter's obsessive commitment to music. He didn't really care about anything else. I understood that and they didn't. That was why it was me and not them.

Carter rarely talked about his family. What I knew, I had to piece together from campus gossip and the internet. He had an older brother and sister and it was easy enough to search his dad, a big Republican donor who appeared in news photographs with senators and members of the Bush clan. Perhaps not coincidentally, the Wallace family company, a behemoth with tentacles in construction, logistics and energy, had expanded since 9/11, helping America prevail in the War on Terror. Toilet blocks in Afghanistan. Airstrips and PX's. Known these days as the Wallace Magnolia Group, they supplied earthmoving equipment, built freeways, laid pipelines. Carter's dead aunt's name was on a new lecture theater, which, given his near-total lack of interest in academic work, may have been the price of his admission to our not-quite-Ivy school. Carter knew what the Occupy crowd said about him, the no-blood-for-oil crowd. He told people he'd been disinherited, but that wasn't strictly true.

Together we went on record-buying trips to Cleveland and Detroit. He had a 1967 Ford Galaxie, Candy Apple red, which handled like a boat and drew him into conversations with admiring gas station attendants and diner patrons. We drove that ridiculous car round a circuit of thrift stores and basement record dealers, looking for sixties soul on local labels like Fortune and Hot Wax, techno twelves on Metroplex and Transmat and every other style in between. We took chances on weird private press releases that

usually turned out to be lounge singers cranking out Sinatra covers or school bands doing shaky versions of seventies bubblegum
hits. We found gems (a cache of mint BYG/Actuel free jazz albums
still in their shrink wrap, a blue copy of the UR "Z Record") and
dropped money on turkeys, bad records with one good track, rare
records that turned out to have no good tracks at all.

▼

MORE THAN A MONTH WENT BY before I finally played back the recording of the chess players in Washington Square. We had an old Roland Space Echo that sounded beautiful while it was working, but kept cutting out. It was a simple problem, a loose connection in the power supply. I wasn't going to trust it to the clowns at the repair place. We (I had fallen into saying "we") had rented a loft in Greenpoint, in a building that had once been a Catholic church. We watched TV in a room whose floor was spangled rainbow colors by old stained glass. I sat up on the roof with my soldering iron, wearing headphones and shades, the heat reflecting off the cladding, baking my shirtless back red as I retraced the meandering path I'd walked that evening, up Orchard and into Chinatown. I heard Cantopop songs and electronic jingles, fading in and out as I turned off Canal and crossed that little park behind the court buildings where all the old Chinese people go to gamble. Dominoes slapping down on tables, buskers sawing and plucking at stringed instruments with plaintive tunings. Back across Canal. Traffic noise and a cop shouting at someone. On Mott I had passed two women having an argument. At the time I couldn't hear what it was about. Now I could. One was accusing the other of taking something from her purse; coupons, it sounded like. She'd stolen coupons her friend was saving to get groceries. One-fiddy on Huggies, shouted the victim. And a dollar off motherfucking Cheerios. They were drowned out by a fire engine, ten seconds of distortion that took me into the echo of an empty loading bay, a guy talking Spanish on his cellphone, then silence, more traffic noise as I crossed Broadway, someone's comedy ringtone and one side of a conversation. Dude, she said she would so she gotta. You tell her. Washington Square had been full because of the heat. By the fountain there were break-dancers drumming up a crowd, yelling, applauding themselves, doing backflips to "Billie Jean." Under the arch a young busker was ineptly singing Dylan. Then the chess game, the crowd grumbling as PJ lost to the stranger. I stopped soldering, a sudden nervousness in the pit of my stomach. When the voice came, I couldn't believe it. I couldn't understand how I hadn't heard it the first time, when the singer was in front of me.

Believe I buy a graveyard of my own

It was a pure voice, quite high, with a rasp when driven, as the singer did on "buy," a word he made into three tones, the middle one spiking into a piercing falsetto buzz.

Believe I bu—u—uy me a graveyard of my own
Put my enemies all down in the ground

Surely, in the presence of such a voice, I'd have paid attention. It would have been impossible to do anything else. But I had a clear memory of a girl skater. Sure enough there came the rumble of skateboard wheels, but no shift in orientation. I hadn't turned to watch her. How could I remember what she looked like if I hadn't turned round? The singer was still in front of me. After the first two lines his words were slightly muffled, as if something that absorbed sound had moved between us. What it was I couldn't tell. But he kept on singing. How was that possible? My memory was clear. Two lines only. Maybe one line. I had been facing in the opposite direction for a few seconds. When I turned back, the tables were empty and the players gone. But this audio recording captured an entire performance, lasting several minutes. Phrases of the lyric jumped out, less muddy than the others. *Put me under a man called Captain Jack.* Something something *down my back.* And a third verse, *went to the captain* something something, something *have mercy on* something. It went on. Several verses.

That evening, I played it for Carter. He listened casually at first, but soon adopted a prayerful posture, hunched forward, his hands cupped over the headphones as if to press the voice further into his head.

—This, he said when it was finished. You actually heard this.

—Some guy who just won a chess game over at the tables in Washington Square. I swear I thought he only sang a few words.

—Jesus, man.

We listened to it again. And a third time, and a fourth. The voice was mesmerizing. We stayed up until six in the morning, cleaning up the recording and deciphering the words. At a certain point, this stops being an aural task and becomes a visual one. You abstract the sound into shapes, start selecting, magnifying. Then it's just a matter of smoothing curves, taking slices out, pasting other slices in. I edited out the skater. I filtered the background noise, brought up the vocal until we had a clear a cappella. Carter was enchanted. "It's beautiful," he kept saying. "Incredible." He was right, but all the same as I worked I had an instinct to cover my ears, to unhear what I was hearing. Several times, I let my finger hover over the delete button, willing myself to press it.

> Believe I buy a graveyard of my own
> Believe I buy me a graveyard of my own
> Put my enemies all down in the ground
>
> Put me under a man they call Captain Jack
> Put me under a man they call Captain Jack
> Wrote his name all down my back
>
> Went to the Captain with my hat in my hand
> Went to the Captain with my hat in my hand
> Said Captain have mercy on a long time man

Well he look at me and he spit on the ground
He look at me and he spit on the ground
Says I'll have mercy when I drive you down

Don't get mad at me woman if I kicks in my sleep
Don't get mad at me woman if I kicks in my sleep
I may dream things cause your heart to weep

We played it one more time, then, in our very different moods, we powered down the equipment and went to bed.

▼

MOST GUYS LIKE US would have formed a band, but Carter was always more interested in the studio. He wasn't a poseur or a show-off; people who say that never knew him. In the weeks after we met at college, I taught him how to use my equipment and we made some breakbeats together. He loved it and immediately began buying gear—stuff I'd been making do without, like good monitors and a copy of Pro Tools that didn't come on an unlabeled disk bought from a Chinese guy outside a supermarket. Then he got in touch with some music students and persuaded them, by sheer charisma, to be our unpaid session men. They followed orders while we fooled around, trying to make them sound like Africa '70 or the J.B.'s.

It's hard to overstate how much of a change this was for me. I was used to being alone. Suddenly I was surrounded by people, at the center of chaotic all-night recording sessions which sometimes turned into parties, as girlfriends and would-be girlfriends and other hangers-on turned up, attracted by the pheromone musk of music. One sign of things to come was Carter's limited tolerance for computers. He hated clicking mice and tapping screens. Soon he was scouring auction sites for old equipment, anything with sliders he could push, knobs and dials he could twist. He spent a lot of money on a nineteen-eighties drum machine and a bass synthe-sizer, legendary pieces of equipment that most people only knew as software emulators. For a while we immersed ourselves in electro and squelchy Acid sounds, imagining ourselves kings of the block party, superstar emperors of the rave.

Until then I'd never given much thought to the difference between the digital sounds I'd grown up with and their analog ancestors, sounds made by variations in the electrical charge flowing through actual physical circuits. Electricity is not digital. It does not come in discrete packets, but floods the air and flows through conductors and shoots from the hands of mad scientists in silent movies. If it is futuristic at all, it is a past version of the future, temperamental, unstable, half-alive. When you start to fool around with old synthesizers, building sounds by setting up waves in banks of oscillators, it's more like a chemistry experiment than the strange Adderall obsessiveness of the digital studio. Carter and I began to consider ourselves connoisseurs of analog echo effects. We were unimpressed by the packages on the internet, so I found some schematics and together we built a primitive spring reverb, which made excellent wobbles and clangings that we used to excess on every track we made. Soon we were trying to reproduce effects we'd heard on music made at Lee Perry's Black Ark studio in Jamaica. That year Perry was our idol, our god. He would make use of anything that came to hand. He'd buried microphones under a palm tree and pounded the earth to make a rhythm. We did the same thing, using a pine tree (this was the Northeast) with indifferent results. He once installed a sand floor in the studio and built a hollow drum riser out of wood and glass, filling it with water. This was supposed to change the sound of the drum kit. We built our own construction and part-flooded the school's new music studio.

We worshipped music like Perry's but we knew we didn't own it, a fact we tried to ignore as far as possible, masking our disabling caucasity with a sort of professorial knowledge: who played congas on the B-side, the precise definition of *collie*. The actual black kids at our school, of whom there were very few, seemed to us unsatisfactorily preppy or Christian or were basketball jocks doing business degrees, devirginating sorority girls and talking loudly in the commons about their personal brand. It seemed unfair. We were the ones who wanted to be at a soundclash in Kingston. We knew what John Coltrane was searching for when he overblew his tenor in the middle section of *A Love Supreme*. There was a Nigerian called Ade who we liked because his short dreads made him look vaguely like a Jamaican singer called Hugh Mundell, who'd been shot dead at the age of twenty-one. Ade smoked a lot of Carter's weed while fielding questions about police brutality, but there was no getting around the fact that he wore suede loafers and a Patek Philippe watch. His old man was an oil trader in Lagos.

Before long we would look back on our college Rasta phase with shame. Carter, who briefly owned a red-gold-and-green beanie hat, lived in fear that pictures of him wearing it would turn up on Facebook. We really did feel that our love of the music bought us something, some right to blackness, but by the time we got to New York, we'd learned not to talk about it. We didn't want to be mistaken for the kind of suburban white boys who post pictures of themselves holding malt liquor bottles and throwing gang signs.

In our senior year Carter and I shared an off-campus apartment. An uncertain and threatening future was visible on my horizon. I could barely pay my half of the rent, even with a job in the college development office and another making wraps and sandwiches at a local deli. My debt was big enough for me to be dreaming about it, icebergs and teetering bookcases looming in my sleep. When Carter "bounced," I knew I would bounce too, back to my dad's place in New Jersey. I wasn't sure I could handle lying awake in my teenage bedroom, listening for dead people in the hallway. I'd been hoarding sleeping pills, in case I needed a quick exit.

I was researching internships in recording studios in New York and Los Angeles. I was ready to accept anything—coffee assistant, cable gimp—that would get me within reach of an actual paying position before one of several different credit providers took me to court. I'd set myself a deadline. If I hadn't found a music job by a certain date, I was going to accept a cousin's offer to set me up with an interview at the engineering company he worked for in Boston. If that didn't work out I'd do technical support, food service, whatever.

Carter, of course, didn't have to worry. He talked vaguely about traveling with that month's girlfriend, a model called Mariam or Miriam. She was African and spoke with a French accent, I think her dad was the Senegalese consul in San Francisco. Carter was going to take her to the Caribbean on a sailing yacht. I wanted to spend time with him, to wring out every last drop of friendship before we went our separate ways. I was convinced that was how it would be: he'd head on into the rest of his glamorous life while at best I'd be chained to a photocopier in some suburban business park, at worst locked in a State hospital, my ass hanging out of a backless gown. I spent long hours in my bedroom, fretful to the point of tears, imagining Carter at pool parties, drinking cocktails on high-floor balconies. I mourned him as if he'd already gone.

Carter quickly got bored of my languishing. He started taking a sarcastic tone, inventing derogatory nicknames for me. I was the robot professor, the tin man. I lacked spontaneity and heart. By then he had stopped listening, not just to the old house and techno we'd once loved, but all contemporary music, anything that used digital sounds. He'd been through a hip hop phase, scouring the internet for twelve-inches by regional producers from the eighties and nineties. Now he only wanted to listen to ethnographic recordings or scratchy 45's of doo-wop bands. The Flamingos, The Clovers, The Stereo Sound Of The !Kung Bushmen. An ever longer list of things was not real enough for him, tainted by the digital sins of modernity. "Just ones and zeroes," he'd sneer, dismissing some recent part of the culture. "Out of touch with the human body." If I hadn't used his expensive drum machines and keyboards, they would have gathered dust.

One night we were sitting up late in the kitchen. I was smoking a joint to get rid of the stink of deli ham and mayonnaise as he plucked distractedly at a new toy which had arrived by courier that morning, a nineteen-twenties Gibson mandolin. He'd deleted his iTunes, he said solemnly, angling the mandolin's body so the starburst finish caught the light.

—I know what you mean. The sample rate—

—Fuck the sample rate. It could be a million hertz, I wouldn't care. It could be all the hertz. This bullshit about lossless. There's always a loss, don't you get that? There is always something missing.

He started lecturing me, a speech I'd already heard a dozen times. Technology was a trap. Modern musicians were locked in a box. Digital sound had an absolute cutoff, a sonic floor that repelled the listener and set an inhuman limit to the experience. You couldn't go below zero, had I ever thought about that? Whatever happened to soul, to the vibration of an animal-gut string, the resonance of lacquered rosewood? Always the stark binary. Zero or one. I admit I stopped listening. He clutched the neck of the mandolin as if physically grasping the elusive quality he sought. He seemed high to me, higher than usual, scratching himself and making agitated passes at the strings, little chops and cuts. I asked him what he'd taken and he gave me a look and stalked off to the spare bedroom that we used as a studio. I heard rustling and scraping and went in to find him pulling cables out of the back of the patch bay.

—What are you doing?

—What I should have done years ago. This is all going in the trash.

—Carter, you're wasted.

—What do you care?

He was brandishing one of the few pieces of equipment that actually belonged to me, an expensive digital delay, hefting the brushed steel case in one hand.

—Please, Carter. You'll break it.

He pouted sarcastically, then went over to the window and threw it out. I heard it smash on the sidewalk. We were on the second floor. Someone could easily have been underneath. I noticed that my breathing had become irregular. I pointed it out to him, that someone could have been underneath. Don't be such a pussy, he sneered. It's just a *thing*.

I tried to remain calm. I'd spent all day working for tips; I'd saved for that machine; someone could have been killed, I'd been working all day, working for tips, I'd saved, someone could have been killed and—I threw myself at him, my hands scrabbling for his throat. At that moment I wanted to kill him. I wanted to scrape away his looks and charm and expose the skeleton of money underneath. People always remember Carter as an imposing figure. That's the psychological power he possessed. Actually he was slightly built. If you saw him coming out of the shower or lying asleep in bed, he looked like a waif, a lost boy.

The force of my attack knocked him over. His long blond locks splayed out across the couch and his eyes opened wide in an expression of *anime* surprise. It was as if he'd never seen me before. I watched myself choking him, kneeling on his chest. I felt as if I'd snorted ketamine and had suddenly been gifted all the time in the world, time to notice the pores in his face and the hole in his right earlobe where he'd removed a stud. I wanted to speak to him, but my mouth was dry. A crust of white powder rimmed his left nostril and I contemplated it, this scurf of whatever he'd been snorting, and I told him *I'm not a violent person,* though I don't think I spoke the words out loud. Then, for a shocking instant I was looking at myself, lying there on the couch, at my own eyes wide open in an expression of surprise. I must have slackened my grip, because he twisted round and shouldered me off onto the floor. I kept hold of him, bunching fistfuls of his shirt, his hands now at my throat. As we rolled onto the carpet, I heard the crunch of the mandolin under my back.

Of course there was some truth in his accusation, otherwise I wouldn't have lost control of myself so catastrophically. I have always respected material objects. Not as status symbols or anything like that. I don't have any particular need to be envied. Carter had never had to yearn for anything, a tool or toy or an instrument, something that would enlarge his possibilities or make his life easier. If he wanted it, he clicked and it came. I'd spent hours of my life, days, weeks at a time, fantasizing about musical equipment that I could not afford to buy. That mandolin was beautiful because it was useful. The sound of it breaking took all the heat out of my attack.

Carter broke my grip and straddled me, pinning my arms with his knees. Then he began to punch me in the face. People always look aroused when they're acting violently. They're abandoned, their guard is down. I tasted blood in my mouth and in my jolted, jumbled state it occurred to me that if I let him beat me unconscious, to death even, all my problems would be solved. It would be easy to fall into darkness, watching the wild expression on his face.

But it didn't work out like that. No beautiful death for Seth. I let my body go limp and closed my eyes but my surrender must have bored Carter because he stopped hitting me and sat back against the couch, breathing heavily and rubbing his throat. I rolled over, coughing. The mandolin was in two pieces, the neck snapped clean through, just below the headstock.

—What the fuck? he croaked. What the actual fuck?

—You shouldn't make everything about money.

—Get away from me.

—You shouldn't do that. You shouldn't do that to people.

—If you care so much about that stupid box, I'll get you another.

—Do what you like, I don't care what you do.

I woke up the next morning to find him gone. I supposed our friendship must be over. I thought he'd come home and tell me to move out. But he never did. Days went by, a couple of weeks. I served customers at the deli and wrote job applications in a state of numb depression. I didn't think about making music. There is a place I sometimes go to where no value attaches to anything. The world is flat. One sensation is exactly equal to the next. Putting your hand on someone's skin or in the flame of a candle. When it's particularly bad, it becomes a visual condition. I can look out the window and see only churn, shapes and colors that don't add up to anything. Visible light of various wavelengths. I can spend hours playing computer games or watching internet porn. Food, when I remember to eat, tastes like ashes on my tongue.

As I waited for Carter to come back and end it, I ran through mazes with a machine gun, masturbated, bombed alien cities flat, and all I really thought about was how I'd burned out my palate and couldn't taste my food. One afternoon, I returned from work to find, among the pizza boxes and dirty underwear on my bed, a brand-new digital delay. Seeing it, pristine in its shrink-wrapped box, I underwent an ecstatic convulsion. I'd been forgiven. Pacing the apartment at night, I had called Carter terrible names, spiteful names designed to push him away. But now he was home and I was forgiven and I danced a fucked-up celebration dance, one hand in the air, the other clutching the waistband of my sweat pants, which were about to slip off. When I got myself together I scooted through the apartment, cleaning up around the sofa where I spent most of my time, picking up soda cans and tipping the contents of several makeshift ashtrays—plates, cans, a small plastic bottle—into a grocery bag. I took a shower and examined myself in the mirror. When I sucked in my stomach, my jutting hipbones framed a concavity. I could count my ribs. I wondered if Carter would notice.

I'd done the dishes and was mopping the floor when he breezed in, a joint drooping from the corner of his mouth. He had been staying with friends in California and was sporting—I think that's the word—a porkpie hat and an army jacket and vintage Nike sneakers and two fistfuls of silver rings. I hadn't seen any of it before. He must have spent all his time in California buying hats and jackets and sneakers and rings.

—Hey brother, he said, all Superfly.

I resisted the impulse to hug him and modulated my voice to match.

—What's up?

—Expressing with my full capabilities. I got you another box.

—I saw. Thanks, bro. About the mandolin—

—Don't sweat it. I ordered another.

And with that, the fight was over. Often it was like that with Carter. By mutual agreement, we would close the trapdoor on a thing and never speak of it again. That same night he asked me if I wanted to move to New York with him. I couldn't believe it. Reality had inverted itself. I had been so full of despair, and now I was going to live in New York with Carter. I was one of the Lord's anointed.

A CIRCUIT OF SHOWS AND CLUBS AND PARTIES. Parties in basement bars, on midtown rooftops, in Bushwick warehouses with water streaming down the walls. Me at the very center of it all, beckoned past the velvet rope, given the nod, the wristband, the drink tickets, the bump of coke. We cycled to Coney Island. We tripped on Chinese lab chemicals in Prospect Park. It seems absurd now that we had so much time to waste. I could make a coffee run and a round of record stores last all day.

Rich young people have usually been taught, either by their parents or bitter life experience, that certain things can be a barrier to forming relationships. Certain things being a euphemism for money. Carter hated to have it mentioned. One stray remark could end a conversation; he'd just turn his back and walk away. By the time we made the move to New York, I'd adopted a religious attitude towards the many benefits that came to me: bow your head, open your hands, silently give thanks. Money was Carter's invisible helper, a friendly ghost making things happen in the background. Cars arrived, restaurant tabs got picked up. When it was time to change scenery, money dissolved the city into a beach or a ski lodge. The thing was never to point out that this was happening. Since I couldn't work out how I came to be there, why I was Carter's faithful squire instead of some other studio engineer, none of it seemed real. It was all illusion, red dust, shit turning up in FedEx boxes.

When Carter decided we were going to set up a recording studio, it just sprang into existence. He came into my room one day with the keys to a building by the water in Williamsburg. We cycled over and there it was. Contractors were already at work, installing soundproofing, building partition walls. The gear was magnificent, none of it new, always with a history, everything at least forty years old, tube amps and sixties fuzzboxes and a desk certified to have once been installed at Fame studios in Muscle Shoals. Vocals went through a pair of nineteen-fifties AKG C12's that cost fifteen thousand dollars. When the remodeling was finished, we plugged in and started looking for business. Six months out of college and I was in New York, running a fucking *studio*. Carter had a very particular idea about what he wanted to do. We were billing ourselves as audio craftsmen, artisans of analog. We would even offer to record to quarter-inch tape, if that's what the client wanted. He knew a place that could press from it, so we could make vinyl records of new music that hadn't been digitized at any stage of production. Ye olde stereophonicke sounde. Step right up.

Carter cut off his dreads and began to dress as if the year was 1849 and he was heading west to pan for gold. He wasn't alone. At that time Bedford Avenue was full of hobos and mountain men and Pony Express riders. They were our first clients, pioneers and gunfighters hunched over drum kits, tweaking guitar pedals. I gradually realized they weren't nineteenth-century revivalists at all. They were sixties revivalists, revivalists of the western revival of the nineteen sixties. Their girlfriends wore ponchos and wide floppy hats and everyone photographed each other with olde-timey filters, sepia and bleached out yellow.

In his personal music taste Carter was hovering around 1950, in some Houston basement with Lightnin' Hopkins singing through a guitar amp. That's how he wanted everything to sound just then. Hollow, buzzing and raw. There was a song called "Black Cat Bone" that he'd play over and over. It sounded terrible, as if it had been recorded in a coffin. To him, it was the apogee of audio perfection. His record collecting had taken on a new level of seriousness. If he was beaten at an auction, he would scream at the screen. We spent evenings throwing down shots and doing lines on the coffee table while he told me how he *needed* such and such a record. How I would never understand (being Spock, the tin man, etcetera) the emotional gravity of his loss.

Meanwhile we began to lock into a production sound. This organ. That handclap. Put the guitar in a cave and the vocal raw and breathy, right up front. Add surface noise, a hint of needles plowing through static, throw the whole thing back in time. Rock bands loved us. We did a record with some punk chicks from LA who were fans of the sixties Detroit girl groups. Big hair and sailor tattoos, that whole deal. We blew up their harmonies into towering melodrama, sprayed on the fuzz and pressed onto pink vinyl. It sold out in a week. After that the internet began to pay attention and we got hired to do some tracks for an album by a big British band. I hated their music and the whole Rolling Stones junkie troubadour bullshit that went along with it, but it was an opportunity and we made sure we didn't screw up. The present is dry, but add reverb and you can hear time reverse its flow, slipping on into the past, into echo and disaster. It's a trick, usually, just clever technique, except when it's not. *Twenty years ago. Thirty years ago* . . . Distance can create longing. It can open up the gap into which all must fall. When they heard what we'd done to their generic three-chord songs, the Brits were overjoyed. You made me sound amazing, the singer told us, in his nasal London drawl. Timeless. You made me sound like Skip James.

There are ways you can use a studio. Things you can do that open up impossible spaces in the mind. You can put the listener in a room that doesn't exist, that couldn't exist. You can put them in an impossible room.

▼

WHEN DID I LOSE TOUCH WITH THE FUTURE? I remember how immi-
nent it used to feel, how exciting. The old world was dissolving, all
the grime of the past sluicing away in digital rain. The future was
reflective, metallic. Soon liquid drops of mercury would reconsti-
tute themselves into spacecraft, weapons, women and men. Now
I would say the future is behind me. It is, in any case, out of my
reach. It would be easy to put the blame on Carter, on his melancholy attachment to the crackle and hiss, but I bear my share of
responsibility. I let my guard down. I let myself fall. *Nostalgia:* from
the Greek "nostos"—*homecoming*—and "algos" *pain* or *ache: the pain
a sick person feels because he is not in his native land, or fears never to see
it again.* Now I am nostalgic for the future, which was my native
land.

One weekend my dad came to town. He wanted us to bond, so
he took me to "Sunday jazz brunch" at one of the clubs in the Village, the ones that trade on the fantasy that as you eat your bad
burger you'll be transported to the wild and swinging bebop era
and all the city breakers and European backpackers at the tables
around you will magically morph into angelheaded hipsters burning like roman candles in the night. Not that my dad even liked
jazz. I don't know what he liked. I think he thought that place was
my scene.

It was an act of duty, most probably. My brother was living in Las Vegas. He hadn't been in touch. Dad mentioned, as he sometimes did, that he had "promised to hold the family together for mom." He was making an effort. We drank watery Bloody Marys and I tried to tell him about the studio. All he could think to say was, so he's rich, your friend. He tried his best, hammily nodding and tapping his fingers on the table, demonstrating that he "liked something I liked," that we had "shared interests." Some loser took a busy, vibeless tenor solo and a leathery blonde who would never be Julie London, let alone Ella or Billie, scat-screeched oooon-a-cleeear-daaay and I prayed for release because that wasn't music, it was the death of music, what happens when people repeat the same gestures for forty years after they lose all meaning.

When we said our goodbyes on the sidewalk outside, we knew that was it. Nothing happened. Nothing that would make a story. We were always going to lose touch.

A few days later Carter and I were asked to sit down with a major label. We found ourselves in a midtown office with a view of the Hudson, talking about a famous white hip hop artist who wanted to pay his dues to the tradition by releasing an album of classic covers. The executive running the meeting had walnut skin and a facelift that made him look like a pilot in a centrifuge, a clean-cut American hero experiencing some large multiple of earth's gravity. He tried to impress us by telling an embarrassing story about doing coke with Sly Stone. His assistant was so beautiful, I didn't dare meet her eye. She should have been on a yacht. The executive told her to bring us drinks and when she bent over to put the tray on the coffee table, he leaned back to check out her ass and made an insufferable *I know, right?* face at Carter, who looked back at him blankly. I was worried about Carter. His head wasn't in the game.

The rapper arrived with his people and the room rearranged itself around him as he perched on the edge of a lounger, cradling a chai and explaining that he essentially considered himself a curator. He was a sincere young man from Maine, who'd had a *Billboard* number one with a song about drug dealing and had recently (according to a magazine someone left in our bathroom) purchased a nice-looking beach house in St. Barts. Onstage he was like one of those internet videos that illustrates the whole history of something in ninety seconds. Hyperactive, encyclopedic. Between verses he did James Brown dance moves, all slides and splits and theatrical sexual fainting, snapping into more modern styles: breaking, pop and lock. In person he was surprisingly low-key. He was always giving quotes about feeling "humble" or "in awe" of one or other canonical black star. Now, he explained, in a half-whisper that forced everyone to lean forward slightly, it was time to take his humility a step further. Every track on his album was to be a tribute to a particular period and style of African American music, from ragtime through fifties RnB to eighties boogie. Nineteen ninety, the year of his birth, was the cutoff. He was not going to cover other people's songs, but remix his own material in other styles, the styles of the great artists of history. As the executive explained:

—It'll be like my man was born in different time periods.

—*My Past Lives*, said the rapper. Am I right?

I said I thought it was a good name.

—I've decided vinyl only, he added. The executive said they would talk about that. I thought we were pitching to do one track, but it became clear that they wanted us to produce the whole album. It was a career-making opportunity. The rap star loved our *precision*. He loved our *patina*. Our *patina* was on a *whole other level of precision*. He told us he thought of us like those Chinese oil painters who turn out perfect reproductions of Monets and Cézannes to sell on the internet.

Expressing enthusiasm wasn't my job, Carter was the one with the social skills, but instead of complimenting the rap star and closing the deal, he was staring out the window, tapping on his knees and humming the chess player's blues under his breath.

> *Put me under a man they call Captain Jack*
> *Put me under a man they call Captain Jack*
> *He wrote his name all down my back*

He'd been humming it for days. I'd hear the track on repeat, the a cappella voice singing its threatening, melancholy lyric. A year earlier, that voice wouldn't have had such an impact on him. It turned up just when he became receptive. All postwar music had vanished from his life. The electric guitars and thumping rhythms of the nineteen forties and fifties had faded into prewar blues recordings, lone guitarists playing strange abstract figures, scraping the strings with knives and bottlenecks and singing in cracked, elemental voices about trouble and loss. Lately, he'd set up a 78rpm turntable in his bedroom. He would sit on the floor close to the speakers. It was as if the chess player's blues had risen up to meet him, as if he'd summoned it into his room.

A lot of people find early recordings unlistenable. I did too. The audio quality is so poor, instinctively my brain wants it cleaned up. Carter had explained that some of the records were so rare that only single copies were known. In some cases that lone copy was worn out. The pressings had been bad in the first place, companies skimping on shellac, using too much clay and cotton filler in the mix. Even in mint condition, some of them sounded as if they'd been scoured with sandpaper. I suppose it was inevitable that, sooner or later, Carter would run into those old singers. They were as far back in audio time as you could go. He'd been following their traces through downloads and vinyl compilations to a wooden box lined with green baize that he was gradually filling with expensive original 78's. He had begun to talk about songs by referencing their catalog numbers, scouring want lists and dealer sites for work by musicians so obscure that even their real names were in doubt.

The rapper had been talking about his respect for The Last Poets, who he kept referring to as The Last Prophets. Carter cut across him and spoke directly to me.

—I can't believe you're not out looking for him.

—Looking for who?

—You met him at the chess tables, right? Maybe he plays there regularly.

I was thrown. It took me a moment to realize what he meant.

—Let's talk about this later.

The executive asked if Carter needed anything. People always told me, said the rapper, with the air of a man trying to cut through bullshit to the realness within, they said pull up your pants and act white.

I said I understood.

—I spent hours with my notebook, just honing my skills. I went to parties way out in the hood.

Carter scowled. The executive tapped him on the knee and told him that his assistant would get him anything. Anything at all, double underscore. Somehow we stumbled through another fifteen minutes, but the meeting had essentially fallen apart. We left with a lot of hugs and complicated handshakes, but without a definitive agreement to do the record.

I knew we could make a killer album. I had a lot of unused material that I didn't know what to do with. Because of Carter's voracious and well-funded collecting, I was sitting on super-rare breaks that would lose their value the instant someone else ripped them off. We could make tracks that sounded like 1973 because we *had* tracks from 1973, hyper-rarities no one else possessed. Secret knowledge. Gnosis. I couldn't understand why Carter wasn't excited. Outside on the sidewalk, I confronted him.

—What the fuck was that? I asked. He lit a cigarette.

—He can kiss my ass.

—He's huge. Everything he does charts.

—So? We're doing him a favor even talking to him.

—Come on, man. Don't screw this up. It's what we've been dreaming about.

—This is *our* music, Seth. We live it. We feel it. He thinks he can just swan in and buy it off the shelf?

—Do you know how insane you sound?

He shrugged.

We stood around, awkwardly, smoking and shuffling our feet. Then he summoned a car on his phone, got in it and drove away.

▼

I DIDN'T SEE CARTER AGAIN until the next morning. I had slept badly, so when he burst into my room, I was groggy and disoriented. He pulled the sheet off the bed and made an announcement: his brother Cornelius was having a weekend party at the family place in Virginia and we were going.

—Taking off from Teterboro in three hours, so pack a bag.

—What?

—Corny chartered a six-seater for his friends, and some of them dropped out. My God, you look disgusting. Were you drinking last night?

—No.

I sat up, yawning and picking gunk out of my eyes. I didn't want to know why he was suddenly so charged up when he had been completely apathetic at our meeting. He was operating at an atypically high intensity, full of plans and designs, stalking around the apartment wearing a dress shirt and neat khaki slacks dug out from God knows what forgotten corner of his closet.

Put me under a man called Captain Jack, he sang. *Wrote his name all down my back.*

I padded into the kitchen and fumbled angrily with the coffee machine.

—Why are you dressed like a Mormon? I thought you hated your brother.

—I never said that, Seth. I would never say that.

—Pardon me for asking. Look, are you OK?

—Sure. Come on, hustle hustle, finish your cereal. One thing, the guys traveling with us are douchebags, but you can relax because Leonie is coming too.

Leonie. A wound in my side.

I only met Carter's sister after we came to New York. We went to an opening at a little storefront gallery on the Lower East Side. The place had been a leather goods wholesaler, and the signage was still on the window and over the door. *Bags, shoes, belts, fancy goods.* The sidewalk was blocked by smokers, bikes clamped to every sign and lamppost. I shouldered my way in behind Carter, fishing for the last few bottles of beer at the bottom of a giant bucket filled with mostly melted ice. Leonie was an artist. Or trying to be one. Carter couldn't decide how seriously to take her. She's very solemn, he warned. She drops a lot of French names. We squeezed through a crowd of kids in thrift store clothes ironically referencing the nineties suburbia they'd escaped to come and make it in the city. Here and there were signs of money: an older couple protected from the rabble by a slick young man who I assumed was the gallerist, another couple smoking outside, studiously ignored by everyone around them, an instantly recognizable musician and her actor boyfriend.

It was almost impossible to look at the show, which had work by a dozen young artists, but since the place was so small Leonie's contribution wasn't hard to find. She'd made a video of herself dressed in exercise clothing and ski boots, stomping about in a studio, crushing pills and capsules underfoot. She kicked about bottles of vitamins and nutritional supplements. After a while, she started to pour big tubs of protein powder on the floor.

—How long did that take to make, Carter fake-whispered. Ten minutes?

—Oh, *much* less.

Stricken, we turned round. There she was, making a sarcastic face at us. Her tangled blond hair was tied back with a scarf. She wore jeans and a battered biker jacket, downtown uniform for someone who doesn't want to look like they're trying too hard.

I'd seen pictures, but the sight of her and Carter together was still a visual shock: the same high cheekbones and straw-blond hair, the same blue eyes contradicted by heavy darkish brows. A single image, strobing. As I looked more closely, I saw that her mouth had a slight irregularity, a warp or cast that pulled up her top lip and exposed her teeth, marring what would otherwise have been classical Northern European perfection. It was as if she'd heard unpleasant news, a betrayal or disappointment that had left a permanent trace of sourness. She was three years older than Carter, and though his remark had clearly annoyed her, she leaned over and kissed him in the time-honored gesture of indulgent big sisters, bringing her hand up under his chin and squeezing his face to make his lips bulge.

—You're an ape.

Carter said sorry.

—I liked it, I said, distancing myself from his rudeness. She looked starkly at me and turned back to her brother.

—If you make the right gesture, craft doesn't matter. It could take ten seconds.

—You know you're just covering your ass because you can't draw.

She punched him hard in the shoulder.

—Go fuck yourself, you're supposed to be here to support me, not give me a crit.

—So are you going to stay on here for a while? Or do you want to go get a drink?

We ended up at dinner with a big crowd, a waiter's nightmare of people shifting seats, going outside to smoke and take calls, arriving late and disappearing early. All Leonie's friends seemed to be from somewhere else, some other city in some other country. It was the first thing they talked about, their geographical otherness. They found Carter intermittently charming, asking him questions about music and listening intently to his answers, yet there was something patronizing about their interest. The conversations were not sustained. Me, of course, they treated with barely disguised contempt. In the pecking order of that table, it was clear who was on top. A trio of artists in haute redneck attire, with full-sleeve tattoos and unruly facial hair, were ordering steaks and expensive red wine, roistering, playing to the crowd. When they spoke, the others turned to listen, particularly when the alpha, a bearish man with dark circles under his eyes and a drinker's paunch, began to enumerate his beliefs about art. They seemed standard enough to me—he was for tearing down the old and bringing in the new—but he delivered his platitudes as if they were important and shocking, something to be shouted through a megaphone at a Happening. When he finished, his trucker buddies refilled his glass and clapped him on the back like a soldier returning from patrol. In the momentary silence, Leonie tried out a joke.

—I have a simple aesthetic. As long as my mother hates something, I know it must be worth doing.

She sat back, expecting laughter, but the table took its cues from the important painter and he seemed irritated.

—You show your mother your work?

—No, of course not. What would she say? She likes the Impressionists. She carries round a little bag she bought at Giverny.

I thought this was funny, but only one or two other people smiled. The important painter shook his head.

—You probably went there, right? To see the waterlilies.

—Yeah, so? I went to Giverny with my mom.

—She probably took you to Florence too, and the Parthenon and Basel and Venice for the Biennale.

—You want to see my passport?

—No, I don't have to. I'm saying that, you know, everyone has a role. A position. Maybe you should bow to the inevitable and get into collecting.

The table treated this as a killer punch line, a zinger. Leonie didn't show she was angry by anything she said or did, but I could see a cord of muscle standing taut in her neck, and her laughter wasn't well-acted. Soon afterwards she left. Carter sat there, rocking slightly in his seat, giving the important painter filthy looks, rehearsing putdowns he was too tongue-tied to deliver.

It was a thing you soon noticed about Leonie, how she would bring up her mother at inappropriate moments, always to mention some difference of opinion, some disagreement. For Carter, the parent he needed to overcome was his father, but the differences between these two were clear-cut. It was obvious the son would never sit on a board or manage a business. Leonie's lines were less distinct. I would later find out that her mother was an amateur painter, a patron of DC galleries and museums. Art school was something they had agreed on.

After that evening, I always tagged along when Carter was going to see her. We went to more openings, a dinner in someone's loft. I was fascinated by her arcane social rituals, the ever-changing pecking order of artists and curators and collectors that governed where she went and what she said there. Before I met the Wallaces I had no idea any of that even existed. Carter, who grew up flicking finger food at movie stars and captains of industry, thought his sister's scene was lame. Full of Eurotrash, he said. A lot of nobodies pretending to come from money.

When Carter told me Leonie would be traveling with us to Cornelius's party, my face must have betrayed me, because he laughed.

—Now you want to go.

I knew my interest in his older sister was ridiculous, but I didn't like to be mocked. I grabbed a book from my nightstand and threw it at him. It went wide, clattering against the door. As he sauntered into the kitchen he sang:

> *Went to the Captain with my hat in my hand*
> *Went to the Captain with my hat in my hand*
> *Said Captain have mercy on a long time man*

Then he changed out of his teenage church clothes into something more like his normal attire, jeans shorts, a broad-brimmed hat that made him look like a Rough Rider, and a poetic linen shirt with big sleeves gathered into the cuffs. With the car waiting outside, and me in the living area, a weekend bag packed and a coffee in a thermos mug ready in my hand, he shut himself in his room and didn't come out for forty-five minutes. As usual, the driver had my number as the contact, and he kept calling to warn me that we couldn't be late for wheels-up. I went to the door to knock and heard Carter hissing under his breath. He was having an argument about money with Betty.

—Did you try the other account?

I was never sure how much I was supposed to know about Betty. She handled things. Booked travel, researched, offered options. Carter only talked to her when he thought I wouldn't overhear. I'd never met her, never even found out where she was located. All I had to go on was his hand cupped over the phone, the shameful masturbatory hunch of his back as he tended to the logistics of his charmed life. Later he told me, in a casual tone of voice, that the reason we were going down to Virginia was because he wanted to talk to his older brother about investing in the studio.

—He'll be cool, he said, half to himself, as we were driven through the Midtown Tunnel. He won't want to be hanging around in the control room. He has no actual interest in music.

—He'd be like a partner?

—God no. At worst we'll have to get him and his asshole friends comped at some clubs, so they can come on to chicks by telling them they're in the music business.

In the five years we'd known each other, Carter had never invited me to his family home. There were other houses (in Aspen, on the Mississippi Gulf Coast, Paris) but his parents lived in this place for much of the year, in a DC exurb that was popular with wealthy government and business people. Carter occasionally disappeared there on summer weekends, hungover and grumbling, required to appear at some clan summit. I imagined an informal lunch, a lawyer dropping by. Documents to sign over coffee.

—The trouble with my family is there's always some angle.

The tunnel lights flickered in the window.

—It's the company. It poisons everything. You know. Different people have different levels of control. None of us can speak to each other, not really.

—What about you and Leonie?

—Especially me and her.

The car pulled up at the airport, and a doorman with an earpiece showed us into a modest terminal, furnished as blandly as a regional hotel lobby.

—Finally!

Carter didn't enter Leonie's embrace, raising a hand in limp benediction.

—In your usual fragile mood, I see, Carty.

—I wish you wouldn't call me that.

—Seth, I'm so honored you're here with us to celebrate our older brother's surgical transformation into our father.

Leonie always used my name in a vaguely insulting way, as if testing it for impurities. She turned her eyes away and I felt as if my face had been seared on a grill. I tried to make bright conversation.

—So what's the occasion? Is there a reason for this party?

Carter smiled at his sister.

—He *is* a great son.

—*Such* a great son.

—I mean *really*.

—No *really*.

—*So* great.

—A *great* son.

Neither of them answered my question. I didn't mind. I always loved to hear them talk like that, finishing each other's thoughts. I would have gone on expeditions, waited hours and days in a camouflaged hide.

—The rest of your party is here, said the pilot, who had been hovering in the background. This way.

Corny's three friends had all been at Princeton with him and now they were in finance. That was about as far into their lives as I cared to go. They didn't like the look of us either, and after introductions were made and interest faked, we all stood around, not making eye contact. Then the pilot escorted us to the plane and waited patiently as each of them took a picture of himself and set about posting it to social media. Hashtags #flyprivate #highlife #goodlife. No doubt their feeds also had pictures of their watches and bar bills.

Leonie handed a large straw hat to the hostess, who put it in a locker. We settled into the cavernous calf-leather seats.

#wheelsup

—What can I get you gentlemen to drink?

The hostess knew the answer before they said it. She opened the champagne and the bros clinked glasses, congratulating each other on whatever it was they thought they were experiencing.

—This is it!

—The shit!

—The *shiznit.*

Carter and Leonie hunched down instinctively in their seats. Leonie asked for a mineral water. Carter, one-upping the bros, rolled and lit a joint, which made the hostess instantly nervous. She conferred with the captain, who closed the cockpit door. Poker-faced, she produced an ashtray. I nursed a cold beer and looked at Leonie, at the sunlight streaming in through the Gulfstream's window onto the contours of her face. Carter prodded her with his foot, to get her attention.

—You go first. Why are you here?

She rolled her eyes.

—Why get into it?

—Because I want to know.

—I'm just here to congratulate Cornelius on his important new job.

—Oh, sure.

—Get off my back. Anyway, what about you?

Carter gave a theatrical shrug and pursed his lips. We sat in irritated silence, listening to Corny's friends talking about bottles and models. Once the champagne had kicked in, they began to pester the hostess.

—Got any beats?

—Now you talking!

—We should have some sounds all up in here!

Leonie turned round sharply.

—No beats. No music. No nothing. This isn't some shitty beach party.

They had zero comeback. Not a squeak. For the rest of the short flight they sat and sullenly checked their phones.

We landed at a small airport somewhere outside Washington.

The young bankers got into a waiting limo van, which Carter and Leonie ignored, stalking across the tarmac to a car rental place, where they picked up a little Japanese convertible. I crouched in the bucket seat with the bags, holding Leonie's delicate hat on my lap to protect it as we drove at high speed out into the suburbs, past farmhouses and white fences and flagpoles flying the Stars and Stripes. Carter switched on the sound system and the car was flooded by the last thing I wanted to hear. *Believe I buy a graveyard of my own.* I asked if we could have something else, but Carter pretended he couldn't hear me. *Believe I buy me a graveyard of my own. Put my enemies all down in the ground.* Eventually after a few repeats, Leonie leaned over and switched to a DC hip hop station.

Gradually the fences got higher and the houses vanished from view. At last, Carter took a sharp corner onto a side road, then up a driveway barred by a wrought iron gate. He spoke into an intercom and the gate slid back to reveal a scene like an eighteenth-century print, a tree-lined avenue winding away towards an unseen house.

Gravel crunched beneath the wheels; solitude unfolded over us.

To my surprise, when it revealed itself, the house was on a modest scale, more like a summer place than the enormous mansion I'd been expecting. Old, though. Not old-style or "olde" but actually old, with white plaster columns along a wide porch and little windows set in the gables of a tiled roof. A vivid lawn ran downhill towards woodland that blocked all view of the outside world. The earth rolled pleasingly, as if landscaped solely to frame that view. I think the meaning of private property had never quite sunk in for me until then; its weight, its peculiar authority. Privacy was disconnection, the power to take a section of the world offline.

—It's not that we own it, said Carter, as if reading my mind. We're just maintaining the asset for future generations.

We parked the car, and a man in a golf cart came to take our bags down to the guesthouse, a two-story building screened by trees. As we ambled down towards the pool, I wondered idly what kind of electronic security measures were in place. Did motion sensors cover the green lawn? Were there cameras in the hydrangeas? Whatever they had was artfully disguised. The pool itself looked like a pond in a fairy tale, with lily pads and a weeping willow and great rounded mossy boulders on its banks. Around it, thirty or forty people were hanging out on chairs and loungers. Most were in their twenties and thirties, dressed in casual clothes and swimwear. A few of the younger women wore bikinis, posing and laughing to attract the attention of the men, who were mostly engaged with their phones and their drinks. Here and there I spotted older faces, a cluster of substantial sixty-somethings at a picnic table, two skinny middle-aged women stretched out on loungers like a pair of lizards, eyeing up the boys from behind their dark glasses. A large grill was tended by three sweating black chefs, wearing tunics and white gloves to turn over steaks and burgers. At the bar, they were serving juleps and iced tea. Two men were lining up tequila shots, watching the girls in the pool.

—How many hours a week on the stair climber?

—Not enough.

—That one, though.

They looked Leonie up and down as we came in. She put on her hat and turned away from them, effectively masking herself from view. She was more beautiful than the women they'd been appraising, and they were offended that she was making no effort to please them. I watched their sexual interest curdle into a desire to hurt her, take her down.

—Where's Corny, Leonie asked Carter, apparently unconcerned.

—Up at the house. He's probably watching us through his binoculars.

As Leonie laughed, I tried to record it. Not literally. I tried to imprint on my memory the unforced rise in pitch, the broken descent. I would treasure it, house it in a place of honor, like the relic of a saint. I was aware of the pathetic figure I cut. Sometimes, late at night, I Googled her, looking at the same half-dozen party shots, Leonie with her arm round a curator, a musician, the owner of a West Village restaurant. When I imagined myself in their place, being the man who took her home and made out with her in the taxi and finally, in the privacy of some luxurious apartment, slipped the straps of an expensive dress over her shoulders, I was brought up sharply against my own physical meagerness. The contrast between us was so grotesque that I could never enjoy the fantasy.

Once in a while in New York we went over to her TriBeCa loft. It was a peculiar place, in a doorman building with a marble reception desk and fresh-cut flowers in the lobby. When you got out of the elevator, you felt as if you'd been teleported. Her books sat on metal warehouse shelving. She slept on a mattress on a little plywood platform. The walls had been stripped back to brick, and the floor painted heavy-duty battleship gray. It was a facsimile, a simulation of the kind of place other artists lived in, many stops away in the outer boroughs. Everything about her domesticity was apparently careless. Ashtrays and dirty plates. Bags of recycling propped up against a wall. Part of the huge open space had been crudely partitioned by a plasterboard wall that didn't meet the ceiling, a white box inside which she sometimes painted or shot photographs. We would hang out at her fake squat with its panoramic view of the Hudson and I would watch the sunset and listen to her friends talking about this show and that fair while she sat cross-legged on the floor in a pastel jumpsuit or a lurid eighties sweater, transparently hoping that someone would ask about the bubble-wrapped C type prints stacked in neat rows against the far wall. Somehow they never did. I never did. Not because I didn't want to. If I'd dared, I would have asked about her pictures.

Excuse me, she said, and made her way to the other side of the pool, where she bent down and greeted a man in his fifties, one of a group sitting and eating round a picnic table. He had an outdoor tan, sailing or skiing, ruddy around the nose with white bands at his temples where some kind of goggles had blocked the sun. His hair was swept back in a gray mane. She kissed him on the cheek, and he let his hand linger on her shoulder. As she talked, rocking animatedly from foot to foot and playing with the brim of her hat, he sat, half-turned on the bench, his eyes dipping down and back up again, scanning her from knee to breast. There was something raffish about him, a whiff of the bohemian that stood out against the conservative golf wear of the other men at his table. The linen pants, the popped collar on his shirt. I was offended by all of it, his boyishly tousled hair, his air of well-fed hedonism. I waited for her to move away, but she didn't.

Carter disappeared to take a call, and I hovered by the grill, eating a burger. I couldn't see anyone who might be willing to talk to me, so I drifted into the pool house, a quaint old building with a tiled roof and cedar siding that had weathered almost to black. Inside it smelled of chlorine and wet towels. A huge pair of oars hung from the roof, trophies of some long-dead varsity crew. The walls were hung with photographs of swimming parties dating back eighty years. Recurrent faces, remixes of Carter and Leonie in baggy woolen suits with rubber rings and drinks in their hands.

Guglielmo Marconi, the inventor of radio, believed that sound waves never completely die away, that they persist, fainter and fainter, masked by the day-to-day noise of the world. Marconi thought that if he could only invent a microphone powerful enough, he would be able to listen to the sound of ancient times. The Sermon on the Mount, the footfalls of Roman soldiers marching down the Appian Way. I clapped my hands, listening to how the report was absorbed by the walls, but reflected by the concrete floor. The pool house had a strange tone, a particular blend of interior and exterior that made me suddenly wary. I retreated back out into the party.

People sat on lawn chairs or stood waist-deep in the pool, bonded in impenetrable social rings and hexagons. Things had gotten looser while I'd been inside, louder. Drinking and the summer heat. By the grill, one of the servants was cleaning up the shards of a broken bottle. My phone went off in my pocket. Carter was calling me.

—Get a ride and come up here.

—Where?

—To the house. Cornelius wants to meet you.

Two staff members were leaning against their carts at the foot of the hill. I walked up to them, but they didn't acknowledge me. I trudged upwards, reaching the top in a flop sweat. Unsure if it was OK to go in through the front, I walked round to the back porch. Finding the screen door open, I picked my way in over a clutter of boots and hats and tennis rackets.

—Hello, is anyone there?

Crammed tightly together on the walls of the hallway were old prints and maps. I had a glimpse of a small room, not much more than a walk-in closet, containing what looked like a server rack, black modules with red winking lights.

Carter appeared in a doorway.

—There you are.

—So what does Cornelius want with me?

—You're my business partner. He wants to look you over, see what he's buying into.

—So no pressure.

—Don't blow this, is what I'm saying.

—Jesus, Carter. Are your parents here too?

—No, they're in Europe. It's just Corny.

We found him in a study or office, standing in front of a huge oak desk on which sat no fewer than five screens, showing market data, news tickers, surveillance views of the property. Leonie hadn't been joking about the binoculars. Dressed in the awkward smart casual of men who spend their lives in suits, Corny was standing at a bay window with a view downhill toward the pool, his legs braced, training a pair of German precision lenses on the party like a commodore on the bridge of his cruiser. As he formed his first unfavorable impression of me, I got a closer look at the binoculars. They were the military kind that incorporates a laser, returning various kinds of range-finding information. Beautifully engineered. Reluctantly, I made eye contact again to confirm that Leonie's sneer was playing across a face decorated with Carter's nose and cheekbones. The recombinant quality of this stranger in a button-down shirt was uncanny; a hostile alien intelligence animating the features of people I loved.

—So is this going to work? he asked.

—Sure, I said hesitantly, turning to Carter and silently cursing him for leaving me so unprepared.

—Seth's kind of a wizard. What he doesn't know about music technology isn't worth knowing.

—And you think New York isn't a mature market?

We both shrugged, at a loss.

—It's like, too mature, said Carter. It's decadent. People want to get back to the source. The old school. They want things they can touch.

I waited for him to say more, to give me a clue as to what we were trying to sell, but he trailed off into silence, scuffing the rug with a foot. The contrast between the two brothers was instructive. Corny, neatly put together, impregnably respectable. Carter's bare legs, the tattooed skulls on his chest, visible in the deep V of his poet's linen shirt. Corny spoke slowly, savoring his own patronizing restraint.

—I meant, are there other people who offer the same service? What is your competition?

I'd never seen Carter blush before. Sure, he mumbled. Of course.

—So there are?

—No. We're the only ones. We can do, like, a lot of stuff. No one has what we have. I mean, in terms of equipment. And talent.

—Did you actually do any research? Or do you just know?

—Man, get off my back! Give me this one little area, at least. One tiny little area where I'm the one who knows.

—Please don't call me "man."

Carter threw his arms up in exasperation. Corny made a pantomime of thinking about his investment decision.

—If I do this, will you wash your hair?

—Fuck off.

—And wear underwear, and stop taking drugs?

—I knew this was pointless. Jesus, for a moment I actually thought you weren't going to be a dick.

—I am serious. You're a goddamn disgrace.

—Seth, let's get out of here.

Corny chuckled.

—God, Carty, don't get your panties in a bunch.

He took a large leather-bound checkbook out of a drawer, produced a pen.

—Like shooting fish in a barrel. How much, again?

—Fifty.

He sat down to write, arranging his materials with fussy formality.

—I'm satisfied you can't be in that much trouble. If you had a drug habit or you owed money to the mob, you'd have promised to wash your hair.

Carter took the check and stuffed it into the back pocket of his jeans

—Like I said, this isn't charity. We'll hook you up, no doubt.

—Dad would tell you to live within your means.

—That would involve Dad finding out my number from his assistant.

—Such a martyr. And don't take it out on Betty when you run out of funds.

—Why not. She's paid to deal with my shit.

—She's only authorized to go up to a certain limit.

—But she's paid, right. I'm her job.

—You're all our jobs, Carter. Everybody does their share.

Corny made an ironic face, to show that he was waiting for the thank-you he didn't expect to get. He held it for a second or two, then let it drop.

—So, I'm bringing some polo buddies into the city next weekend.

—Sure. I got you. Whatever you need.

—Great. I thought you might want to congratulate me, though. You know Dad's made me VP of Correctional Services?

—Really?

—Really. I'm in charge of the whole Walxr operation. Fifty-eight facilities. All the ancillary services. Effectively I'm the CEO of my own company within the Wallace Magnolia Group.

—Feet fitting the big shoes, huh?

—Be as sarcastic as you like, but you know he'd love to do something for you too. If you cared enough.

—You are truly fucked in the head, Corny. You never take me seriously. I don't need a job. I have a job. I make music.

—You shouldn't leave it too long. Don't get stuck in that life.

He waved a hand at me, casually dismissing the visible manifestation of "that life" like a tasteless shirt or an earring, a kid brother's foolish and transient choice. Carter sighed.

—Come on, Seth. We're done here.

We hopped on a golf cart and pit-stopped at the guesthouse, where we smoked a joint, leaning out over the balcony. I was aware that the check was still stuffed into the back pocket of Carter's jeans, and I asked him if he wanted me to hold on to it. Carter handed it over and I filed it in the pocket of my laptop case. He asked if I really wanted to stay the night. There was probably a scheduled flight back later on, we could get on it. I told him I didn't mind. Whatever he wanted to do was fine. He seemed despondent, all the morning's manic energy broken on the jagged rocks of Cornelius. There was something intimate about the moment that made me feel I could risk a question.

—I know it's not my business, but why are you having to do this?

—Do what?

—Go to your brother. We're making some money. You don't need to bow down before him.

He said nothing. I tried to work out if he was offended.

—I'm sorry. It's just—we're not in trouble, are we? Financially.

He shook his head.

—There's stuff I want, that's all.

—Stuff?

—Records. What else? Things have been put on shellac that I was born to hear.

—What records?

—I have one or two things going on. Deals I'm trying to swing. Don't worry, you'll get to hear whatever I buy.

Then we went back to the party. While we'd been away, afternoon had collapsed into evening, and the staff were setting out tables for a formal meal, lighting lanterns and hanging them in the trees. A four-piece band set up on a little stage and began to play jazz standards. People had disappeared to change, and were reappearing in cocktail dresses, jackets and ties.

Carter looked at the table map and moved our place cards so we were sitting with Leonie. only to find that when the meal started she sat down at another table, next to the man she had been talking to by the pool. The guests at our table were all twenty-something lawyers, eager young folk whose firms were attached to the Wallace Magnolia Group like barnacles on the hull of an oceangoing tanker. After a round of perky introductions, it became clear that I wasn't worth talking to and Carter was ignoring them, so they made conversation amongst themselves. Carter sat with his phone between his legs, checking an auction on eBay. I ate my diver scallops and my duck and looked up at the lanterns in the trees, listening to the band amble through "Now Is The Time."

After the main course had been served, Cornelius Wallace stood and gave a speech, acknowledging various people at the party and thanking us for "sharing this milestone" with him. He made a joke about being named the youngest member of the Magnolia board and claimed to be very thankful to have "Roger and Bill and Harry" to help him find his feet. Somehow he made his thanks sound like a threat, as if Roger and Bill and Harry would soon find themselves clearing their desks if they didn't swiftly demonstrate loyalty to the new regime.

They served coffee and dessert and people began to move around. Some of the lawyers vacated their places and Leonie and her friend came over to sit with us.

—Carter, this is Marc.

Marc shook Carter's hand, then sat back with placid self-assurance, crossing his legs and shooting his cuffs and adopting the expression of a man ready to be fascinated.

Carter said hi. There was a drawn-out pause.

Marc's smile did not waver. Instead, though no one had asked, he told us how he knew Leonie. From downtown, he said, with a knowing underscore that made him sound almost archaeological. I did some quick calculations. Young in the eighties.

—Actually, I bought one of her videos.

Is that what you do, asked Carter. Collect videos?

—No, I have a software company. Lately some other projects too. I have an environmental nonprofit that takes up some of my time.

—Oh God, you're that guy.

Marc was measured in the face of this unexpected aggression. Leonie looked furious. Carter sighed and scraped his chair back from the table.

—Ones and fucking zeroes. Excuse me, I need to piss.

He stalked off. I wondered if I ought to go too. The silence became awkward. Leonie filled it by introducing me to Marc, who shook my hand and gave me his ready-to-be-fascinated face. Up to that point, no one had acknowledged me.

—It was such a wonderful surprise to find out Marc was going to be here. It's positively made my evening.

Leonie's smile was almost as radiant as Marc's. She behaved as if she and I were the greatest of friends, apparently hoping that I would help cover for her brother's rudeness. Then she and Marc told each other again and again how pleased and surprised they were to see each other at the party, until I became convinced that they had arranged to meet, perhaps as part of some subterfuge. I looked on his hand for a wedding ring, but didn't see one. As they played out their little scene, I shrunk further into myself. A silence descended which I made no particular effort to fill, and they began to look around for ways to move on.

There was whooping and shouting, and then a splash. Corny's friends from the plane had met another half a dozen young men as moronic as themselves, and together they'd pushed a girl into the swimming pool. Leonie used the opportunity to pull Marc away. I watched them go, his hand brushing the small of her back as they made their way towards the house. More than twenty years older. Probably twenty-five. I felt very bitter, brimming with a poor young man's outrage against the old and rich. His thickening body against hers, his knowing unworshipful hands.

Around me, the party was bifurcating, one faction already saying good night, giving out business cards and promising to be in touch, the other gearing up for some real fun, shots and powder and sneaking in and out of rooms. Carter reappeared and told me not to talk to him, because he'd lost the auction he'd been following and now it was all he could do not to punch someone. A complicated cascade of transactions had depended on him buying a hillbilly record, some Appalachian fiddle band. The fiddle band record would make some kind of set or package with two others he already had, and the three together might lure someone he'd been talking to online to part with a worn but playable copy of

Mississippi John Hurt's "Spike Driver Blues." But he'd been outbid. He'd not been paying attention. Someone else was using sniper software, so no John Hurt record. It wasn't fair. The loss had put him in a foul mood. I knew from experience that it wasn't a good idea to be around him. All he'd want to do was pick at his wounds and work up an excuse to lash out at me.

—What's the deal with Marc, I asked, cautiously.

—Oh him. He's another collector. Emerging artists, blah blah blah. All so he can impress his Teva-wearing tech buddies with tales of urban exploration.

—What about him and Leonie?

—Is she fucking him? I don't even want to know.

I said I was tired and I'd probably go to bed. He went to the bar and for a while I walked desultory circuits of the pool, listening to the band race through "A Night In Tunisia." From somewhere nearby I heard the sound of a helicopter taking off. I don't know why I chose to go back into the pool house.

Inside, the noise of the party was muffled. The moon shone in through a high window, throwing a slanted band of light over the wall of photographs. The dead people in their swimsuits and tennis whites crossed their rackets and raised their glasses in an ironic toast to my social failure. Behind me was a row of changing cubicles. From inside one of them I began to make out the sound of breathing. A man's breathing, ragged and deep. Then, quite distinctly, I heard the man groan and a woman's voice telling him to shut up. It was Leonie. There was silence, and then a series of tiny, wet, noises. The man's breathing got deeper again. I was trapped by what I was hearing, my feet glued to the ground by a sort of vile abjection. The groans increased in urgency until, with a soft exhalation, the man came.

I hid in the darkness.

A moment or two of scrabbling around, the clink of a belt buckle. Only when it was too late did I realize that I should have left, that it would only deepen my self-disgust to see the cubicle door swing open and Leonie come out, adjusting her cocktail dress. I attempted to compose myself, to form some emotional structure that wouldn't collapse. Then she stepped into the shaft of light and I saw her flushed face, her disordered hair. Marc followed, buttoning his shirt. I don't know what made him look towards me, whether I made a sound or gave some other clue. He saw me trying to bury myself in the damp beach towels hung on pegs on the wall behind me. For an instant he looked shocked. Then he broke eye contact by checking an expensive diver's watch, its steel bracelet half-buried in his grizzled arm-hair. Excuse me, son, he said, allowing himself a half-smile. He followed Leonie back out to the party.

▼

WHEN WE GOT BACK TO NEW YORK, Carter asked me for the audio I'd made on my walks around the city. By that time he was claiming to friends that he didn't even own a computer anymore, so this was surprising. He usually wanted nothing to do with my environmental recordings. I put them on a drive for him and forgot about it.

The studio sucks up time. I wanted to lose myself, disconnect from my obsessive thoughts about Leonie. Despite Carter's behavior at our meeting, the hip hop star was still interested in working with us, and I closed the door on the world and trawled through recordings of thirties dance bands, collecting samples for a demo. McKinney's Cotton Pickers, Cab Calloway, The Harlem Hamfats. Days passed, taking me further away from that pool house, the shame and confusion I'd brought on myself. My plan was to do a mix that sounded like you could have heard it at the Cotton Club, all banjos and muted trumpets. I had the files for one of the hip hop star's hits, the one about "going uptown" to "see what the dark side brings." I was basically trying to make it sound like Duke Ellington's "Creole Love Call," without getting mixed up in a lot of complicated arrangements.

Carter wasn't interested in helping. He communicated his preferences by shrugging whenever I brought the project up. He was busy with something else, something he didn't seem interested in discussing. I thought perhaps it was a girl. One evening I was collecting a burrito from a delivery guy at the studio door when Carter appeared behind him, wearing sneakers and white earbuds. For a minute, I thought he'd been jogging. None of this—the shoes, the headphones, physical exercise—was normal. I put the food on the counter of the kitchenette and asked him if he wanted any. I hoped he'd ask to hear the mix, which I thought was sounding good. He didn't answer, too absorbed in whatever he was listening to.

Eventually he gave up and held out the earbuds. I put them in and heard a mariachi band playing on the subway—nasal harmonies, a jaunty accordion, guitar. There was a change in the acoustic as the doors opened, a muffled announcer's voice saying something about the train running express.

—This is my file?

—You remember where you were?

—The C train, I think. Uptown C.

—Oh. I guessed wrong. I thought it was the six.

He looked disappointed.

—You're retracing my walks?

—You heard something, Seth. There might be other things.

—This is what you've been doing? All week?

—Mostly.

—There's nothing on those recordings. I pulled out anything worthwhile.

—So you say. You could have heard things you didn't know you heard.

—You understand how much work we have to do, right? We're on deadline.

—Let me get my laptop. I'll prove it to you.

We sat down and he made me listen to audio that I'd recorded somewhere in Bed-Stuy, an old homeless man shuffling up to me, asking for money. I remembered him. He'd done a sort of lolloping tap dance; he had a comic pitch: *hey man hey brother make a donation to the United Negro Bacon Sandwich Fund.* I heard myself laughing. Then he began to shout at me. You could tell that he was close, right up in my face, snarling *pay me pay me what you owe me motherfucker.*

I remembered the man, but I had no memory of that.

—Who was the guy?

—I have literally zero idea.

The beggar's voice was changing stereo position, as if he or I had been moving around. I could hear my own breathing, labored and uneven, as if I were agitated or making a physical effort, but I wasn't saying anything. A man was shouting at me in the street and I wasn't responding at all.

—You know who that was, right?

Carter sounded as if he expected an answer.

—Some old guy. I have no clue.

I remembered the first part, the amusing part, the shuffling, the pitch.

—Hey man hey brother? You don't hear his voice?

I knew what he meant. The very idea was frightening. But why couldn't I remember the rest? How could my mind have erased something so intense and dramatic?

—Carter. It wasn't the same guy.

—What did he look like?

—This was an old guy, an older guy. I'm telling you it wasn't the same person.

But in spite of myself, I started thinking: Seth, you didn't see his face, you can't remember his face. There was something avaricious in Carter's eyes. It was as if he thought I was deliberately keeping some nugget from him, a piece of valuable information.

—So what about our Vanilla Ice tune?

The way he changed the subject felt tactical. He was throwing me a bone.

—Come on, Carter.

—What? You've been working to meet the important deadline for MC Snowy Snow. Let's hear it.

—Don't call him that. Don't mock him while we're working with him.

—Fuck does it matter when I mock him? Let's hear it.

We sat on swivel chairs in the control room. The lyrics chugged nicely along over the big band syncopation. It worked. Carter asked why I'd kept the bass so far to the front. It sounded too modern. He wanted to hear more of the clarinet, that would be more authentic. I agreed enthusiastically with all his suggestions, pleased he was giving input. I wanted to be less worried than I was. I wanted him to be thinking about something other than a man playing chess in Washington Square.

After we'd played the demo a couple of times, he got up from the desk and collected his things. He had stuff to do, he told me. He would see me back at the loft. When we opened the door to the street, I was surprised to find it was dark outside. That wasn't so unusual—we often lost track of time in the studio—but just then it seemed ominous. I needed to feel rooted, to remember things instead of forgetting them. We stood for a while, smoking and breathing in the humid air, until Carter's car pulled up. As he got in, I caught sight of his expression, an external blankness that wasn't passivity or peace or even simple tiredness. It was like a lid on a boiling pan, masking some spirit-consuming interior battle.

I ran back inside, grabbed the bag that held my recording equipment, set the alarm and quickly wheeled out my bike. I locked the door and waited impatiently for the beeps to end. Then I cycled over the bridge into the city, to Washington Square.

I looked for him through the evening crowds, the people milling around by the fountain and watching punk kids making chalk drawings on the flagstones. A bluegrass duo—a girl with a nose ring who played upright bass and sang, a mullet-haired guitarist—was busking under the arch. He was not watching them. On one of the benches near the dog run, a well-dressed man rocked backwards and forwards, shouting anguished obscenities to himself. I found Carter by the chess tables, talking to the hustlers. I chose not to approach him. I wanted to eavesdrop, to hear how he spoke when he thought I wasn't there. I'd brought a small parabolic, a professionally made handheld device, much less cumbersome than my old hacked satellite dish. I hovered around, far enough away to be discreet, which was easy enough in the darkness. In this way I picked up snatches of his conversation. He was throwing twenties at people, asking if they knew a singer. A chess player who could sing.

—I can sing. Sing anything you want. Show me the money.

—No, this is a particular guy.

—I told you, Imma sing for you. Want to hear me sing?

Two informants. A third.

—Dark skin. Maybe a gold tooth.

—Sure I know the dude. Bring him right to you.

They took the money. None of them came back. Carter waited, shifting from one foot to another and playing with his hair. Even from a distance you could tell he was on edge. He looked like he was trying to score drugs. This neediness worried me. I'd never seen him like that. He was someone who was careful only to want things, never to need them. To me, he looked like he was unraveling. I didn't know what to do, who to tell. What, in fact, was there to tell? I wanted to go to him, but I didn't dare show myself, because then he would know that I'd been spying on him. In the end, I left him there. I waited up at home, watching TV in the living area, but he didn't come back that night.

For the next few days, I worked on a second rough for the hip hop star. I was using one of our rarest breaks, an obscure record from a short-lived Philadelphia label that had cost Carter a pile of money back when he was still interested in the seventies. By some miracle it hadn't been reissued, so for the moment it retained its value. I was chopping it up with a guitar sample from an equally rare Afrobeat cassette. The work was absorbing, but it wasn't enough to keep me from my thoughts: Leonie, Washington Square, things I had forgotten, buried things that I ought to remember but couldn't bring to mind. One night, just after I'd gone to bed, Carter called me from the studio and told me he had something I needed to hear. I was overjoyed that he was working, but also nervous. It was 4 a.m. He sounded more than usually amped up. I hauled myself out of bed and cycled over.

The first thing he told me after he unbolted the door was that I should prepare to cry. He'd cried. He'd been crying for two hours straight. He told me just to sit and listen—I wouldn't be the same after. He turned to the desk, and through the studio speakers came the sound of a New York street. Traffic, the sound of footsteps. My footsteps. I quickly recognized Tompkins Square in the East Village. I could hear barking from the dog run, skaters panhandling by the benches. He turned up the volume. I heard myself walk past the skaters into a sort of aural dead zone. The street noise faded, the dogs too. The only significant signal was the sound of a guitar, someone fingerpicking in a weird open tuning that made the instrument seem to wail and moan. It was mesmerizing, the performance of a musician struggling with inexpressible pain and loss. The recording was completely clear, unmarred by voices or traffic. I must have been standing directly in front of the guitarist for several minutes.

And yet I couldn't bring to mind his face, or even picture the scene.

—Now, said Carter. Listen to this.

He leaned over the desk and pushed a fader. Suddenly the chess player's vocal was laid over the guitar.

> Believe I buy a graveyard of my own
> Believe I buy me a graveyard of my own
> Put my enemies all down in the ground
>
> Put me under a man they call Captain Jack
> Put me under a man they call Captain Jack
> Wrote his name all down my back
>
> Went to the Captain with my hat in my hand
> Went to the Captain with my hat in my hand
> Said Captain have mercy on a long time man
>
> Well he look at me and he spit on the ground
> He look at me and he spit on the ground
> Says I'll have mercy when I drive you down
>
> Don't get mad at me woman if I kicks in my sleep
> Don't get mad at me woman if I kicks in my sleep
> I may dream things cause your heart to weep

They fit together. In fact they were perfect, as if they were two halves of a single performance.

—What do you think of that?

What did I think? I was terrified. I felt dizzy. My hands were cold. If before my fears had been vague and inchoate, now they were definite. This was a message. Someone or something was addressing us.

—It's like—I don't know what to say. I don't like it.

—But it sounds real, right?

—Yes. It sounds real.

—So go do your magic.

—What magic?

—Seth at the controls.

—No Carter.

—What are you talking about?

—I can't. Not on this. I don't want to work on this.

—Why not?

—What do you want me to do, anyway? Clean it up? It's pretty clean already.

—No! Make it dirty. Drown it in hiss. I want it to sound like a record that's been sitting under someone's porch for fifty years.

He wanted me to do it and I couldn't think of any reason to refuse, except that it scared me, and that didn't seem good enough. I tried to tell him how I felt. I begged, but it was as if he couldn't hear me. He kept on bullying me until finally, exhausted by his hectoring, I got to work. I played it out through a tinny little speaker salvaged from an old transistor radio, re-recorded it and buried it in crackle. By the time I'd finished, it sounded like a worn 78, the kind of recording that only exists in one poor copy, a thread on which time and memory hang.

Carter was ecstatic. He played it again and again.

—It's perfect, he kept saying. It's is the greatest thing we've ever done.

Slip, drop it, and that memory lies in pieces. Smashed, unrecoverable.

I DIDN'T KNOW Carter had put it on the internet, until he came into the control room and thrust a laptop in front of me. On the screen was a page from a file-sharing site, all penis enlargement ads and animations of girls taking off their tops.

KG 25806 Charlie Shaw Graveyard Blues
Type: Audio > Music
Files: 1
Size: 3.1 MiB (3250585 Bytes)
Tag(s): 78rpm blues oldtime

Uploaded: 20—- 07-01 18:32:41 EST
By: Anan51

Seeders: 12
Leechers: 67
Comments: 27

Info Hash: 699D60E19FBA114E24798C15A588B44687559D0D

Above it was a scan of an authentic-looking label, scuffed and faded, informing me that the song was vocal with guitar accompaniment and the disk had been "electrically recorded in the USA." The words "Key & Gate" appeared above an image of a pair of ornamental iron gates, half-open, with a key hovering above them like a UFO.

—What's this?

—Look at how many seeds.

—But what is it?

—It's our tune. The chess player's blues. I made a label and everything.

—Right. I see that. Who's Charlie Shaw?

—Just a name I made up.

—What the fuck, Carter. What are you doing?

—It just came to me. Looks authentic, right? I posted it to a couple blues sites too. Check out the comments. They're losing their minds.

Sure enough, in the tiny confines of the prewar blues internet, it was like someone had dropped a bomb.

Hidden gem!!!

What about the b-side

bw?

bw?

thanks op u rock

WHO POSTED THIS I HAVE TO KNOW

There were even offers to buy the record, sight unseen. One poster mentioned five thousand dollars. There were inquiries from Germany, Australia, a badly spelled one from Japan.

—Why would you do this?

—They believe in it. Isn't that amazing? We made that and they believe it's real.

—Is this really a wise idea?

—What do you mean? It's the best idea! These fuckers think this music was made in 1928, but actually we made it. We made it, fools! We made that shit last week! So who's the expert now? Who knows the tradition? We do! We own that shit!

Carter was so exultant that I began to get a contact high. Together we looked at the feverish discussion on the comment boards. It was amazing. No one had the slightest sense that it wasn't a genuine recording. Not only that, but it was being hailed as a masterpiece. Words like *feeling, artistry, classic* were being used. Several collectors were trying to get in touch with *Anansi*, the account Carter had used to upload the file. One message caught my attention. The guy—had to be a guy—sounded like a lunatic, wrote in all caps:

> JumpJim at 20—- 07-01 20:11 EST:
> WHO SOLD THIS TO YOU DO YOU KNOW WHAT YOU HAVE
> DO YOU YOU MUST CONTACT ME !!! IMMEDIATELY!!! VERY
> IMPORTANT INFORMATION WE HAVE TO TALK

—Who's that?

—I don't know. Some retard. Dude's posted the same stuff everywhere I uploaded the song. Every single thread. He's obsessed.

—What does he actually want?

—How should I know?

He smiled.

—Why don't you ask him?

—Me?

I tapped out a question.

> EVP_Seth at 20—- 07-02 22:32 EST:
> what u want JumpJim?

He came back almost at once.

> JumpJim at 20—- 07-02 22:34 EST:
> WHO ARE YOU

EVP_Seth at 20—- 07-02 22:35 EST:
my record

JumpJim at 20—- 07-02 22:35 EST:
WHERE DID YOU GET IT

EVP_Seth at 20—- 07-02 22:36 EST:
thriftstore pls turn off all caps = shouting

JumpJim at 20—- 07-02 22:36 EST:
SOrry where?

EVP_Seth at 20—- 07-02 22:36 EST:
nyc ftw

JumpJim at 20—- 07-02 22:37 EST:
bullshit I live east side nothing worthwhile in those places
since 1950s

EVP_Seth at 20—- 07-02 22:37 EST:
ORLY

JumpJim at 20—- 07-02 22:38 EST:
?

JumpJim at 20—- 07-02 22:39 EST:
dont understand

Carter nudged me away from the keyboard.

EVP_Seth at 20—- 07-02 22:41 EST:
ur such a loser

EVP_Seth at 20—- 07-02 22:41 EST:
such a lil bitch u been pwnd

JumpJim at 20—- 07-02 22:42 EST:
dont understand

Carter started messing with him, claiming to be offended, issuing ridiculous rap-battle threats. It was dumb, but funny. I began to offer suggestions.

—Tell him we're going to find him, fuck him in the ass.

After a few posts JumpJim went offline. I thought we'd frightened him away, but when I checked out the thread the next day, he'd been leaving conciliatory messages. He must have been old. It wasn't so much that he didn't understand half of what we said or the weird mention of thrift store record shopping in the fifties, which had to be bullshit. He just sounded cranky, irritated by having to type his questions, like an old man who has given up trying to understand new things. I almost felt sorry for him. We'd been saying nasty stuff, how we were going to rip his head off, pull his tongue out a hole in his throat. We probably went over the top. I posted once more, just in case.

> EVP_Seth at 20—- 07-03 23:11 EST:
> you still there JumpJim?

I made coffee. When I came back and refreshed the thread, he was online.

> JumpJim at 20—- 07-03 23:18 EST:
> please don't want to do this on the computer much better
> talk like human beings

> EVP_Seth at 20—- 07-03 23:19 EST:
> what about? you want to buy the record

> JumpJim at 20—- 07-03 23:20 EST:
> you selling. how much?

> EVP_Seth at 20—- 07-03 23:20 EST:
> $$$ its rare I want $50k for it.

> JumpJim at 20—- 07-03 23:21 EST:
> maybe someone will give you that not me though

> EVP_Seth at 20—- 07-03 23:22 EST:
> so why are we talking

> JumpJim at 20—- 07-03 23:23 EST:
> what do you know about Charlie Shaw

> EVP_Seth at 20—- 07-03 23.23 EST.
> not much

> JumpJim at 20—- 07-03 23:24 EST:
> you got other KG 25 series

This foxed me. I called in Carter and he took over the account, diving into a conversation about catalog numbers, session dates, the various qualities of Vocalion, Electrobeam Gennett and Victor pressings, how Paramount cuts got clearer as the tracks went on, that kind of thing. Collectors are like dogs. They have to sniff each other's scent, establish bona fides.

> JumpJim at 20—- 07-04 00:04 EST:
> ok so you are not total amateur

> EVP_Seth at 20—- 07-04 00:05 EST:
> true

> JumpJim at 20—- 07-04 00:06 EST
> ? does it say SJH anywhere on the label anything else

—Carter?

—No idea.

—But he seems convinced by the label.

—I don't know why. I just found an image on the net and Photoshopped it.

—Really? I didn't know you knew how to do that.

—I'm not a moron. Say something or he'll get bored and go offline. Answer his question.

EVP_Seth at 20—- 07-04 00:07 EST:
   No SJH or anything just serial number keep saying

JumpJim at 20—- 07-04 00:07 EST:
   b/w

JumpJim at 20—- 07-04 00:08 EST:
   WHAT'S ON THE OTHER SIDE

That, neither of us could answer. Carter shrugged.
—It's kind of an obvious question, I suppose.
—Should I make it up?
—Give me a moment.
We stalled.

EVP_Seth at 20—- 07-04 00:09 EST:
   Do you know what's on other side?

JumpJim at 20—- 07-04 00:10 EST:
   Your record you tell me.

That was stalemate.
—I'm too stoned to think of anything. Tell him we'll meet him.
—Really?
—Why not?
—Well, you know. The internet. We don't know anything about
him.
—What's he going to do to us? Maybe he'll have records to sell.
He seems to know a lot about Paramount pressings. I'd pay good
money for high-numbered Paramounts, better than he knows.

EVP_Seth at 20—- 07-04 00:11 EST:
   Let's talk

JumpJim at 20—- 07-04 00:11 EST:
   Great. Will you bring record

I couldn't exactly refuse, so I just lied.

> EVP_Seth at 20—- 07-04 00:11 EST:
> OK

He named an Irish bar on 14th Street, almost at the East River, a spot I'd never heard of. Streetview showed a windowless joint wedged between a dry cleaner and a dollar store, the kind of place you could walk past twenty times and still miss. He wanted to meet there at eight-thirty in the morning. What kind of bar was open before nine in the morning? We told him that was too early. He wanted a morning meeting. He was very insistent. We settled on ten.

> JumpJim at 20—- 07-04 00:12 EST:
> Deal. Now I will tell you something. Before you posted that song, I had not heard Charlie Shaw since 1959.

I showed the screen to Carter, who made crazy person circles with his finger against his temple.

▼

AT NINE THE NEXT MORNING I was showered, dressed and working my way through a cafetière of strong coffee, trying to stop checking the time on my phone. Carter still hadn't come home. Even though he couldn't be bothered to make the meeting, I knew he'd be angry if I missed it, because it was a collecting connection and—as he often reminded me—there weren't so many people who were in it at his level. Maybe fifty worldwide, was his estimate. I don't know if that was boasting. He said you couldn't be choosy about who you dealt with. People didn't put together serious collections by being nice and well adjusted. So I felt obliged to go. I sent him a final where-are-you text and got on my bike.

It was already hot. I pumped up onto the bridge, standing up on the pedals and telling myself I had options, promising myself that I wouldn't get drawn in to anything. Then I freewheeled down into the smell of gasoline and uncollected garbage. Delancey Street in summer: light particulates, the tar spongy at the cross-walks. I turned north and rode through the projects towards the white chimneys of the power station. Locking the bike to a street sign on 14th, I chugged some water, toweled off and changed my shirt, which was soaked in sweat. I walked along until I found the doorway between the dry cleaner and the dollar store and stepped down a flight of stairs into darkness and air-conditioning and a long skinny bar lined with alcoholics of various ages and professions, steeling themselves to go outside to smoke.

I was wearing a cap pulled down low over my eyes. My plan was to blend in and watch for a while before I identified myself, in case JumpJim looked threatening or insane. I admit I was curious to see this man who was so convinced by Carter's fiction. Some loser collector, no doubt. They all had that look, that basement-dwelling look. I didn't know what to have so I ordered bourbon. I didn't want a bourbon, it was ten in the morning. The crinkled bills on the counter, the Irish tchotchkes, the bartender's halter top and shitty Chinese character tattoo; the whole place was marinated in sadness. Ten in the fucking morning. You could feel the furred carpet making its way up the legs of your stool, seeking to become one with your ankles.

A candidate came in. Dressed in regular old-guy clothes. Slacks, a dress shirt, everything comfort fit. Good thick rubber soles on those sneakers, sir. Good grip. I started the recorder in my pocket, assuming this was him, but he took a stool and started talking to the bartender in Russian and I got bored and looked down the row into the dark colon of the bar only to realize that the guy, the real guy, had been there all along, watching me from a booth. Shock of white hair, thick black eyeglasses that scanned as fashion until you checked the raincoat with the grubby collar, the unpleasant-looking scab on his forehead. Exactly who I did not want to meet. Very slowly, he raised an index finger and pointed to me, a gesture like firing a gun. Carefully positioning a coaster on top of his drink, he eased himself off the vinyl bench and hobbled my way.

I need a cigarette, he said, and crooked that long nicotine-yellow finger. *Follow.* How old was he? Eighty? Older? He looked embalmed. I got off my stool and we went upstairs. We stood there on the street watching the traffic, me sweating in the heat, him wrapped up in his long coat like a man expecting bad weather, a man prepared for the worst. Certain other peculiarities of dress: hiking sandals over some kind of orthotic socks, polaroid lenses on the glasses. In the July sunlight it was like two security gates dropping down, twin black screens. He procured a tin from his coat pocket, rolled and lit a cigarette. Then he came right up to me, toe-to-toe like a boxer, and jabbed the cigarette at my face, holding it between thumb and forefinger and using it as a pointer. You, he said.

I took a step back. He took one forward.

—I don't see any record.

It seemed the cigarette had played its part. He flicked it at a passing dog walker ("fuckin' yuppies") and headed back inside. I followed. I didn't know what else to do. The carpet in his booth was sticky underfoot. He pointedly emptied the slush from his glass, his hands trembling.

—Why don't you get us two more of these? Then we can talk about why you didn't bring the record.

—I'm not sure this place takes cards.

—Young man, I am wrestling with my disappointment.

—Take my drink. I haven't touched it.

—The hell I will.

Chastened, I went to the bar and bought him a whiskey. He flexed his hands and cracked his knuckles as I returned to the booth.

—That is more like it. And you are?

I didn't want to give my real name.

—Dan Smith.

—I just can't believe you didn't bring the record, Dan Smith. It is a blow, I don't mind saying. It shakes my confidence in you.

—Well, what about my confidence in you?

—Don't you worry about that. I'm kosher. Genuine certified.

—You haven't brought any records with you either.

—Whenever did I say I'd bring records? To a bar, are you out of your mind? Think of the environmental hazards. The stuff they use to clean these tables is highly alkaline. Put a disk down and straightaway that'd be the surface gone.

I switched on the recorder in my pocket.

—So you must have a great collection, right?

—Slow down, jitterbug. We'll get to what I've got and what I've not in due time. I'm more concerned with what you got. You do have a copy, correct? KG 25806, Charlie Shaw, "Graveyard Blues."

You must have, unless you're not the one who put it out there. You *are* the one with whom I've been conversating?

—Yes. I am.

—Good. And you know what you have?

—Sure.

—Sure is not what I would call an encouraging word, son. Sure is not what you should be, because right now you are out on a limb.

—I have no idea what you're talking about.

—And that's not so good either. Not that I can solve anything. I make no claims for myself. You only have to look at me to know I'm not a powerful person.

He appraised me again from behind his smudged lenses.

—Oh, I see now. I see how it is. *Fuck*. He made the word into a long lizardy croak. You actually have no goddamn clue. That—He trailed away into a sigh, rubbed his palms wearily over his face. That is really not encouraging. The name Bly mean anything to you at all?

—No.

—Chester Bly?

—No.

—And you're supposed to be a goddamn collector?

—Well, to be honest, there's two of us. There were two of us online.

—And you're the other one.

—That's right.

—You're shitting me.

He banged the table with his fist, suddenly furious.

—So why the fuck am I talking to the other one? Jesus Christ, what a mess. What a goddamn mess!

—Hey, calm down. I don't know, OK? I don't even know why I'm here. Look, I'm sorry I wasted your time.

I got up to leave. I really did want to leave. He didn't have anything for Carter and I needed to be outside in the open air, under the sun.

—Hold on!

He spread his hands, and for a fleeting moment I saw a tell. Of what, I wasn't sure. Something about those trembling, beseeching hands.

—Please. Take a seat. I believe you. You represent whoever you represent. I'm not here to pry into your business. If you've got the record, you'll know what I'm talking about. I'm not a powerful man. I was just a kid who liked to listen to old music.

—Honestly, I've got to go. I'm meeting someone.

—Look, I'm not involved, and I don't want to be. In fact, I'm not a collector at all anymore. Not the kind of collector who would want that record. But I do have questions. I'm curious. Surely that's forgivable.

—Come on. You want the record.

—Oh no. I'd never want to own that record. No thank you. All I'm asking is that you sit down and tell me about it. Just for five minutes. Tell me where you got it. I won't ask anything personal. I won't pry into areas that aren't my concern. Look, you didn't even drink your drink. I'll get you another. Something different, perhaps? Lyuba's piña coladas are famous.

All I wanted was to leave. I knew Carter would press for his joke to go on as long as possible, to run through as many losers and suckers as it could, but I didn't have the heart for it. There seemed no point, nothing to be gained. What fun was there in messing with a semi-homeless old man?

—Look, sir. I'm sorry to say this, but you made a mistake. It's all a joke. A hoax. Whatever record you heard back in the day, this wasn't it, because my partner and I—we put it together literally last week. It's just field recordings and some surface noise. That's all. I'm sorry, but you wasted your time.

His pleading expression became a snarl.

—Stop lying to me! I'm trying to help you out here. It's obvious you know nothing, less than nothing. What is in play here is highly, and I mean *highly*, complex. You may think you're still moving forward, right now. You may feel safe.

—I'm sorry. We made it up, the whole thing.

—You're a bad liar. You're already slipping, you don't even know it.

—Look, I'm going to go now, but just in case—do you own and if so do you wish to sell any high-numbered Paramounts?

—Why?

—My friend wants to buy 12900 and up. He'll pay for anything in good condition. That's the only reason I came.

—This being your partner, the one who is a real collector but sadly can't be here with us today? Does your collector friend mean good as in generically good or specifically good as in G condition or higher on the VJM scale?

—I have no idea.

—Tell him I have what he wants, many E, even E+. A few unplayed. Not a complete run but near as makes no difference. Tell him 13099, Willie Brown, "Window Blues" and "Kicking In My Sleep Blues." That'll get his attention.

—So you have records.

—I have records. Repeat it. I want to check you have it correctly.

—Willie Brown, "Window Blues."

—13099, Willie Brown, "Window Blues" and "Kicking In My Sleep Blues"

—13099, Willie Brown, "Window Blues" and "Kicking In My Sleep Blues"

—But he has to come in person. And he has to bring the Charlie Shaw record.

—Come where?

—Here. If I'm not around, Lyuba will know where to find me.

I left him in his booth and half-ran up the stairs, back out into the light.

▼

IT WAS IMPOSSIBLE to get Carter to listen. I tried to describe it, the bar full of sad morning drinkers, the smudged fingerprints on the man's filthy eyeglasses, but the only thing he seemed able to hear was thirteen thousand ninety-nine Willie Brown. Did the guy really say thirteen thousand ninety-nine? Yes he did. Definitely that serial number. Yes, I could prove it. I'd been recording. He wanted to hear the whole conversation, spinning round impatiently on the control room chair as I scrolled through, looking for the file. I must have screwed up, because all I had was some audio I'd made a few days earlier, out in Queens, walking through one of the cemeteries in Ridgewood. I was angry at myself for making a mistake. I was usually very careful.

When I told him I had accidentally deleted the file, Carter had a tantrum. He threw a pair of headphones at me, then went into the live room and started kicking over the mic stands. I could see him shouting on the other side of the glass, his snarling face in dumb-show. I wondered what he'd taken. The pupils of his eyes were like saucers. I pushed the button on the control room talkback, so I could hear.

—Do you even know about that record? Paramount thirteen thousand ninety-nine. You asshole! No one has that record! There are no known copies!

I muted him. The same avaricious expression on his face. The collector asking about Charlie Shaw. The same beseeching hands. He spent a long time in the live room, much of it lying on the floor, one arm flung over his face as if he were exhausted or in physical distress. Later, after he'd calmed down, we started drinking. We took a bottle of vodka out of the freezer and ordered chips and soda from a bodega. It was an old routine, one of the ways we reconnected when things were going wrong. Dogged consumption of alcohol. One of us always said something, eventually. One of us always broke and began to talk.

—You don't understand what that record means. If I had that record, people would deal with me. I would count for something. These fuckers are tribal, man. You offer them good money, even ridiculous money, and some of them still won't sell to you. It's like you have to *deserve* the music, some shit like that. They're all old too, the big ones. Old white dudes. No one who wasn't already doing it years ago can get a foot in the door. Tell me, what else has the guy got? Did he mention any other names?

—Bro, come on. He hasn't got your Willie Brown record. He hasn't got anything. He's just an old man who lives on his own in a room that probably smells of piss and cat food. He's just trying to get you to go see him.

—Why?

—How the fuck should I know? Because you're a baby millionaire and you have money coming out your ass?

—Don't talk like that.

—He's just trying to get mixed up in your shit.

—It doesn't mean he doesn't have records. You'd be surprised who has records.

—If it's not about money, then he wants to hear the great lost Charlie Shaw, who—just as a reminder—doesn't exist. He already thinks we're holding out on him. He thinks he heard it before, but obviously he must have heard something else.

—Here's how it works. He thinks we've got something he wants. That's leverage. I can at least get in there and hear what he's got. If he has mint condition thirteen thousand Paramounts he could easily be sitting on other stuff. Did he say Gennett to you? Vocalion? Black Patti?

—You are obsessed.

I started getting ready for bed and he went into his room, leaving the door half-open. From the record deck, crackle and hiss. A strident voice singing about *That bad man, Stagolee*. Later, I saw him counting money on the bed. Thousands of dollars, stacks of twenties and fifties zigzagging across the covers. Willie Brown, he said as I went past in my dressing gown. Thirteen thousand ninety-nine. And he gave me the thumbs-up.

Willie Brown, Charlie Shaw. What kind of names were those? Ten thousand dollars. Fifty thousand dollars. No-names. Scottish or English or Irish. Common and blank. Names that didn't match the voices looming up out of Carter's records, testifying through the static.

Early the next morning, still mostly asleep, I went to the bathroom. Carter's door was open. The bed hadn't been slept in. I didn't know what time it was. A gray hour just before dawn. It wasn't anything out of the ordinary.

▼

MY PHONE SAYS 4:47 A.M. People have been muttering on the other
side of silence, just out of range. Leonie's name on the screen. It's
hard to make out what she is saying. She's sobbing, taking great
gulps of air. Half-asleep, I find myself drifting, wondering how she
got my number, feeling pleased she has it, the thrill of speaking to
her overriding what she's actually saying. That something has happened to Carter. Something very bad.

—Where did you say he was?

—The Bronx, the Bronx, why don't you listen?

—What was he doing in the Bronx?

—How the hell should I know? They took him out of his car and
beat him up.

—I don't understand. He got carjacked?

—He won't wake up. He's unconscious, Seth, I'm not in the city.
I'm in Montauk. You've got to go there for me.

She gives me the name of the hospital, or a version of it. I tell her
I'm on my way.

A driver, speaking to some friend or family member in French
creole, punching buttons on the radio, hopping from Naija pop to
light classics to some ranting religious phone-in show. The street-
lights are faint and watery against the lightening sky. I have a terrible feeling that I've missed something, that I ought to know more
than I do. Distracted by his conversation, the driver leaves the dial

between stations, and I ride uptown bathed in static that soon gives birth to all the other things, the whistles and moans and urgent whispering. If Marconi was right and certain phenomena persist through time, then secrets are being told continuously at the edge of perception. All secrets, always being told.

By the time I get to the hospital, a grim brick slab in the South Bronx, the sun is up. The scene in the ER is chaos, and it's hard to make myself understood. They keep saying they don't have Carter as a patient. I insist, until the nurse at the desk tells me that if I keep bothering her she'll call security. Finally I phone Leonie, who takes a long time to answer. Her voice is slow and thick. I wonder if she's sedated. They moved him, she tells me. New York Presbyterian. He's in surgery. You should have called me, I say, making my voice gentle, hiding my anger. She does not apologize. I ask if I should go to New York Presbyterian. Sure, she says. He'd like that. Then she hangs up.

I have to wait thirty minutes for a car, then some drunk takes me back downtown in a rattling old Crown Victoria that smells of vomit. By the time I get there the sun is over the horizon and when I phone Leonie from the hospital lobby, it goes to voicemail. The receptionist isn't supposed to give out any information, but I beg and she takes pity on me, pity on the state I'm in. She can't tell me much. Carter is alive, but in critical condition. I push. What happened? Did the police say what he was doing there? She asks if I'm a journalist. If I'm a journalist, I will have to leave. A representative of the family has told her to be on the lookout for the press. She uses that phrase. *Representative of the family.*

—My advice, go home, get some sleep. If they want you here, they'll let you know.

—Are they here? Is his sister in the building?

—His father and brother, I believe.

I can't get any more out of her. I keep calling Leonie, but she doesn't pick up, so I walk to get coffee, then hang around the lobby. The receptionist gives me the evil eye, whispering to her colleague. Finally Corny comes out of the elevator, talking on his phone. He is not happy to see me.

—What are you doing here?

—How is Carter? Is he OK?

—Look, I don't have time to go into the details of his condition with you, Damien. It's Damien, right? Just hold yourself available. The police will want to ask you some questions.

—The police?

—My brother was taken from his car and attacked. He has severe head injuries. Right now he's having pieces of his skull removed from his brain. I would say there's a reason for the police to be involved, wouldn't you? Now, could you please step aside? I need to take this call.

—What's your problem, Cornelius? Can't you just talk to me for a minute? I'm as worried about him as you are.

—You seem to have a very high opinion of yourself. Of your importance in the scheme of things.

He bustles out of the building, ignoring the receptionist, who is jabbing a finger at a large "no cellphones" sign on the wall. I'm left reeling from his hostility, from the disorientating thought of Carter lying under a green cloth with surgeons peering into his skull. I am a participant in this, I want to tell him. He's my best friend. This is my story too. Out on the street, it seems impossible. People are going about their business, shopping, heading to work, while Carter is up there in an operating theater, on the verge of death. *This is my story too.* I would shout it out loud, but no one would listen.

▼

HE MUST HAVE STOPPED AT A LIGHT. Maybe someone flagged him down. They pulled him out of his car and beat him unconscious. The police had a witness, a woman. Two, possibly three assailants. She wasn't sure. They had hammers and a baseball bat. Afterwards they got into his car and drove away, leaving him there, spread-eagled on the ground in the middle of the intersection.

Unexpectedly, Leonie hugged me. My body went rigid under her touch. Her hair smelled of cigarette smoke and burned plastic. She was swathed in a black shawl, like a Spanish widow. She looked exhausted. We sat down at a filthy Formica table in a sandwich shop near the hospital, jostled by impatient office workers as they stood in line to pay for lunch. I was eye level with some woman's oversized bag, which grazed my face every time she turned to talk to her friend. Leonie's skin had broken out round her mouth. She had a raw, uncared-for look.

—Have you seen him?

—He's out of surgery. They have him in the ICU.

Hunts Point. I'd never even been to Hunts Point. I barely knew where it was. Why would Carter drive all the way out there? Leonie spoke so softly that it was hard to hear her over the soundtrack of the lunchtime rush, top forty radio on little blown-out speakers. I had to strain to catch her voice, though she was only two feet away.

—She's a hooker, the witness. The cops think that's what he was doing, looking for sex.

—You're joking.

—I know you're, like, his sheltered friend, but you have to see how it looks. Why else would he be in Hunts Point? That's, like, beyond the hood. He wouldn't be stupid enough to try to score on the street up there. You guys have a number, right? A guy who delivers?

—He was going out to buy records. He had a lot of cash.

—There's some twenty-four-hour record store in Hunts Point?

—From a guy, a collector. But he doesn't live up there. He's in the East Village.

—How much cash?

—I don't know. Corny wrote him a check at his party for fifty thousand dollars.

—Corny did that? You're sure? As much as that?

—Carter told him it was an investment in the studio.

—What was he thinking?

—I'm not sure I follow.

—Tell me the truth, Seth. I won't bite your head off. Believe me, you'd be surprised who uses hookers.

—What truth?

—Is this something the two of you do together, drive up to the Point and bang crack whores? Is it, I don't know, part of Carter's black thing?

—His what?

—You know what I'm talking about.

—He isn't some degenerate.

—Yes he is. Just be honest with me. Do you get up to this ghetto shit with him?

—Of course not. I swear.

Leonie, asking me that question. I felt nauseous. I couldn't hear properly. That was the problem. I couldn't hear.

—Can we please go outside?

She looked up at the people in line, porting their plastic clam-shells of salad. A man was calling out his sandwich order over the distortion. Pastrami, he was shouting. On a croissant. Leonie picked up her bag and we left.

I was relieved to be out on the street.

—I want to see him.

—It's family only, for now, Seth. You understand. I ought to go.

I still felt sick.

—Hold on. How do I get news? No one else will tell me what's going on.

—You can call me. Or I'll call you.

She walked away from me down the street. A ghost in jeans shorts and a black mantilla. Lost in the dirty white light.

▼

TOXIC 14TH STREET. Gum melted into the sidewalk at the crossings, volatile hydrocarbons lacing the air. I don't know what else I can do. There's no other move I can make to help Carter, so I'm shouldering open the door of the bar and stepping down into the darkness, down where the damned sip their drinks and watch cable sports. The air conditioner rattles, an insect buzzing that almost drowns the commentary. Was Carter here last night? Did he sit at the bar or in one of the booths? Did his eyes take time to get accustomed to the low light? I squint to pick up a trace of him, some sign on the worn linoleum floor, reflected in the glazing of the framed fight cards.

—You must know the guy. I was in here with him. Old guy. He said you mix a good piña colada.

The bartender looks at me balefully and pours a shot of rum over ice, topping it off with something yellow out of a can. Around me are people from the Reagan era, warehoused in sweat pants and sneakers, wreathed in cigarette smoke, drinking themselves to death. I peer into the darkness. The TV is showing a fight. *Hagler's now shaking those right hands off, Al. He was stunned a little earlier and he's normally a slow starter.* I can't see the collector anywhere. I decide to wait. It's what everyone else is doing.

What will I do if he comes? How can I confront him? What

would I even say? I sit through the afternoon, but nothing gets clearer. I keep ordering Lyuba's piña coladas. After the first couple, they aren't bad.

He doesn't come.

Back outside on the street it's dark, but the heat hasn't gone out of the air. I wait to cross, a little unsteady, staring down at the black lesions baked into the concrete skin.

▼

MY MIND WAS A JUMBLE. Something bitter and mucoid lay at the back of my throat. The next thing I really remember was being in bed, trying to sleep. My phone was buzzing next to my pillow.

Leonie sounded jumpy, wired. I'm outside, she said. In a cab. Can I come up?

I pulled on shorts and a shirt, buzzed her in. I watched in a sort of trance as she threw down her bag and flopped on the sofa. It was—I checked—two in the morning, and Leonie Wallace was in my living room.

—What have you got to drink?

—Is vodka OK? I don't think we have wine or anything.

—Vodka is perfect. Sorry to get you out of bed.

—Has something happened?

—No. No, nothing like that. The surgeon says we just have to wait. I just, you know. I could have taken a pill, but I didn't feel like taking a pill. Not right now.

I went to get ice and soda water and we sat, listening to the tiny clink of the cubes in our glasses. She was wearing the same clothes. Though the air-conditioning was making little impact on the humid air in the room, she kept the shawl wrapped tightly around her shoulders. My head felt terrible. I noticed that she was spattered with dark gray paint, tiny flecks on her clothes, her face, her bare legs.

—What have you been painting?

—The studio floor.

She saw the look I was giving her.

—Why not? You have a better fucking idea?

She lit a cigarette and breathed deeply, her tension producing a perceptible body tremor as she exhaled. Still and in continuous agitated motion.

—Did you see Carter?

She didn't know how to answer that question.

—Yes.

—How is he?

—Not so good.

I waited for more. She lit another cigarette, topped up her drink. She fished about in her bag for gum, leaving the cigarette burning on the edge of the coffee table. Then she began to cry, wedged into a corner of the sofa, hugging her knees. After a while her strength gave out and she slumped sideways against me. I transferred the cigarette to an ashtray, and awkwardly held her, smelling the smoke in her hair, feeling her back quiver as she cried, uncomfortably aware of her bra strap under my palm.

After a while she sat up.

—Can I see his room?

So we went in to Carter's room and climbed up onto his bed, leaning our backs against the big iron frame. Sitting like that we could see ourselves in an old full-length mirror Carter had propped against the wall. The silvering had flaked off, and we were hazy, flecked with gray, a daguerreotype of two people on a bed. Leonie Wallace and an orc. What's all this, she said, indicating Carter's steampunk music setup, the brass and vacuum tubes, the polished walnut box.

—He collects blues records. 78's. You didn't know?

—Like fifties, sixties stuff?

—They were generally releasing 45's by then. I suppose you could say his focus is on the late twenties and early thirties. More or less stopping at 1934. A few things later than that. You could say 1941, to be definitive. Or perhaps 1942. Pearl Harbor.

She looked at me as if I'd spoken to her in binary code. I understand that my precision amuses people. I just don't know how to mitigate it. It takes effort to be vague, to fuzz up your answer so as not to appear threatening or self-absorbed. I was half-asleep. Sometimes you just have to talk how you talk.

For my pains, another difficult silence. She lay down for a while with her face buried in her brother's pillow. I wondered if she was crying again, and debated whether it would be appropriate to touch her, perhaps to stroke her back. At last she rolled over and fumbled in her bag for something or other which she couldn't find. She stared defeatedly at the ceiling.

—OK, I'll bite. Why 1934?

—You don't need to ask me questions. I won't be offended.

—Don't be like that.

—If you actually want to know, it's when the best material was recorded. They introduced electrical recording in the mid-twenties, which made it easier to reproduce quieter sounds. Fingerpicking guitar and so forth. You couldn't record that very well before, when you had to play into a horn. Then most of the companies doing it got wiped out by the Depression. So there was only a small window, really.

—A small window.

—Of time.

—A small window of time. In that case, I suppose you ought to play me something.

I chose Carter's pride and joy, Victor 38535, Tommy Johnson's "Canned Heat Blues," recorded in Memphis in August 1928. I slid it out of its sleeve, feeling the heft of the shellac as I placed it on the turntable and lowered the needle on its counterweighted tone arm. Then I sat down beside Leonie. Johnson's guitar rose up out of the crackle, followed by his strange, lamenting voice.

> *Crying mama mama mama*
> *you know canned heat killing me*

It flipped up into an uncanny falsetto:

canned heat don't—
crying babe I'll never die

The strange high vibration of *I* and *die.* I had listened to that record many times, but it was as if it had never broken my skin. The air was rent open by the sound; darkness poured in. *Babe I'll never die,* he sang. I'd always heard the line as frightened, the alcoholic singer afraid of the death he is swallowing: Sterno brand camping fuel strained through a cloth. But now I heard something else. A veiled threat. If what I've already swallowed doesn't kill me, nothing can. You will never be able to stop me, babe. I'll just keep on coming.

The needle hit the runout groove and I lunged forward, terrified that it would skate. I didn't dare turn my head to look at Leonie. Only when I'd secured the record, sleeved it and returned it to the box did I finally steal a glance. She seemed agitated, angry.

—That's it? That's what he loves?

—I know the sound quality is poor.

—That doesn't help me.

—I'm sorry.

—It's the opposite of helpful.

—I'm sorry, I don't understand.

—Why would he listen to this? It's so morbid. Everything about it is dead and buried.

—I didn't mean to upset you.

She seemed to be making an effort to pull herself together.

—It's not your fault. I'm just upset. Look, you can go back to bed. You must be tired, I got you up. I'll sleep here.

I thought about warning her not to try and play any more records. Carter's deck was temperamental and she was more than a little drunk. But she'd said she hated the music, so I judged that there was little risk of her damaging anything.

—Really, she said. It's OK. Go to bed. I'm just going to crash.

—Do you need a towel?

—Sure.

—I'll just leave it outside your door.

—OK.

Even with the air conditioner on high, the heat that night was oppressive. As I got ready for bed, I was aware of her presence across the hallway, asleep so very close at hand. I got up twice. Bathroom and glass of water. I tossed and turned in a tangle of damp sheets. I kept my door open, in case she called out.

▼

THE NEXT MORNING I got up early, expecting to have the place to myself while I tidied. In the kitchen I found Leonie wandering around in one of Carter's shirts, eating cereal out of the box. I started grinding coffee and washing glasses, keeping busy so I didn't have to endure the full hormonal shock of her. Leonie Wallace, wearing a dress shirt and a pair of black cotton underpants. Leonie Wallace's legs. Either she was dealing with a hangover or she hadn't been to bed. Either way, she was irritable.

—You said he was going to buy records? So what does he spend on a record? A hundred bucks? Two hundred?

—More. The one I played you last night is worth about four thousand dollars.

—Four thousand dollars for that?

—More, possibly. Maybe a little less. That's what he told me he paid for it. There are forty copies in the world, perhaps not even that many.

—So he could have taken a lot of money with him?

—I guess. He got fifty thousand dollars from Corny as some sort of investment in the studio. He told me he was going to spend it on records.

—Why would he do something so stupid?

—I suppose he doesn't see it that way.

—Not Carter, Cornelius. What was he thinking, trusting Carty to hold on to that amount in cash?

—I don't really understand. It's not like your brother is ever short of money.

She gave me a straight look.

—Actually he's on kind of a tight leash, financially.

—What? Really? It never seems like that.

—Sure, he's got his allowance, he can buy toys.

She saw that I didn't understand.

—Seth, Carter's had a few problems in the past. Maybe you know about that. He doesn't make good decisions. We try to avoid anything which would stress him out.

As I was trying to process this corporate "we," the doorbell rang. The entry phone showed two men on the street outside. Ties and shirtsleeves. One of them held up a badge to the camera.

—Maybe you should put some clothes on. The police are coming up. Go into the bedroom and I'll talk to them while you get dressed.

—Relax, Seth.

—But it's the police. You don't want them to see you like that.

—This isn't Saudi Arabia.

Reluctantly, I buzzed them in. Leonie hopped up on the kitchen counter and struck a centerfold pose, arching one eyebrow sarcastically at me. They stepped out of the elevator, professional intruders. I was in a state of sexual panic, aroused and humiliated. It was too much to bear, the way she made them look at her. One, maybe both men knew who she was. The shorter one, who looked Latino, knew for sure. He didn't take his eyes off her, swiveling left and right, up and down, checking out her ass, her legs, the shape of her breasts under the shirt. Helping himself. The taller one, the white one, was big and doughy, too physically somnolent to really feel her provocation. He turned to me and said blandly that they needed to ask some questions about the attack. Sit down, he said. It'll only take a few minutes. The Latino detective gave way to autoeroticism, compulsively stroking his little French beard. Her point made, Leonie got down from the counter and leaned against the sink, her arms folded, making no further eye contact with him.

—Miss, said the white cop, glancing balefully at his partner. Why don't you finish getting dressed and give us a minute with your friend?

I thought Leonie was going to say something smart. Instead she walked away and shut herself in Carter's room. What could I do but comply? I sat down at the table and answered their questions. The short cop was angry with his partner for embarrassing him, so to compensate he went in hard. Why was Carter at Hunts Point? Did I realize it was a known haunt of prostitutes? A "known haunt of prostitutes," a period phrase, strange out of his mouth. I told them that Carter didn't use prostitutes. I basically told them the truth. They pressed and the short cop raised his voice, maybe for his partner's benefit, maybe for Leonie, hiding in the bedroom. When I told them about the money, they thought they'd made their case. Did I understand there was a possibility that he was targeted because of the cash he was carrying? Who knew about it? Cornelius. Leonie. Who else? I must have mentioned it to someone. I needed to think. Was his understanding correct that we were in the music business? A moment of hesitation. We probably socialized with—he hesitated again, hunting for the delicate term—*hip hop guys.*

How could I tell them what I really thought? The money wasn't the reason it happened. It was bad luck he had it, but whatever happened to Carter had to do with the song, with the three minutes of darkness we had released into the world. That's what I believed, but I had no justification for it, nothing I could put into words. Just my fear, the acid knot in my gut that had persisted for days and would not go away, no matter how much stomach medication I poured on top of it.

—Just to refresh my memory, sir, where were you that night?

—Here.

—All night?

They mentioned phone records, a search of the apartment. I told them I had nothing to hide.

Just then, Leonie appeared in the living area, dressed for the road, carrying her bag.

—I'm going now. You should tell them about the guy, Seth. The record collector guy.

—He's downtown.

—But you said you thought Carter might have gone to see him. The detectives looked concerned.

—He intended to visit someone? Sir, I think you need to be more frank with us.

Leonie left. They made no attempt to stop her. I wondered if they had instructions not to bother Carter's family. Reluctantly, I told them about JumpJim. I said nothing about "Graveyard Blues" or about the fact that I'd met him. I just said that he was a person Carter had met on the internet, that in my opinion he had no records to sell.

—And you think Mr. Wallace may have gone to meet him?

—It's possible.

—You never found out his name?

—I guess not.

—Or where they were going to meet?

—No.

—We're going to need access to his laptop, if he had one. We have his phone. What email system did he use?

They took down details. I told them I couldn't give them his possessions without permission from the family. They weren't happy about it and the Latino detective went into the hall and made a phone call. They left, saying they would be back with paperwork.

As soon as they'd gone, I got on my bike and cycled over the bridge into Manhattan. I don't know if I was tired. Perhaps I made some kind of mistake. I took the same route as I'd taken the previous day. I chained up my bike to the same lamppost. But though I walked that stretch of 14th Street several times, it seemed confusing and unfamiliar. Between the dollar store and the dry cleaner, where the bar ought to have been, was a clinical white space selling frozen yogurt.

▼

THE LANGUAGE. *Blunt force trauma. Bradycardia* and *hypotension. Impairment of neurological function secondary to mechanical impact.* They had surrounded Carter with this language, lowered it over him like a wire cage. Later the police came back with a warrant to search the apartment. By that time I'd collected anything that had to do with drugs and thrown it in a dumpster behind a nearby restaurant. They found the old laptop he used to check and send mail, and took it away in an evidence bag. After a cursory look at the walnut box of records, they left it alone.

Then Leonie texted me. If I wanted to see Carter, I should come by the hospital. She was going over there. She would sneak me in.

It was hard to look at him like that, attached to a ventilator, his hands a mess of tape and plastic vents and drains. His head was tightly wrapped in bandages and the few exposed sections of his face were horribly bruised. Both eyes were closed up, puffed out by fluid. Plugs of blood-soaked cotton stuffed his nose. Something else had happened, some indefinable sliding of his features, as if they'd been smeared, pushed sideways. Sensors were taped to his chest and clipped to his finger to monitor vital signs. The audio output on the machine by the bed was turned up high, presumably so staff could hear alerts when they were outside the room. Inside, the volume was punishing, the thump and squelch of his amplified heart an industrial bassline, some other parameter indicated as a high-pitched pulse, like a car alarm.

I held his cold hand, stained orange by some kind of antiseptic, trying not to cry at the sight of the plastic tags circling his thin wrists. The previous summer, he'd collected festival passes like fluorescent friendship bracelets. I wanted to play music to him but they said I couldn't use my phone, so I sat there, listening to his amplified vital signs, watching paper scroll out of a plotter onto the floor.

—Did they find his car?

Leonie shook her head. She was leaning over the bed, stroking her brother's matted hair.

—I still can't believe what an ape you were. Going up there in that stupid fancy car. Bright red. I mean, Carter, come on. You're supposed to be the streetwise one.

A nurse passed the door and frowned. Visitors were only allowed on that floor by special permission.

Carter wants to trust people, I said.

—That's the trouble. My brother thinks the world is fundamentally a safe place.

The nurse passed the door again, still scowling. You could see she was itching to tell us to leave.

Leonie took out her phone and framed herself in a picture with Carter's bandaged, swollen head. I must have looked surprised because she told me not to freak out, she was on airplane mode, she wasn't going to short-circuit his defibrillator or whatever. The phone made its fake shutter sound. I wondered why she wanted the picture.

—We ought to go, I think my mom and dad are going to stop by.

Too late. We met her parents as they were getting out of the elevator. I recognized her father from photographs, the precise wedge of gray-blond hair, the prognathous jaw. In person, he had a particular quality, not exactly visible, the unbreachable membrane of legal decorum that only politicians or very wealthy men of business possess, the suggestion that everything he did was correct because he did it, that your impertinent questions could not touch him, would in fact only rebound on you. Pictures didn't convey his raw, unwholesome physicality. The skin around his jaw was rough and pocked, as if he'd survived some childhood disease. Above a blunt, heavy nose, a nose like a ship's bridge or a gantry, two pale eyes surveyed me with displeasure.

—Hello Leonie, he said, addressing himself deliberately to his daughter.

—Hello Daddy.

—Who is this?

—This is Seth, Carter's roommate.

—I see.

The children had this man's unholy features sanctified by those of the mother, a birdlike blonde with an air of startled perfection. How do you do, she said, just a trace of a southern accent. A limp hand extended like a sea creature putting out a feeler.

—I'm surprised to find you here, Seth. I'd given instructions to the staff to let only family members see my son.

Up to that point I'd been holding up OK, but, caught by those eyes, I lost my nerve. I became hyper-conscious of my baggy board shorts, the grubby soles of my sockless feet. My right calf began to itch, in a spot where I had a persistent patch of eczema. No obvious response to her statement came to mind.

—It's not the hospital's fault, mother, said Leonie. I snuck him in.

Don Wallace turned his eye on me.

—Why would she do that for you? Who are you to my son?

Why hadn't I put on a pair of shoes instead of going out in flip-flops?

—Sir, he's my best friend. I was—I am worried.

Don Wallace carried on looking at me. I couldn't say he scrutinized me, because that would imply a level of engagement which simply was not there. He just rested his eyes on me as he might on any phenomenon in his visual field—a stone, a spreadsheet. I am often accused of lacking emotional response. In fact I think that what I lack is emotional spontaneity. It takes me a while to release my reaction, for the feeling to bubble up from below. That man was what people think I am. He made me afraid.

—I didn't mean to intrude, I said, instantly disgusted by my cringing tone. I was rolling over, baring my throat.

—And now you've seen him, said the mother, in a tone that suggested I would not be doing so again. A very refined threat. She must have been the prize of whatever town Don Wallace found her in. Miss Magnolia, Cotton Queen. Waving at all the little people in the parade.

Leonie took my arm. I held my breath at her unexpected touch.

—I'm going to walk Seth to the lobby.

We got into the elevator. My calf was on fire and I reached down to scratch. Leonie was visibly upset, chewing a strand of hair and scuffing the sole of her sandal against the floor.

—Stupid me, she muttered. Stupid stupid me.

—Why?

—He's going to get them fired, those nurses.

—Seriously? Your dad can do that?

—I don't know. Probably. He's all about consequences. My mother will make sure he does something.

—I should go back and talk to him. Take responsibility.

—Believe me, that would only make it worse.

I left her in the hospital lobby. Later, she texted me and we got dinner in Chinatown, silently slurping noodles in a place with wobbly plastic tables where the lighting turned everything green and a Cantopop karaoke video played on a screen over our heads. She didn't seem to have anywhere to go. I wanted to say to her, where are your friends? All those people who sit for hours in your apartment? Where is Marc and his billion-dollar tech company? Like the previous night, we ended up back at our place, sitting in Carter's room and listening to records. *I'm leaving baby crying won't make me stay.* We were crying to make him stay, trying to cast a spell with our crying. The records were all sending messages, now I had ears to hear. Crying leaving crying leaving leaving. The hiss and crackle of worn surfaces, the constant chirping of our phones. Ignored alerts, word about Carter getting around.

▼

THE FOLLOWING DAY I took a call.

—Hey Seth, it's Lewis. How have things been?

Fine, I said.

—Look I was so sorry to hear about Carter.

I talked to the guy for a minute, trying to work out who he was. I agreed that it was terrible. I said I hoped the police would find whoever attacked him. I ended the call without ever quite working out who I'd been speaking to.

Just after midnight, Leonie came round again. I'd spent the day cycling along 14th Street, through the East Village, over to Washington Square. I was disturbed. Everything was slightly off. It wasn't as if the city had changed, exactly. Perhaps my memory was at fault. Leonie was in party clothes, all hair and heels and bag. Her hands were a blur of motion as she opened the fridge and made herself a drink. She knew the whole thing had been a mistake, she said. What had she been thinking? Her friends had insisted, but it was such a bad idea. It was hard to follow her train of thought. I gathered that she'd been to an opening.

—The asshole gallerist went to the bathroom and obviously he Googled me. I mean what would it cost him to be nice, to acknowledge my work, the fact that I *make* work, but he comes back and all of a sudden he wants to sell me a picture. He's talking about how legacies get made early and touching my arm and I want to say I sent you slides, remember, only last month, why don't you talk to me about my slides, and then I flash on Carter lying there with a fucking tube in his mouth, tubes all in his arms. He's up there in the ICU and I'm making nice to this asshole for what? For my *career*? How sick of a person am I? Then, well, I just couldn't anymore. I wasn't dramatic. I didn't raise my voice or throw things around. I just told him I thought he was a dick. And still everyone behaved like I took a dump on the floor.

She fought back a sob, swallowed it with a slug of vodka soda. I was bold enough to put my arms around her for a moment, a friend to Leonie Wallace, a confidant. She plucked distractedly at the collar of my shirt and looked up at me with genuine warmth, her eye makeup running in black streaks down her cheeks. For a brief instant we were lit up by romance, like a couple in an old movie.

—Let's go in to his room, she said, a husky note in her voice. We sat down in our usual places on the bed and she told me the news. None of it was good. *Low scores* on the *Glasgow Coma Scale. Elevated intracranial pressure.* I held her again. Her head lay on my chest, her breath moistening the shirt fabric over my collarbone. I could not grasp what was happening. I was holding Leonie with such tenderness. Carter was in a coma.

—I think he's going to die, she said.

She sat up. I tried to compose myself. Then we made more drinks and listened to Carter's records and made more drinks again until she swung her legs down off the bed and sat slumped forward for a moment, her hair falling over her knees like a damp towel on the head of a defeated boxer. The covers were a mess of cracker crumbs and spilled tequila. I checked the records in case there was something I'd forgotten to re-sleeve or return to the box.

—Gotta piss.

She left the door open. I could hear her urine hitting the toilet bowl. It's cliché—the idealistic suitor who can't believe his lady love is a human with a body—but I can't pretend I wasn't shocked. Again I felt the mixture of insult and arousal that came from her physical unselfconsciousness in my presence. I pulled myself off Carter's bed, then took my own turn in the bathroom, with the door shut. When I came out, she was on the phone. I had the feeling that I sometimes had with Carter, a sort of giddy wonder at being around her in conditions of such intimacy.

—I've decided I want to look at it, she said. You're coming with me.

—Coming where?

—Where they attacked him. Hunts Point.

—Why do we need to do that? There's nothing there. If you want to see it I can show it to you on StreetView.

—Are you his friend?

—Of course I'm his friend.

—Then you should want to face it. To look at it, where it happened.

I didn't really grasp her logic, but she seemed determined and I was too drunk to argue. A pattern was emerging in our communication, a kind of premature ease. I was falling into being for her what I had been for Carter, the sister a substitute for the brother. I could tell she was feeling it too, an unearned intimacy. I would follow where she led, that was already understood. Her phone rang.

—Car's downstairs.

We got into the elevator, slumping against the walls as it lurched down.

The driver did not like the idea of going to Hunts Point.

—Why you want? Is no good there.

We gave him a dummy address to put into his GPS, a taquería near the intersection where Carter had been attacked.

—You get food somewhere else, plenty other places.

Leonie leaned into the gap between the front seats and flashed him a smile.

—Come on, man. We aren't going to rob you.

The driver looked angry.

—Maybe you get out my car.

—I got a deal for you. You go off the clock. Just say you rejected the fare. I'll give you two hundred cash to take us up there and just drive around. Two hundred dollars.

—I'm a working man, you know.

—We aren't going to give you any trouble. Look at us.

—I not say anything, but—

He made an "alcohol" sign, putting a thumb up to his mouth and drinking.

—It's cool. We're cool. I know what you're thinking. I see how your mind is working. We won't throw up in your car. Look, I'll pay a hundred up front. OK, I see now I don't actually have cash, but we can stop at an ATM.

—A hundred now.

—Just drive us to an ATM. Then another hundred after. All we want you to do is take us up there, drive us around and take us back again.

—Sure. OK, miss. Sure.

Once the money was in his pocket, we traveled at speed up the FDR, past the UN and the stacked lights of the projects on Roosevelt Island, then slalomed through a tangle of bridges which ejected us into the Bronx, where I had never once been during my years in New York. Manhattan, cross-river patches of Brooklyn and Queens: I had the same reduced geography as all my friends. Hunts Point was entirely off our map. It was as if Carter had chosen it deliberately for its remoteness from our white world, a way to force a confrontation. There is always more to New York. More than you've seen or care to see.

—Sir, is it OK to smoke in your car?

—No.

—Sure. I respect that. That's fine.

Leonie dropped her cigarettes back into her bag.

—I feel like puking anyway. Ask you a question, Seth? Carter had been good lately, right?

—Yeah.

—You know what I mean, don't you? You see him every day.

—Good?

—Chill. Not too hyper.

—He's been kind of preoccupied.

—About what?

—About a song. I don't know if you remember, but he played it to you in the car on the way to Corny's party.

She looked blank.

—He had it on repeat and you switched it off?

—What kind of a song?

—Something we made. A blues. It probably sounded real, but it wasn't.

—What do you mean, it sounded real?

—It honestly doesn't matter. Carter wanted to make something that sounded authentic. That sounded genuinely old.

—I have no idea what you're talking about.

—I think he wanted to show—I don't know any more. It was something that got hold of him. I couldn't understand it.

We came down off the expressway into a bleak streetscape of yards and lockups. Auto parts, tires, scrap metal. Graffiti throwups on gates and shutters.

—Slow down, Leonie said to the driver.

Here and there we saw people standing on street corners, young men, a woman in a mesh dress that showed her underwear, another woman wearing high boots and leggings, who walked backwards a few paces as we passed, did a little shimmy. Near the intersection where Carter had been attacked, someone had parked a flatbed with dozens of portable toilets strapped to the back.

—We'll get out here, just up ahead.

The driver wasn't sure.

—You want get out?

—Just for a moment.

A deathly quiet. Loading bays, a yard with a chain link fence, a shuttered cash-and-carry.

—Here.

—Remember, there's another hundred for taking us back.

—OK, but I don't want wait here very long. This is not a good place.

We got out. A truck crawled down the street past us, the driver eyeing Leonie. There was a clunk as our driver locked his doors. I followed Leonie to the middle of the intersection, into the gathering silence.

—There's nothing here.

Without warning, Leonie lay down, stretching out in the middle of the intersection.

—Don't do that. Please get up.

She didn't reply, just lay there with her eyes closed and her arms by her sides. I knew exactly what she was doing. Being Carter, trying to feel what he felt, putting herself in his place.

I looked and listened for traffic. Then I saw a glint of light. On the corner, tucked in by a fencepost, was a candle in a dish, sitting on the sidewalk next to a bag of rotting fruit. I left Leonie and knelt down in front of it. It was one of those religious candles sold in bodegas and botánicas, with a picture of some saint on the side. The place could not have been more desolate, yet someone had lit it, kept it alight. Did they do that for Carter? Perhaps shrines just spring up after any act of violence, anywhere there is some energy that people want to harness or ward off. For months, a cluster of candles and empty liquor bottles had marked a patch of wall in our neighborhood where a teenage boy got shot. Perhaps the candle had nothing to do with Carter. Perhaps it was none of my business.

Leonie got up and brushed herself down. The driver hesitated before he let us back in to his car. We drove downtown in silence. I couldn't shake the memory of the eerie shrine at the crossroads. I wanted to talk about something, anything. I wanted to hear Leonie talk.

—You told me Carter's not trusted with money.

She nodded. She was fiddling with her phone. I pushed.

—I didn't know. I mean, I don't know the background to that.

—You never noticed? Come on. The highs and lows? The bursts of manic energy?

—I know that he had some kind of diagnosis. When he was a kid. That your parents sent him to a doctor.

—That's what he told you? Seth, your friend Carter has episodes. He finds it hard to keep his shit together, particularly when he's under stress. Though apparently it's been fine lately, since you seem to have no clue that he's even sick.

—Not everyone has the same definition of normal.

—Give me a break. There's a woman he phones, a counselor.

—Is she called Betty?

—I don't know. Maybe.

—I thought she was his PA.

—Well, she is. But she's also a licensed psychotherapist. She authorizes his expenses, keeps him on track. There's some kind of trust. Your apartment's probably owned by that. I know the building where you have your studio belongs to Corny. He owns that whole block. Carter had to beg him for it, for, like, two years.

I'd always thought of Carter as the most independent person I knew. Someone who was truly autonomous, free to follow his desires. As I heard her talk, something bleak and dark began to draw a grid over the sky. The flickering candle, the bag of rotten fruit, the new picture of my fragile, watched-over friend.

I assumed Leonie would direct the car to drop her off home in TriBeCa, but instead she came back with me, shoving some bills at the driver and half-tumbling out onto the sidewalk. Once again we sat on the big iron bed, facing the mirror. We played records. I heard little hisses and clicks as she smoked. Little intakes of breath.

> Make me a pallet on your floor
> Make me a pallet on your floor
> I make sure your husband never know

Again she slept in her brother's bed. My door was open all night.

▼

THE FOLLOWING EVENING I was preparing for her to come round. The loft was clean and tidy. I'd chosen some records I particularly wanted Leonie to hear. I'd been to a fancy deli in Williamsburg and bought cold cuts, olives, some Italian cheese.

—Buzz me in.

I unlocked the door and set about opening a bottle of white wine that I had chilling in the freezer.

—Page Six? You asshole.

I turned round, confused. She was standing in the doorway, staring at me in disgust.

—You piece of shit.

She looked at the table setting, the neatly arranged dishes of appetizers.

—What the fuck is this?

—I knew you were coming over.

—You have to be joking. What, you think this is some kind of date?

She said I was no friend to her brother. She called me a series of vile and hurtful names. She wouldn't believe that I didn't understand what she was talking about, but she waited while I got my laptop and went online. To my horror, beneath items on a diet guru's divorce and a domestic violence charge involving two RnB stars was a post headed *Coma heir "cruising for sex." What was a young music producer with a glittering career doing at 3am in the industrial wasteland of Hunts Point?* It was clearly at least partly based on the conversation I'd had the day before. *His roommate claimed . . . according to his producing partner . . .* It was picture-bylined *Lewis Carolle,* who seemed to be a preppy young black guy in tortoiseshell glasses and a bow tie.

A gossip columnist. I'd been so stupid. He had seemed to know everything anyway. Like an idiot, I'd confirmed what must only have been a rumor. I'd given him his whole story. Leonie didn't want to hear my explanation.

—You sleazy bastard.

—I swear I didn't know he was a journalist.

—Yeah right. Did you still not know when you told him where to send the check?

—Come on, Leonie. I wouldn't do that.

—Oh really? You cheap little fuck. How much did you sell my brother out for? I bet it wasn't even a thousand bucks.

—That's not fair.

—If anything changes with Carter, someone will call you. But don't call me. I don't want your number coming up on my screen. You took advantage of my brother, riding around on his coattails. I won't let you do the same to me. So stay the fuck away.

I'm sorry. I never. I didn't. I wasn't.

Leonie, I didn't know.

She walked out and slammed the door, leaving me with my small plates, my bottle of wine, the fresh linen I had put on Carter's bed.

In the days after Leonie cut off contact, I underwent a sort of collapse, like a tower caving in on its foundations. The loft seemed hollow, cavernous. The pressed tin panels on the high ceilings, the great round stained glass window that flooded the space with spiritual light, these features had once seemed magical to me, signs of my charmed New York life. Now they just looked expensive. Without Carter, the light was merely an amenity, one that did not belong to me. I drank and looked at porn. I felt raw and frightened, my slug underbelly exposed.

The white rapper's record label was leaving messages. They were sorry about Carter, but they were on a schedule. Did we have anything for them to hear, or should they look elsewhere? No, there was nothing for them to hear. There would never be anything for them to hear. I knew that. I was hopelessly lost, stunned into immobility. I spent most of my time in Carter's room, putting 78's on the turntable, sitting on the bed in front of the speakers.

> *Can't tell the future, can't forget the past*
> *Lord it seems like every minute going to be my last*

> *See see rider see what you done done*
> *You made me love you now you trying to put me down*

Why had Leonie treated me like that? She was being unfair. I'd never wanted much, I'd meant no harm. It was worse, somehow, that she'd let me get so close before pushing me away. I conducted conversations with her, arguments. I pleaded my case. Sometimes it was almost as if she were there in my head. Yes, Seth. I understand. I see what you mean.

> *Don't get mad at me woman if I kicks in my sleep*
> *I may dream things cause your heart to weep*

▼

I DID NOTHING, or next to nothing. I couldn't work. I didn't answer the phone or go online. I cut myself off from the world. Carter could have been alive or dead, I had no way of knowing, but I felt we were the same, each in his own coma, dislocated, floating free. One afternoon I was asleep in his bed, wrapped up in his antique patchwork quilt. By the time I heard the thumps and voices, the movers must have been working for at least an hour.

In that apartment, we put bills and bank statements and anything else official in the jaws of a stuffed coyote that sat in a corner by the door. When there were too many envelopes to fit in the coyote's mouth, Carter stuffed them into a FedEx box and sent it to Betty. I never handled anything administrative. In terms of paperwork I was almost invisible. Perhaps there had been a letter. The state I was in, even if one had been addressed to me, I probably wouldn't have opened it.

I came out to find all the furniture gone from the living area. The contents of my room were being boxed up by a crew of surly Russians or Ukrainians, big pale men with unempathic eyes. I couldn't get any sense out of them. They shrugged at my questions, shook negating fingers. No English. They pointed out the boss, who showed me a work order. He had keys. His instructions were to empty the place and put everything in storage. I told him he had to stop and put it all back. I told him to get his guys and leave. It escalated from there. I don't remember getting Carter's bat. I just found it in my hands. The boss said if I touched him, he'd call the cops. Go ahead, I said, swinging the bat. Call them. Then I locked myself in Carter's room and tried to get Cornelius on the phone. His assistant said he was unavailable.

The police turned up and shouted at me to open the door. I was expecting to get arrested, but they didn't want to get involved. One actually told me that I had more rights than I thought. My landlord needed a court order to get me out. He told me to phone a lawyer. The cops and the movers talked for a while. The movers agreed to leave.

Finally, I was alone again. Almost everything was gone from the apartment. Furniture, kitchen equipment. I now occupied an empty brick box, with dusty boot prints all over the hardwood floor. A well-proportioned bunker. My room had been mostly emptied. Card-board boxes were piled in a corner which seemed to contain books and not much else. My bed was gone, so were most of my clothes. Only Carter's room was untouched. I made his bed and generally straightened things up. His treasure chest of 78's was still sitting in its place by the record deck. I phoned a locksmith and gave him Carter's credit card number. While he worked, I looked at the small things that had been left behind on the floor. Restaurant flyers, paperclips, pennies. It would be hard to reconstruct our life from such frag-ments, to know what had been said and done in that space. I kept trying to reach Cornelius. After the third time, the assistant told me not to call again. She would be in touch if and when Mr. Wallace was available to speak to me. She suggested I send an email detailing "my concerns" and "sit tight" to await a response.

The movers came back a couple of hours later. They banged on the locked door and cursed at me in their language. After a while they went away. Only then did it occur to me to think about the studio. I ran down the stairs and cycled over, arriving drenched in sweat. I fumbled with the key in the lock. As I had feared, it didn't work. I banged on the door with my fists, calling out to Carter, as if it was all a terrible misunderstanding and he would shamble to the door and open it up and let me in and everything would be the same again, just like before.

▼

—CORNELIUS? I'M LOCKED OUT. Yes, that's right. What? What do you mean? That's ridiculous. We have projects, contracts. Yes, I've got proof. Of course I've got proof. I don't understand why you would do this. Cornelius? Hello?

Please take notice that a judgment has been made in the above pro-
ceeding giving Wallace Magnolia Properties LLC possession of the
premises now occupied by you.

—Surely I have some rights in this situation. That's not fair. He's my friend. I would never. Well, it was a verbal contract. No. Of course not. That's completely unreasonable. If I want a what? What? Of course I don't want to make a claim against your family. This is my life we're talking about. I need to get into that studio.

An order of eviction has been issued empowering the marshal to
remove you and your belongings

—I have nowhere to go. I'm your brother's best friend. That's not true. How can you even say that? I am not. I resent that. No way.
    Your problems are not my problems, Cornelius says in his imper-meable voice. The family has been advised that it is unlikely that

Carter will wake from his coma. They see no reason to wait to put his affairs in order. It's not the family's fault that I didn't respond to earlier attempts to contact me. If you wish to bring suit, you should feel free to have your lawyer call mine.

I am unable to separate one thing from another. It all comes at me in a swirl, a storm. The casual way he says that Carter will never wake up. The knowledge that I have nothing, that at a stroke he has taken it all from me. The way he can tell me all this in his unreachable, impermeable voice.

as provided by law the undersigned will execute such order of eviction

—Goodbye. Please don't use this number again.

▼

WITHOUT ACCESS TO THE STUDIO, only two threads connected me to Carter: his records and a copy of the picture Leonie had taken in the ICU, the selfie with her bandaged intubated brother. I'd got hold of her phone one evening while she was in the bathroom and sent it to myself. Beautiful Carter smashed and punctured, his mouth open for the ventilator. Back at the empty loft, I pushed his bed against the door of his room and spent long periods, sometimes hours at a time, staring at it as I listened to his records. It had a terrible beauty. Brother and sister in extremis. Carter wired to drips and monitors, Leonie staring into the lens as if it were the barrel of a gun.

Since my clothes had been taken by the movers, I began to dress in Carter's, which fit me well enough: his selvedge denim jeans, his soft cotton shirts, work boots I padded with two pairs of socks so they didn't slip. I packed some of his clothes into a small back-pack along with a few toiletries and some other useful items from his room—a little hunting knife, a pocket flashlight, forcing myself out of my prostration to prepare for what I knew would eventu-ally happen. I locked my bike to a railing at the other end of the block, so I wouldn't be left without transport. Then I took the wal-nut box of records and moved it to a locker in a nearby storage unit. The varnished wood was slick in my sweaty hands as I walked to the storage facility, an old industrial building with bricked-up windows and primary-colored signage facing the street. I focused on the need to be careful, to be precise in each step, to avoid obstacles, objects on the ground or uneven paving slabs. Technically this was theft, but I was the only person who understood the significance of Carter's collection and I felt this gave me some kind of moral right of guardianship. Though the records were worth thousands of dollars, I had no interest in their market value. They were a vital clue to what was happening to us, what I had begun to think of as a jinx, a curse that had put Carter in the hospital and was grinding my own life to powder. If Cornelius took those records, I would never be able to save his brother. It was imperative to keep them under my control. I zipped the storage unit key into a small pocket in the backpack. Every time I went to get groceries (this was the only reason I left Carter's room at all during those days) I took the backpack with me. When Corny's men finally broke in and changed the locks, leaving me outside on the street, I was ready.

As I was trying to fit my key in the door, two men got out of a car and began walking towards me. I ran, but they didn't follow. I was on my own. A bike, a few clothes. The records, though I had nothing to play them on.

After that, waiting became my life. Waiting outside the hospital where Carter was being kept, waiting outside Cornelius's office. Waiting on the sidewalk outside Leonie's building, in the basement bar with the fights playing on the bulbous black-and-white TV. I sat on a bench in Tompkins Square. I hovered on the corner near the studio. I slept in various places. It was summer: you could put a camping mat or some cardboard down on the sidewalk and no one would bother you, as long as you picked a quiet spot.

I stood on the sidewalk opposite Leonie's building and waited for her to come out. I waited outside her building, standing on the sidewalk. Two hours the first day, three the second, until my feet hurt and my bladder was swollen full.

At last she came out. So quick, it would have been easy to miss her. The doorman helped her into a town car, which immediately pulled away. I got on my bike and followed the big black Lincoln uptown through heavy traffic. Past Houston it pulled away, disappearing up Tenth Avenue. I stepped on the pedals, skirting potholes and bumping over the lips of those giant metal slabs that utility companies throw down when they're excavating the road. I was streaming with sweat by the time I spotted the car in Chelsea, parked on a block lined with art galleries. I could see Leonie herself, waiting on the curb in the heat, tenanting a small patch of shade and smoking a cigarette. I leaned on the handlebars as I watched her, trying to gulp enough air into my lungs to slow my racing heart. I could smell the hot stink of my unwashed body, the telltale scent of the outsider. A second car pulled up and a man got out. I saw the wavy boyish hair, a pair of dark glasses pushed up into it like a headband. Marc. So Marc was still in the picture.

A white-walled former warehouse with a sealed concrete floor. Quickly past the woman at the desk, too preoccupied with her email to look up. The cavern contained a single row of vast paintings, monuments of banality, wallpaper patterns stenciled in metal-flake car paint and fields of dots that on closer inspection turned out to be candy. I didn't dare get very close to Leonie and Marc. I didn't need to. I had my recorder, my binaurals. The mics in my ears could pick up her voice.

—It's very impressive.

Marc said he'd been offered another from the same series, almost identical. He wasn't sure the work would hold its value. She told him she thought it was good. Challenging, yes, but some of the artist's best work. He was a friend of hers, in fact. I recognized the name, the bearded loudmouth who'd insulted her at dinner.

As they left, they walked straight past me, as if I wasn't there. I think Leonie genuinely didn't see me, but I had the sense that something more was at work, that my ordinary insubstantiality had intensified. I picked up a short conversation on the sidewalk. Marc making a half-hearted promise to call Leonie, her telling him he'd better, trying to sound casual and sassy. You better, she said, pointing pistol fingers at him, a self-conscious gesture that she held for a moment, then withdrew. You better call. He drove off and left her on the sidewalk.

Silence. The phone echoing in the high-ceilinged gallery, sound waves bouncing off the great big shiny surfaces of the art.

I stepped forward, ready to say please Leonie. I stepped forward in the gallery, on the sidewalk outside the gallery. Please Leonie, let me explain. The ringing phone, the shiny paintings. But she got back into her own car and it pulled away, leaving me alone in my sweat and stink. After that I drifted through the city on foot, recording. That was the summer I drifted through the city. Did I already say that? Everything I saw had a subtle but unmistakable doubleness. Each pace was reminiscent of some previous pace, not just because I knew the streets well and had walked them before, though this was true, but because I'd already taken that particular pace. My present had somehow gone before me and was already irrevocably in my past. All the sounds I could hear, slightly amplified and somehow picked out or defined, were no more than echoes, their presence freakish, their availability to me as exotic as a radio signal from a long-ago war.

Each moment, as I lived it, had already been used up. I could not connect things together. They happened to me, they had already happened to me. The helix that spans from birth to death, the unbroken thread of habit and progress that makes a person a person, a self whole and entire, had become as discontinuous and insubstantial as a chain of smoke rings.

▼

SO THEN IT WAS EVENING and I was cycling down Avenue A, my heart racing, the street treacherous and provisional under my tires. Before or after I saw Leonie and Marc? I could not have said. He crossed in front of me, the old phantom, running as fast as he could into Tompkins Square, chased by a gang of punk kids.

I dropped my bike and ran after them, swerving past trash and piles of building rubble. Up ahead I saw him fall, his black coat flapping in a momentary gesture of surrender. He curled up as they swarmed him, kicking, punching, beating him down. As I ran up, they scattered, a quick flurry that slowed into a saunter with insolent speed. They didn't come back for me, just loped away laughing and high-fiving each other. They had patches on their denim jackets: *Savage Skulls*. I looked down at JumpJim, who lay on the ground groaning and cursing.

—Little fuckers. Snot-nosed bastards.

—You've been avoiding me.

When I spoke it seemed to me that I did so without heart or spontaneity, the words ritual, a recitation of some previous speech. I helped the battered old crow to stand and he pressed his hands into his chest and stomach, feeling for damage. A rich meaty smell rose up off him, and I wondered if, like me, he had nowhere to sleep.

—Why did they do that?

—Broke my fucking ribs.

—You need to go to the ER?

—No, all I want is for you to get me to my front door.

So I was wrong. He had a place. We limped through some kind of tented encampment, two wretched figures clinging together as we stumbled through the wreckage. Homeless men sat outside shelters patched together from tarpaulin and cardboard. A fire was burning in a trash can. I wondered vaguely what had happened to the dog run, the primary-colored climbing frames and slides in the newly opened playground. When I'd last been in the park it was a cheerful, bustling place. Somehow I had never noticed how many of the buildings in that neighborhood were empty, burned out.

Secrets are told continuously at the edge of perception. Nothing ever goes away.

Even injured, JumpJim had a frantic walk, all knees and elbows. From time to time he threw his arms out in a sort of involuntary spasm. People gave us space on the sidewalk. We stopped at a graffiti-covered door, between a bodega and a Chinese takeout.

—OK, you can leave me here.

—I need to talk to you.

—Sorry, but you can see I'm hurt.

—It'll only take a minute.

—I don't know you, man.

—Yes you do. It's about my friend.

—I don't know you or your friend. Just be on your way. I need to get to my bed.

—Carter Wallace. You knew who he was, right? A Wallace. The Wallace Family. You knew how rich he was.

—Let go my arm.

—A minute of your time.

—Just be about your business. I said I don't know you.

—I'm going to make you fucking talk to me. You saw him, or he came to see you. About—I don't know how long ago. Recently.

—I didn't see anyone. I make a point of it. I don't get involved in other people's business. Look, you're a witness to what just happened to me. I was the victim of a vicious and unprovoked assault. You ought to show more concern. You're hurting my arm.

—I swear I'll break it.

—OK, OK. Hold up.

He looked infinitely old and weary.

—No need to push me around. You shouldn't push people around. Sick people. You shouldn't fucking do that, man.

Around me the buildings were in flux. The same buildings, not the same. Night had fallen and I was surrounded by a city made only of its cold places, all the basements and alleyways, the airless back rooms.

—You better come up.

—My friend Carter got attacked. He's in a coma.

—I don't know anything about that.

—Really? You don't know anything at all? He was my best friend. You understand what I'm saying? My best friend.

—Just come inside the damn building. I'll talk to you.

JumpJim pushed at the door, which had no lock. I almost tripped on a broken tile as I stepped inside and as I turned slightly to right myself, I caught a glimpse of the street, the window of a chic-looking patisserie, a woman walking a French bulldog, a scene so cosmically remote from where I was, the dark hallway, the smell of garbage and the closing door, that my mind found the two things impossible to reconcile.

The door closed. I picked my way up flights of stairs into a fetid red darkness, keeping one hand on the wall and listening to JumpJim's asthmatic breathing. We groped our way around corners on unlit landings of uncertain size. On one floor I heard Fania salsa filtering under a door, on the next there was a smell of fish and the sound of an argument in what might have been German or Yiddish. The stairs seemed interminable, the plaster of the wall warm and slightly damp to the touch, like the hide of some amphibious beast. Though we were climbing up, I had the illogical sense that I was descending, so that when, at last, I heard him futzing with a key, it felt to me as if I had been swallowed by the city, and was somewhere down in its pulsing, volcanic belly.

He led me into a stifling apartment filled almost to the ceiling with books and papers. An orange sofa with cigarette burns on the arms, a sticky rug underfoot. Shelves were fitted on every wall, lining the vestibule. Those that weren't overflowing with books, and the front few inches of those that were, had been filled with small objects arranged in ranks or groups: netsuke, tarot cards, wind-up toys, postcards of freeway rest areas. There were old keys and chopstick rests, painted eggs, swatches of fabric, each collection meticulously arranged, like letters in some high-level language. He had a gas ring, a great humming fridge, some kind of murky bathroom. He'd nailed scarves over the windows. The light was submarine. There was, as far as I could see, no bed. And no records.

It came to me that I too had been carrying a box of records. I had been carrying Carter's box of records, careful not to slip. Where had I been taking them?

—I sold them all years ago, too dangerous.

He was talking to me. I must have asked him a question.

—Seventy-eights. I see you scanning the shelves. That's what you're looking for. I sold my whole collection. I did keep a few other things. For example, for example. Aha! You'll find this interesting when it comes.

He took off his coat and began to rummage through a pile of books.

—Damn, where is it? You want tea. I can definitely offer you tea, while I'm hunting this out.

—But you told me you had a rare Willie Brown record.

—I lied. I don't have any records. Not a one. Haven't for years. So do you want tea or not?

—No.

I felt spent, as if I'd run some kind of strenuous race and now the only thing left was to come to terms with losing. I slumped down onto the sofa, which exhaled a barely perceptible breath of dust.

—Just tell me about Carter.

—I really want to find this—ah, here it is!

He brandished a battered little book, covered in red paper, and began to leaf through it.

—"Musician. To dream you hear one play foretells grief and sadness. Eight, eleven, eighteen and twenty-three."

—What?

—Those are your numbers. Eight, eleven, eighteen, twenty-three.

He flipped the cover in my direction. *Aunt Sally's Policy Players' Dream Book.* Some kind of murky woodcut of a woman.

—At least if you played the numbers, you might win a little something. That'd be a consolation prize, am I right? To tide you over your feelings of grief and loss?

—This is all a joke to you.

—No joke, son. All the wisdom of the ancients is between these tattered covers.

He threw the book onto a pile and flopped down on a metal-framed kitchen chair, gingerly palpating his ribs. I saw that one of his eyes was red. A large bruise was forming below it. I tried to remember whether it had been light outside when they were beating him. I couldn't hear anything, no street noise, no neighbors. The place was a womb. A rotten womb.

—I want to know if you met Carter. I think you did. I think you sold your collection to him.

—You are barking up the wrong tree, son. I sold up years ago, before you or your friend was even born.

—You're mixed up in this, whatever is happening here. You know what's happening.

—Hold your horses.

He made a gesture that incensed me, a sort of soothing pianistic fluttering of the fingertips, wafted in my direction. As if he were dispelling me, shooing me back to my place between the pages of his dusty books. I stood up and balled my fist. I told him that if he didn't stop with the games, I would kill him. He scrambled out of the chair and adopted a fighting stance.

—Don't threaten me, you little fuck. I know jiujitsu.

We stood there for some time, pantomiming aggression. Then he adjusted the waistband of his pants and tipped some newspapers off another chair so he could sit down again.

—He got hurt, you say, your friend? Badly?

—He's in a coma. How does that sound? Does that make you happy?

He shrugged noncommittally. I could have strangled him.

—He had a lot of money in cash and I think he came looking for you. He wanted to buy that Willie Brown record you talked about.

—Thirteen thousand ninety-nine. I only said that so he'd come. I don't have that record. Who in the world has that record? It's a unicorn. I needed to talk to him, was all.

—Talk to him? You mean get someone to rob him.

—No.

—Carter came here.

—Not here. He came to the bar. And I tried to warn him what he'd gotten himself into. Look, you're giving me palpitations, looming over me like that. I'm not in the best of health. Come on, sit down. Drink a cup of tea.

—What was it, then? What had he got himself into?

—Sit down.

He looked so pathetic hunched in his chair, quivering, holding his fists in front of him like tiny baubles. The idea of hurting him seemed absurd. I sat down. As he pottered about, making tea, I stared at the sickly yellow-green light filtering through the curtains, willing it to grow stronger. I wanted the sun to burst through. I wanted to be bathed in daylight. Once again I tried to tell him how it had happened. The guy singing in Washington Square, the guitarist in Tompkins Square. How we sewed the two parts together and made a song. Shakily, he set two china cups and saucers down on a pile of encyclopedia volumes that was serving as an occasional table. Then he sat down on a kitchen chair and took off his glasses, so as to fix me with a straight look.

—Son, you may think that story's true. You may have persuaded yourself it is, but you didn't make up Charlie Shaw. Charlie Shaw is real.

—It's just a name. Carter chose it at random.

—Charlie Shaw chose you, more like.

—You may know some guy called Charlie Shaw. It's not the same

guy. I'm telling you, this is just bullshit. A misunderstanding about
a name.

—I stepped away from the collecting scene after what happened
to Chester and I don't want to get back in. It's not even safe for me
to be talking to you, most probably, but I can't help myself. I'll be
straight with you. Cards on the table. I'm curious. Killed the cat,
right? But this thing has been nagging at me for so many years. I
only want to know one piece of information. What's on the other
side? Graveyard Blues on the A, so what's on the flip?

—Will you not get it into your head? There's no flip. There's no
record. I don't have any damn record. It's a .WAV file, if you even
know what one of those is. You probably have it compressed as
an MP3.

—I don't have it as anything and I can't honestly say I know what
the hell you're talking about.

—Just give me your laptop, I'll show you.

—Laptop?

—Your computer. You have a computer stashed away somewhere
in here.

—Does this look like Bell Laboratories? Be a sport. I'm not even
asking to hear the damn thing, let alone handle it. I just want to
know what's on the flip. Why is that so hard?

—Because it doesn't exist.

—What is with you? I know your story. It's just like mine. I was
the sidekick, same as you. Chester was making all the running. At
the time you feel you're just going along, am I right? Going along
to get along. Making yourself useful. But Charlie doesn't care about
that. He doesn't make those kind of fine distinctions. Which one
is the alpha dog and so on. So why would he want your friend?
That's the question you ought to be asking. Because it sounds like
he got him.

—He was robbed and left for dead in the Bronx. I don't know
why he would go there or what he was doing. He had no connection to anyone in that part of town.

—I certainly didn't send him out to the Bronx. He came to the
bar, showed me a lot of money. I could tell right away the boy was

a lost soul. I'm not a bad man. I tried to talk sense into him, but what can you say when someone's like that? When they've got the collecting bug? I'm the same as you. I'm not a powerful person. But I learned my lesson. I don't mess with any of it anymore. The boy was angry that I didn't have any records. Wouldn't listen to a word of what I was trying to tell him, which was get the hell out right now. Same as I tried to tell you, only you wouldn't listen either. He kept running his mouth, saying he'd pay top dollar, did I know who he was, so much bull crap, I couldn't follow it all. He even got his cash out on the table. No street smarts. I mean, anybody could have seen it. Anybody could have heard, the way he was rambling on.

—So you're saying someone overheard him at the bar?

—He told me the same stupid story you did. That he'd made up Charlie Shaw. Wouldn't listen to a word I said. I told him, Charlie Shaw wants something from you, and it's something you probably don't want to give. You've crossed the line and now you have to prepare yourself. He just kept on saying catalog numbers. Paramount this, Okeh that.

—I don't understand.

—That's not news to anyone, son. It's clear to even the most casual observer that you and your friend are lost in the dark. If you promise you won't interrupt, I'll tell you. And after I tell you I want you to get the hell out of my apartment, because I barely made it away from Chester's mess all those years ago and I'm taking a risk even speaking the words. You don't know about Chester Bly. No one does anymore, though at one time he had a reputation. I've seen some collectors, but I can tell you he was the smartest and the most single-minded of them all. He would not rest until he had what he wanted in his hands.

▼

THE STORY THE OLD COLLECTOR TOLD ME was so strange that, had I heard it in any other circumstances, I would have dismissed it as a fabrication. And yet it had a force—I would say the force of truth, but that would be too simple. It wasn't that I believed it or didn't believe it, more that it seemed to come from a place beyond belief. Something had attached itself to Carter and me, some tendril of the past, and if we did not detach it, we would be drawn back into death and silence.

The story built up inside me like pressure in a lab vessel. I couldn't contain it. But who could I tell? The only person who would possibly understand was Leonie, and I doubted she would even hear me out. I used a guest pass to get in to Carter's gym, where I had a shower and ripped open the plastic on a fresh tee shirt and a change of underwear. I combed my hair and made sure my clothes didn't have any visible stains. Then I took the records out of storage and waited outside her building, standing on the sidewalk with the walnut box at my feet. I hung around for a long time, almost four hours. I was about to give up when she came out, wearing jeans shorts and one of Carter's shirts. At first she walked straight past me.

—Leonie! Leonie!

She wheeled round, startled. She was in a bad state. I couldn't see her eyes behind her big dark glasses but her hair was lank and matted and something in her posture suggested lifelessness, defeat.

—I told you to stay away.

She slipped one hand into her pocket, as if she were about to pull something out. For a moment I thought she might mace me. I imagined falling to my knees like a singer, clawing at my eyes. Leonie standing over me, delivering the *coup de grâce*.

—Please, Leonie. I wanted to make sure you had these. They're fragile. I didn't know where to take them.

I pointed out the box.

—I could just leave them with the doorman, if you'd prefer.

—So you brought me Carter's death music. Thanks.

—I didn't know where else I should take it. They're valuable. You should store them properly.

She stared at the box. She didn't move.

—I don't want you to think I was going to keep them. I'm not—that kind of person.

—What kind of person? The kind who'd sell information about my brother?

—Please Leonie, I thought he was one of his friends.

—Who?

—The journalist. It was an honest mistake.

—So you're sorry and I should, what? Forgive you?

—I wasn't thinking. It was stupid of me. I should have remembered his—your position.

—What do you want, Seth?

—Nothing, I swear. I just don't want you to think I'm a thief.

—Bullshit. Everyone wants something from us. It'll save time if you just tell me.

She lit and smoked a cigarette. I stared at the paving stones.

—You probably want me to go.

Weakly, she waved her hand.

—You're just going to leave that here? I don't know if I can even handle having that shit in my apartment.

—So where should I take them?

—I don't know. Break them for all I care.

—Break them?

—No, of course not. Fuck it, I suppose you have to bring them up.

Though the doorman offered to take the box, I carried it to her apartment as carefully as if it were Carter's own body. To my surprise she asked if I wanted coffee. I think she didn't mean to; it was the sort of social reflex to which she was ordinarily immune. But she asked, and once I'd said yes, she had to follow through. As she pushed buttons on her machine, I hovered near the riverside window, surveying a scene of minor devastation. Ashtrays improvised out of cups, foil takeout trays and wine bottles on the floor, a deep scar in the brickwork of one wall.

—Did you have a party?

—Milk? I only have soy. I think there's some agave in the cupboard if you want it sweet.

—No thanks.

She handed me a mug. Seeing that I'd noticed the mess in her apartment, she made a sarcastic face.

—Yes, I had a wild party. Definitely one of the all-time great nights.

I couldn't tell from her tone whether she meant that she'd held a party which had gone badly, or that she'd made the mess herself. There were mugs and glasses scattered along the windowsills. The gash in the brickwork looked like it had been done with a power tool, maybe an angle grinder.

Then we were sitting down opposite each other on two prototypes of a famous Danish chair, and the silence was building up, the pressure of my untold story climbing higher and higher. The only thing I could think of to say was how sorry I was. Again.

—Sure.

She followed my eyeline to the damaged wall.

—My neighbors really love me.

—What did you do?

—I don't even know. I was upset.

—That sounds bad.

—Yeah?

—So you know Corny had me kicked out.

—I heard.

Her voice was flat. She didn't say she was sorry or ask where I was staying. I asked how Carter was doing.

—The same. Exactly the same. They say we shouldn't get our

hopes up. It's very unlikely anything will change now. Even if he wakes up . . .

She trailed off. I thought of Carter in a high room over the city, his consciousness scattered under the pressure of blood clots and lesions. I told her I would never be disloyal.

—You mean to my brother?

And to you. I screwed up, I know it, but in revenge Corne lius has locked me out of the studio. I don't care about the apartment. All our work is in the studio. Our files, all our equipment. I don't have any other—we have clients, we've signed contracts. You understand, Leonie? My whole life is in that studio.

—Corny's very angry. He called it a direct frontal attack on the family.

—I didn't take any money, I swear. The guy called me and I picked up the phone. I just need. How can I put this. If he could let me have my property, that's all I ask. My intellectual property.

—Maybe if you got a lawyer.

Her family had most of my possessions, all my equipment, my tools. I had a couple hundred dollars in a checking account. How could I afford a lawyer?

—What I'm saying, Seth, is that I really can't get involved. I can't get in between you and Corny.

I asked if I could use her bathroom. On the way there I peeped round the half-open door of her bedroom. The bed was a midden of clothes and shoes and other things—Q-tips, an open compact spilling powder. Bits of broken mirror littered the floor. It looked like Leonie was sleeping in the living area. Someone had thrown blankets and pillows onto a couch opposite a big pulldown screen, a little survival zone haloed in trash. I locked the bathroom door and sat on the toilet, wondering what to say when I came out. I examined her toothbrush, the flesh-toned silk robe hanging on a hook on the door. Inside her medicine cabinet were rows of bottles, containing vitamins and esoteric supplements. She had prescriptions from a homeopath, a Chinese herbalist. Capsules of freeze-dried thymus gland extract, "fortified with herb activators and naturopathically prepared nutrients for synergistic effect." Something called turquoise aromatherapy color energy blend. A cabinet full of charms to ward off death. I tried to imagine how she must feel to herself as she stood naked in that marble-tiled bathroom, swallowing pills. Hearing death come creeping in, slinking round her ankles like a cat.

I took a couple of caps of something called Acetyl-L-Carnitine and scrutinized myself in the mirror. I barely recognized the haggard face I saw, its cheeks hollowed out by anxiety, by fear. I knew that if I didn't go back out and tell Leonie what JumpJim had told me, then I would break apart, just vibrate until I shattered.

—I am afraid, I said. I am so afraid.

—What are you afraid of?

Of the sound underlying the other sounds, the suffering rising up all around me, the mare's nest of cable I have to untangle if I am going to find the fault. Of the way the past has hold of Carter. Of my suspicion that it has a name and a face.

Help Carter, I sobbed. I meant *help me*.

Leonie help me. I am caught in a riptide. Help *me*, at least. Carter is already beyond our reach.

▼

HOW LONG AGO? That doesn't matter. Far back in time, drowned in the crackle and hiss. I was nineteen years old, living in a sixth-floor walk-up in Greenwich Village and working as a messenger at the *New York Herald Tribune,* running copy between reporters and editors in the newsroom of their building on 41st Street. Long gone, that newsroom, that paper.

I was a jazz fanatic, but I had no time for the modern stuff. No Miles or Coltrane for me, no bebop, which I called Chinese jazz, because it was all splintered and broken up. I was what they used to term a "hot collector," obsessed with the music of the twenties. To me that was the real deal, the source and origin. Like every other dumb kid starting out down that particular road, my god was Bix Beiderbecke. I didn't know a thing. On my lunch breaks I'd hang around at a store in midtown we all knew as Indian Joe's, digging in the crates. I'd buy any old crap for eight bars of Bix.

One day, doesn't matter how, I tumbled to the idea that what I loved didn't come from Davenport, Iowa. As my tastes changed, I started take the subway uptown to Apollo Music at 125th and Lenox, on the hunt for King Oliver or Louis Armstrong and his Hot Five. New Orleans became my city, New Orleans and its great founding myth, the sound of the drummers in Congo Square vibrating through young Buddy Bolden's ears and on into the pulse of America. It was my fantasy to hear Bolden, the one who came before

King Oliver and all the other bandleaders, the one who was never recorded, whose sound was the missing link to the past. Buddy Bolden, vanished into the silence. I dreamed of being the one who uncovered, in some dusty basement or thrift store backroom, a cache of wax cylinders, my ears the first in fifty years to receive the gift of Bolden's cornet, its sweet high tone piercing the veil.

I know that by that time I'd heard some blues—by which I mean country blues, not commercial female nightclub singers backed by jazz bands, your Ma Raineys and Mamie Smiths and so forth. What I'd heard I hadn't found too interesting. To me, Lead Belly sounded corny. All that "goddamighty-I-kin-pick-a-bale-o'-cotton" horseshit. You want the truth, he was still in the pen, metaphorically speaking, while Lomax *père* was leading him round those so-called progressive New York parties. I mean, making him perform in his prison stripes? The poor bastard was still doing time. Point is *I didn't care about the blues*. Not many collectors did. We were troubled by its lack of sophistication. You have to remember, a lot of people thought the worst of the Negro in those days. We thought that kind of rough, low-down music only served to confirm color prejudice. A lot of Negroes thought so too, I might add. Church people wouldn't have it in their houses.

Anyhow, one Saturday I was loitering by the counter at the Apollo and one of the clerks put on a Charley Patton Paramount. Number 12792, "Pony Blues" with "Banty Rooster Blues" on the flip.

> *You can catch my pony, saddle up my black mare*
> *I'm going to find a rider, baby in the world somewhere*

That sound, my God. Like it had come out of the earth. It made my jazz records seem like child's play, like people fooling around in the antechamber, in the vestibule. I asked to hear it again. They sold it to me for a dollar. That's how much the Paramounts cost. A dollar apiece, all new. The Victors were fifty cents. I took it home and played it twenty times, trying to decipher Patton's words, to hear every eccentric phrase he played on his guitar.

Right away I sold every damn Bix and Paul Whiteman I owned.

All I wanted was blues, blues. But the sound I craved wasn't easy to come by. Patton, Son House, Willie McTell, Robert Johnson, Willie Johnson, Skip James, John Hurt . . . The names were traded by collectors, but no one seemed to know a thing about them. No information, not a scrap. They were like ghosts at the edges of American consciousness. You have to understand, when I say no one knew, I mean *no one*. You couldn't just look something up in a book. Things were hidden. Things got lost. *Musicians* got lost.

I subscribed to record collecting magazines. There was *Down Beat* and *Record Changer*. I forget the others. Collectors would run want lists, mostly for jazz. Their contact details were printed on the inside cover. There was one guy with a New York address who only wanted blues, name after name I'd never heard of, recorded on labels I knew little or nothing about. *C Bly, 179 Division Ave, Brooklyn 11, NY.* Sometimes he wrote letters to the editors, correcting some point or offering additional information. His letters were usually more interesting than the articles they responded to. I wrote to him, at the address given, saying very humbly that I was a young collector and wanted guidance. What should I listen to? What was out there? He wrote back, enclosing a three-page typewritten list. Its title was *Chester Bly Worthwhile Blues Records April 195—*. I corresponded with him for some months before he mentioned an extraordinary thing: he also worked at the *Herald Tribune*. Of all the people in that warren of a building, the sports reporters and the city reporters and the compositors and copy takers and the rewrite men and the columnists and the printers and the drivers who loaded the papers into their trucks and drove away, we two were the most alike.

The next day I got in to work early, asked round in the newsroom. Did anyone know a Chester Bly? We smoked in those days. Some afternoons the newsroom looked as if dry ice was billowing through it. Rows of men, hunkered down over coffee-stained desks, battering at ancient typewriters in the haze. These men worked in a slum of spiked paper and cigarette ash, and I had to run between them, taking paper from one to another, from writer to editor and back and forth and over to a sub to write a headline and downstairs to be set. A monkey could have done it but they had me, and it was hard work. To get a break, you had to devise strategies, get yourself sent on long errands, that kind of thing. It was late before I had a moment to myself, a moment to walk through the haze to the jumble of desks where the copy editors sat. Mister Bly? A gaunt man looked up at me from under a green celluloid eyeshade. In front of him was a blank sheet of paper, and an empty wire basket. Otherwise the desk was completely clear. That was not normal. I introduced myself. If he was surprised, he didn't show it.

—I have a lot of corrections to do, he said, but if you're available this evening, perhaps you would care to come by and listen to some music.

Of all the people in the building, we two were the most alike.

▼

WE RODE THE SUBWAY into Brooklyn, getting out in a neighborhood I'd never been in before. As I followed him down a block of dingy tenements, I saw how tall he was, how thin. He was dressed with a sort of threadbare immaculateness. His suit jacket was shiny at the shoulders, but still appeared perfectly pressed, even in the heat.

We entered a hostel for single men, of a class just a hair above the flophouses on the Bowery. No chow line, no dormitory rooms, but when you opened the front door your nostrils were hooked by that bread-line smell of urine and disinfectant and the first thing you saw was a chapel door with some oppressive motto about repentance written over the lintel. Bly was living in a room like a cell. He had nothing in there, not a thing but three wooden crates under his bed filled with records. No pictures, no personal objects. A plate and a knife and a fork on the dish rack. A pair of metal chairs pushed under either side of a card table. A turntable, an amp and a speaker. The man lived like a monk.

He offered me a chair and took the other. We sat, looking over at the turntable.

—So, he said. What do you want to hear?

—I don't know, I said. I don't know what I want to hear.

—Firstly, I'm going to fix up. If you faint easily or have a phobia of needles, I'm happy to go down the hall to the bathroom.

I'd never seen anyone use narcotics before, never been around it, but in the moment his reasonable tone carried me. At nineteen, you can be very accepting, if something is presented to you as normal. You don't know, so you pretend you're experienced, you play along. He produced a little wooden box, rolled up a sleeve and started to cook a shot of heroin. He had some sort of medical-looking rubber tourniquet, which he tied expertly to his upper arm. Chester Bly's madness was deep and fast-flowing but he was a very organized man.

I waited for something to happen, something dramatic like in the "mature adults only" pictures at the Rialto, a spasm, a widening of the eyes, but he just stared glassily at the turntable. After a pause that seemed to stretch for hours, he reached into his box and pulled out a record.

> Blues ain't nothing but a doggone dirty feel
> Got no money in your pocket to buy yourself a meal

An amazing record I'd never heard before. Though I begged, he wouldn't tell me what it was. I was to find out that this was a habit of his—to play things but conceal their identity. I was forever squinting sidelong at spinning labels, hoping in vain to read them.

It was an exquisite record, near mint and as clear as if the performer was in the room, a guitar blues with a vocal that occasionally climbed into a tremulous falsetto. It was followed by other exquisite records, record after record to which Bly listened with his hands steepled and a frown of concentration on his face. When each one ended, he whipped round to lift the needle off the platter. It was as if he snapped out of a trance.

I feel that is very good, he would say. Or, that is a recording of exceptional quality. Always with this measured judicious tone. And I would nod. After four hours, I said I needed to go home because I had work the next day. My head was spinning, round and round, seventy-eight revolutions per minute, and I was finding it hard to hold everything in mind, all the things I'd heard, the flow of recondite facts and opinions. He looked at his watch with an air of disappointment, and showed me to the door.

▼

WATCHING CHESTER BLY walk in to work the next morning, his jacket folded over one arm. Watching him in short bursts, as I raced from desk to desk. Chester Bly coming out of the bathroom with two wadded handfuls of wet paper towels. Chester Bly bent over his desk, carefully wiping the surface, the seat of his chair, its back rest, each of the four wooden legs.

I could not stop to wonder. I had people shouting at me. Copy! Copy! I had to run. Later, when I brought something to one of his neighbors, Bly acknowledged me with a barely perceptible nod. That was as much communication as we had for the rest of the week. I wondered if I'd failed in some way, if I'd said something gauche, mixed up Lonnie Johnson with Robert or Tommy or Willie Johnson. Lonnie Johnson was "molasses," in Chester's opinion, along with more or less anyone who ever played in a nightclub. Molasses was syrup. It was for the herd. The connoisseur knew the corner was the place for blues. The corner or the porch.

Chester's silence was frustrating. I was in orbit, running ellipses round his immaculately sanitized desk, aware at every moment of my proximity to—not to Chester Bly himself, but the thing that had hold of him, the obsession. I was like a child edging closer to a waterfall, wanting to feel the force of it, to stand beside the thunder and the spray. At night I would play my music, the few "good" records I had, and I would listen as hard as I could, but they seemed like minor pieces of a much larger puzzle, meaningless segments of blue sky. All I could think of were those boxes under Bly's bed. Those little spinning labels, the unreadable text, the hands steepled in a posture of prayer.

One day he sent me a letter. Instead of calling me over or stopping me at the watercooler, he chose to write to me at my home address. No preamble, not much you could call personal. Just a couple of lines, an invitation to a listening party, to be held in his room the following Friday.

Five of us were crammed in there. Five collectors, all men. I was the youngest, Tom and Hal perhaps ten years older. The oldest was Mr. Pinkus, who didn't seem to have a first name and was probably in his sixties. Each one had a specialty, string bands or Scottish reels or Flamenco or Javanese court gamelan, but each also loved the blues. None were naturally social, and Chester made no attempt at hosting, beyond providing the paper cups that we filled and refilled with cheap California jug wine.

I've not seen a second copy of this, Chester would say, pulling out yet another incredible record, another forgotten performance by a lost genius.

> Laid down last night just trying to take my rest
> My mind got to rambling like wild geese in the west

Sometimes, if one of the collectors knew the right question to ask, Chester would reveal the name. But if pushed, he could push back. He had a sharp tongue. He kept us in a state of cowed admiration. Sometimes, one of us would have heard something before, and would signify his claims with an outward display of appreciation, nodding or tapping his knee or gesturing with his pipe.

—What is that, Chester? It's Mississippi, right? It's got to be Mississippi.

—Jesus, Tom, if you can't hear Texas you've gone deaf.

—Texas. Right, Texas.

—Yes, Tom, like Chester says. Listen to the guitar figures.

—Pipe down, Pinkus. People are trying to listen.

—Sorry, Chester.

The next week, he invited me again. Some new things had come in the mail, he said. I didn't need a second invitation. Bly did not shoot heroin in front of his other collector friends, but whenever we listened to music alone, as we began to do at least once or twice a month, he would fix up at the kitchen table, then brood over his record boxes for several minutes, caught in whatever was happening to him, whatever message the drug allowed him to receive. He never offered heroin to me. It was never even a question. The drug ritual was no more than a bodily function, just something he did, and I grew to think of it as a banality. Bly seemed to have no family, no ties to the world. As he freely admitted, all his spare money went on music. He owned little else, and lived in the most frugal manner. His room was always spotless, the kitchen shelf stacked with cans, but outside the hallway smelled of urine and bacon grease and the bathroom on his floor was often swimming in dirty water. He didn't seem to notice these hardships. It was as if his whole soul was directed towards the carefully wrapped packages that he picked up, sometimes daily, from a box at a post office on the next block. I think this was why he lived in that place, to have the post office close by.

Ten-inch cardboard squares, sandwiched around precious shellac. Brown paper parcels tied up with string. I wondered if Bly had been in prison. How else could he make do with so little of the world? By any standards, I was a serious collector, but he seemed to have nothing else, no need to go to the park or the movies or walk round a museum. He was just a vehicle for his obsession, what the Haitians call a *cheval*, a mount for the spirits to ride.

I don't know why I was invited into his solitude. It seemed he wanted to share something of himself. He told me, for example, about his filing system. It was his belief that a man could only properly hold "around four hundred" records in his mind. A collection should be no larger. He had no time for anyone (which was almost everyone, as he well knew) who amassed thousands of records "without regard to quality or importance." There existed what he called a golden number. About this number he could grow quite mystical, but he would never tell me exactly what it was. He would audition many records, but if he wanted to keep one, another had to go. Each new star had to deserve its place in the constellation. It had to be, in a word he always used with great gravity, "worthwhile." For me, who found it wrenching to let go of anything, even music I never listened to and didn't really like, this was impressive. Because of it, Bly was constantly buying and selling records, sometimes stringing together complex deals, acquiring material in which he had no personal interest to use as bargaining chips in some drawn-out game with another collector.

He answered my musical questions, but I knew not to ask too many. It was important to him to keep something in reserve. Some topics he considered public knowledge, part of every collector's basic education. These things he freely told me: how a record lathe worked, how changing the width of your stylus could draw more music from a worn disc. Others, he offered in the form of clues or hints. He had, he said, once met a man who saw Robert Johnson alive during the war, serving as a cook on board a ship in the Pacific, but he would say no more about the man, or Johnson's cooking.

There were certain topics he would only allude to, or rather, there was a mood in which he would intimate darkly that there were such topics, "areas of research" he was not prepared to name. There was some music he'd play and put straight back in its sleeve, refusing to name the players, refusing to discuss it at all.

—Now, now.

That's what he'd say if I was forward enough to ask. Admonishingly, as if I'd brought up something risqué, obscene.

—Why don't we move on?

▼

ONE AFTERNOON IN THE NEWSROOM, I was taking a break, smoking a cigarette and listening to some sportswriters argue over who was the better pitcher, Lefty Gomez or Whitey Ford, when Bly appeared, looming over me, his eyeshade like a great green beak. There was something violent about his sudden arrival. The sportswriters could feel it; they turned away and continued their conversation elsewhere. Without hello or any other preamble Bly asked if I knew how to drive. I said yes. He said he too knew how to drive but did not care for it. He found driving stressful. It was good that I could drive. I agreed that it was. He looked at his hands for a moment, examining the nails. So did I think I could get hold of a car?

I asked him where he wanted to go.

—Mississippi.

I suppose I ought to have known something like that was coming. It was the next step. I could hear the roar, the power coming down. You have to understand, it was July and hot and they were talking, we were all talking, in the coffee bars in the Village, in church halls, in the (inside) pages of our own paper, about The Problem of the South. They were killing Negro boys down there. Still killing Negro boys, despite all the so-called advances. Reckless eyeballing was the name of the crime, and it could get you hung or burned alive or tied to an engine block and thrown in the river. The NAACP were saying something had to be done. The White Citizens Councils were threatening blood and fire. And Chester was proposing to go into Negro neighborhoods in the Delta and knock on doors to ask if they had old records. It did not seem wise.

I was not what you would call a political person. There were plenty around, the earnest folk fans, the gloomy girls with the turtlenecks and the French books, but I wasn't part of all that. I couldn't look anyone in the eye, let alone speak at a public meeting. Don't get me wrong, I believed in civil rights. I thought every man ought to be able to live his life. But handing out flyers and signing petitions didn't seem to make much difference. Sure, I spent all my time listening to the blues, but one of the reasons I liked those old songs, those disembodied voices rising up out of the past, was because they were a refuge from the world. I didn't want them contaminated by current affairs. I had no idea what Chester thought about it. He never passed comment on the condition of the American Negro.

But I also knew I had to say yes. Some things are just fate; you can't step out of their path. I told my boss I was taking a week's vacation and borrowed a car from an aunt on Long Island. It was an old wood-paneled Ford wagon, the kind everyone called a "woody." It looked like a tool shed on wheels, but it ran OK and the old lady didn't mind me borrowing it. I'd drive, Chester would pay for gas, and we would split other costs. That was our arrangement.

When I picked up Chester from his building, I was surprised to find him dressed in his suit, as if he was on his way to work. I thought he was crazy, but as it turned out, like so many things with Bly, his appearance had been carefully thought through. In the places we visited, he was often taken for a minister of religion, an assumption he encouraged by carrying around a large black Bible. People would address him as Reverend and let him into their houses. Chester didn't have much you could call a sense of humor, but he promoted this deception as a huge prank, a cunning and hilarious practical joke. He wedged his suitcase in the trunk, alongside a portable record player and a crate of vanilla seltzer, brought along because he "didn't trust the drinking water."

We drove out of the city, heading south.

▼

WE DRIVE OUT OF THE CITY, heading south, Leonie a passenger in her own expensive convertible, me running my fingers over the soft white leather trim on the wheel as the New Jersey Turnpike slides by. Walnut and lacquer. Adjusting the tone on the eight-track. *I'm a man, yes I am.* Crossing into Pennsylvania, then Maryland. The low sun dazzling me as we barrel into the heat of a long-ago summer evening.

—So, I say. What do you want to hear?

There is only so long you can feel afraid before something cracks. We laugh too hard at things that aren't funny and she tells me another story about how people don't see her, just her name. I understand, I say, as if I too have a famous family name that obscures my reality as a person. It does not seem important what I say. I can be as daring as I like. I am in the moment. What surrounds that moment is fuzzy and I don't feel like looking at it directly, but I am inside completely and it is beautiful. This bubble! Our reconciliation!

How long ago? With each mile we are heading further into the past. This is what I made her understand, that night in her apartment. That we had to repeat something, to go back to meet the force that is reaching out towards us from history.

—It's the only way.

—The only way to what?

—To save Carter. To save ourselves.

We already did this. We already traveled down this road. Now we drive on, laughing, forgetful, and only when we pull over do we touch reality, set foot on the land we are skimming over. Truck stops and little roadside settlements: post office and diner and general store. Early in the evening we cross the line into West Virginia and pull in for dinner at a Chinese buffet restaurant, a great barn off the highway with Formica tables and steaming metal trays of food. A family walks in. The man is a peacock, with long hair trailing over his shoulders, the brim of his camouflage cap carefully shaped. He is trailed by a stout brown wife and three kids. Down from the mountain for sweet and sour pork, white people as exotic to me as any Papuan tribe.

I have been up twice to heap my plate. Leonie is not eating anything, because of MSG. She has a can of club soda and a straw. Her mood has darkened. The mountain family sit down at a nearby table. One of the kids, a little boy of two or three, gets down off his chair and begins to wander around. Suddenly Leonie buries her head in her hands. This is her rhythm. For hours at a time she will make conversation, talk about her friends, movies and books, the things people talk about. Then for a while she will seem distracted, lost in her thoughts, and I know that sooner or later it will come—as it does now—a sudden pang of grief for her brother that racks her body with convulsions. Electromagnetic grief. Mesmeric grief, raising up her corpse and dropping it down again. The little boy watches her, the shoulders lifting, the head thrown back, eyes, mouth and nose streaming fluid. When it is over, she collapses forwards like a doll.

—What you doing, the little boy asks.

I get up to comfort her but she waves me back to my seat. She sucks in air, wiping her nose on the sleeve of her shirt.

—Don't treat me like I'm sick. I'm not sick.

So I drop back onto my chair and we eat. At least, I eat and she watches me, toying with the straw in her can. The sorrow has passed like bad weather, leaving a few traces, blotchiness, a redness to her eyes. She wears an increasingly skeptical expression, the look of someone who needs to be on her guard.

—You are such a weird guy. That night in my apartment you were sobbing, but all day you've been putting out this whole friendship is forever vibe. Like we're on vacation. You were terrified and now all of a sudden it's spring break. Do you see how insane that is?

I just think it's best we maintain a veneer of normality.

—Normality? Nothing's normal about this. I believed what you told me, Seth. I believed you. That you heard a story from a guy about the record Carter bought.

—He didn't buy it.

—That he found, then.

—It's hard to explain.

—Some things can't be explained, I get it. Stuff has been happening to me too. I went to see a psychic the other day, to ask about Carter? She looked at my hand and wouldn't take my money. She told me I had to leave. I believe we're in danger, but you need to talk to me. You need to tell me what it is you know, otherwise I don't see what I'm doing here.

Then it is night, and we are drinking and watching TV in a pine-paneled motel room that smells of lavender disinfectant. I feel knife-sharp, hyperauditory. The room is full of tiny harmonics that connect the wide spectrum hiss of the people next door flushing their toilet to the irregular snare of the air-conditioning and the long sweep of a truck passing on the highway, making the bug screens vibrate. Filaments of order, fleeting hints of meaning. I think about how different Leonie is from Carter, how I have no money to pay for anything, not even in a cheap place like this, not gas, not lunch, nothing, how I have responded by becoming as passive as a baby, how Leonie is sitting there wearing a flesh-pink kimono and a towel wrapped round her hair, how the kimono has fallen open to show me one long bare thigh and her throat is still damp from the shower and she has only rented one twin room, giving me a world-weary look as she put down her credit card at the front desk.

—So you're broke.

At the front desk, in the room. She asks the question simultaneously in both places, muting the TV and looking over at me as the receptionist processes her payment. I shrug noncommittally and pretend I haven't really heard, buying a few moments to compose myself, because I'm not sure where I am, when I am, whether I'm in the room stealing furtive glances at her legs or at the front desk wishing I had money, wishing I wasn't being swept along by events like a twig in a fast-flowing current.

—You don't have money because my brother was paying for everything.

I try to concentrate on the TV. A couple is walking through suburban rooms, dull beige rooms that leave no retinal trace of their passing. They are accompanied by an orchestral score, a string section playing minor key stabs, as if something threatening is about to happen. But it never does and they keep on walking, from room to room to room.

—Seth.

—No. I don't have money because your brother's henchmen locked me out of my studio which is my only means of making a living.

—*Your* studio?

—It's as much mine as his.

—He's the creative one, not you.

—Is that what he said? He actually said that?

She unmutes the TV. Now it's her turn to feign interest in it.

—Leonie, did he say that to you?

—Well, isn't it fair? He told me he was the producer and you were just the engineer.

—Wow.

—So what? Let me guess, it's the other way round? You do everything and my brother's just a spoiled rich kid, a dilettante?

—Look, Leonie, I know what you think of me.

—That you're like, his paid best friend? No offense, but I don't get it. No one gets it. You don't have anything in common.

—That's what you people think.

—Yes, that's what we people think. We don't know why he keeps you around.

—Jesus, I'm not a pet.

—But you're poor, so he always has to look after you, just like a pet. Just like I'm doing. Are you talented? You're obviously clever in an assholish way but it's not necessarily the same thing. So what is it? I'm just being honest. I don't know you, Seth. You're right at the center of my brother's life, but I have no clue about how you got there. As far as I can see, you're nobody.

Nobody.

—I'm just being honest. What's your deal, Seth? What do you actually want?

—I don't know how I can answer that.

—Why? Why would you not be able to answer? It's the simplest question.

—I don't know. I'm sorry. I suppose I don't want anything in particular.

—God, you are always apologizing. One little push and you just roll over. Put up a fight. Tell me to go to hell.

—I don't know what you want me to say. I'm just trying to do what's right for Carter. What's the matter?

—What's the matter? Seriously?

—I mean right now. What's the matter now?

—And again with the drippy concerned expression. You're fake, Seth, that's what's the matter. Why don't you just tell me what you've got going on? You know something you're not telling. It makes me nervous.

—I don't know anything.

—Bullshit. You always try to handle me. We're in this together— I don't know what to call it. This situation. And what I need is for you to be real with me for one minute. A single minute.

—I genuinely don't understand what you want. If I did, I'd try to make an appropriate response.

We watch the television for a while, black-and-white footage of some kind of protest, firemen playing hoses over people huddled against the side of a building. Leonie sighs.

—Actually, fuck it. It doesn't matter anyway.

—Why not?

—I'm saying, it doesn't matter. Forget about it.

—Why not?

—Because this has all already happened, so logically I must already know. You get what I'm saying?

—I'm not sure.

—I know you have that feeling, same as me. Don't tell me you don't. I must already know you're OK, Seth, because otherwise I wouldn't have come.

She changes the channel. The TV shows us a police shooting, yellow incident tape flapping back and forth as a reporter does a piece to camera, surrounded by a jostling crowd. A woman appears in the frame. Why would they kill him, she asks. His hands were up.

Leonie says she's going to sleep. She pulls the covers over herself and turns out the light by her bed. She puts her phone under her pillow. She has a panic button on her phone, she says. Press that button and they will come for her, abseiling out of a clear sky.

▼

WE STAYED IN A HOWARD JOHNSON'S in Virginia, eating an early
dinner in the restaurant. The next morning, Chester banged on my
door at 5 a.m.

—Stop tugging on it! Time to hit the road!

I almost leapt out of my skin.

—What are you sulking for? he asked, as I fumbled with the
ignition key a few short minutes later. I want to put on at least a
hundred miles before breakfast. We've got a way to go.

Around eleven that morning we were somewhere south of Knox-
ville, Tennessee. Chester pored over a gas station map and directed
me off the highway and over a railway line into an evil-looking set-
tlement of shacks and tumbledown cabins. Chicken coops. Fierce
dogs chained up in the yards. Here and there a woman or a child
turned to watch as the woody pitched and yawed its way down
the rutted track. Park up over there, Chester said, and straightened
his tie.

He turned to me, flipping up the polaroid lenses clipped to his
glasses so he could look me in the eye.

—Now listen. Ground rules. There are some records we can dis-
pute over and some I will let you have for your education, but there
are others about which I will brook no argument. I always take the
lead in any kind of negotiation or sales talk. I will banter and put

at ease. You will not speak, unless spoken to. You do not attempt any side deals or in any way indicate that you consider any material valuable or even interesting. That's the quickest way to screw this up. Party line is it's all junk and we're doing them a favor by taking it off their hands. Understand?

I nodded.

—Good. So, let's go see what they have here.

He got out of the car and picked his way through a yard to a shack, knocking on the door and calling out to see if anyone was at home. By the time I'd locked the car, he'd already moved on to a second. He knocked on doors at a furious rate, not waiting for a reply before he turned away. This was Chester's idea of efficiency. If he could have knocked on all the doors simultaneously he would have done so. When anyone opened up, man, woman or child, he'd give them the same speech.

—My name is Bly. I'm traveling in these parts, buying and selling, and I wonder, might I ask if you have any old gramophone records? Under the porch, maybe? Out back? Give you ten cents for every one I take.

Rickety doors, barking dogs. No we don't got nothing like that. No records. No sir. No. All kinds of people opening doors, but only one kind of people. Black people. Black people opening doors, white eyes in black faces, nervous eyes. Two white men on the porch never meant anything good. I found it hard to meet those eyes.

In a couple of places we did turn up some records. A toothless old fellow had a few in the drawer of a broken Victrola, sermons and religious music that Chester declared worthless. Then a woman let us into her home and showed us a stack a foot high sitting under the bed. Among a lot of dull military marches was a copy of Okeh 8455, Blind Lemon Jefferson's "Black Snake Moan" / "Match Box Blues." They had a couple of Bessie Smith Columbias and an unplayable-looking Irene Scruggs. We took the Jefferson and the Smiths. Back in the car, Chester handed them to me. "They're not particularly rare," he explained, "and I don't much care for Papa Blind Lemon."

I was pleased, but also distracted. I had never been inside houses like that. Little shacks patched together with sheet metal and crating. Blackened cooking pots hanging over brick fireplaces, pictures from old calendars pasted up for decoration. I had not thought such places existed, not in America. Honestly, I hadn't known.

We drove all day and on into the night, as Chester "wanted to make time." He was constantly tuning the radio, hopping from one station to another. About the only thing he'd stay with were the religious stations or the ones playing country music. There were songs I would have listened to, snatches of The Coasters and Fats Domino swept away in static. We stopped for coffee at a gas station and he used the bathroom. I think he must have taken a shot because when he came out, he was a different man, all his nervous kinks smoothed out. He found a station and stuck with it, though as far as I could hear, the reedy voice reciting Bible verses was no different from a dozen others he'd passed over in the hours we'd been on the road. *And one of the company said unto Him, Master, speak to my brother, that he divide the inheritance with me. And He said unto him, Man, who made Me a judge or a divider over you?*

—Were you in the army, Chester?

—Navy.

—You get to see the world?

—Sure. Keep your eyes on the road.

But God said unto him, Thou fool, this night thy soul shall be required of thee: then whose shall those things be, which thou hast provided?

By the time he finally decided we could pull in to a motel, I was exhausted. I went to bed without eating, the lights of the cars streaming on behind my closed eyes.

▼

WE WERE IN MISSISSIPPI, driving through rolling hills, then out across the great flat bottomlands of the Delta. Long straight roads, our old Ford ghosted by the dust. High cotton. Fields bounded by stands of hickory and pine. There were signs, Chester said. You could tell the houses where there were records to be found. Lace curtains, flowers on the porch, old jugs or oil cans on poles as nest boxes for the martins. Any sign of old ways or old people. What you wanted was a place where the same family had lived for years.

Driving down long roads. Long dry roads. Instead of goading me to make time, Chester began to consult his maps more frequently, directing me along zigzag routes to small towns, where we'd pass by neighborhoods of neat clapboard houses into zones of tin roofs and patched walls and decay, always some line to cross to get there, a highway or railroad track. Chester, knocking on doors, asking his monomaniacal question. Got any records? Under your porch, maybe? Pay a dime a piece.

—I don't know Rev'nd. Could have.

If there was digging, or lifting, that was my job. Worming under foundations. Dragging trunks and crates out of sheds and barns, while Chester made conversation. He would adopt a bantering manner, laughing loudly, slapping his non-Bible hand against his chest in counterfeit glee. It went over less well than he thought.

Those old pickers and sharecroppers had seen carpetbaggers in their time. I watched faces close down as they tried to work out his angle. They could sense something straining, something violent kept on a tight leash.

There was something secondhand about the way Chester treated those people, as if he'd learned it from a manual. He had no real warmth. But because he was determined, we found records. We grubbed them up out of the dirt.

We found Columbia 14299, Barbecue Bob "Motherless Chile Blues" / "Thinkin' Funny Blues" and Victor 21076 Luke Jordan "Church Bell Blues" / "Cocaine Blues." We found Brunswick 7125 Robert Wilkins "That's No Way to Get Along" / "Alabama Blues" and Brunswick 7166 Joe Calicott "Fare Thee Well Blues" / "Traveling Mama Blues." We had two Pattons, a worn copy of Paramount 12909 "High Water Everywhere Part 1" / "High Water Everywhere Part 2" and a clean Vocalion 02680, "High Sheriff Blues" / "Stone Pony Blues." We had a dozen good commercial female vocals, mostly Ma Rainey and Ida Cox, as well as a number of country records, which was a surprise to me, as I'd thought black people had no interest in the Carter Family or Jimmie Rodgers. Chester was oddly excited by Okeh 8960, The Memphis Jug Band "Memphis Shakedown" / "Mary Anna Cut Off," which he declared he had been hunting for ten years.

We would get to the end of our day, coated in sweat and road dust, and eat at the counter of whatever diner was nearest our motel, spooning up mashed potato and guzzling sweet iced tea. Then Chester would take one of his bathroom breaks. On the road, he never fixed up in front of me. He was, I think, very worried about the police. A child could have seen how we stood out, him in his preacher's black suit, me in the patterned shirt and cutoffs that made me look like what I was, a semi-beatnik northern kid. In white neighborhoods, people stared at us, even more than in black ones. Sometimes the attention was kindly. Sometimes not.

—Where you from, son?

There was a local way of repeating "New York." A special curl of the lip.

When he was floating on his cloud, Chester would lie on whatever motel room bed under whatever picture—Jesus, a waterfall, dogs playing poker—and ramble on about wanting to "suck up every damn record" in some place, the place we were in, a place up the road, a place we'd been or were planning to go. He wanted to leave nothing for the next man. That was his oft-repeated vow. It got old quickly. I would drift off into my own fantasies. Barefoot girls in cotton dresses. Skinny dipping. Sometimes he would touch on other topics, talking about records he had, records he wanted, records he thought ought to be smashed to pieces "to do the world a favor."

—Actually since you ask there are several lady collectors. I have corresponded with a Mrs. Levison in San Francisco. A Mrs. Audrey Levison. She has an interest in polkas. Also Yiddish folk tunes.

Eventually one of us would turn to the portable record player and play one of our discoveries. Voices, rising up out of the hiss.

> *They accuse me of forgery: can't even sign my name*
> *They accuse me of forgery: can't even sign my name*
> *Accuse me of murder, I never know the man*

▼

THIS IS HOW WE CROSS THE LINE. Farms set back from the road. Flat open country, flatter sky. Signs saying *No stopping for next 5 miles* and *Do not pick up hitchhikers,* then a prison, high blocks visible beyond a parking lot. I turn my head to read a billboard.

Walxr: Correctional solutions for a multipolar world.

The perimeter flies past, mute gray sheds inside the wire. Leonie looks over at me, gauging my reaction. You can't choose where you're born, she says, as if she expects me to disagree. You can't choose your family. When you say someone's *from* something, some place or group or category. When you say that, what does it even mean?

She talks about guilt, about how her shrink told her that no one should have to feel guilty all the time.

—My brother feels guilty for being a rich boy. That's why his heroes are always poor or black. I told him, it's not like you're helping anyone by listening to music. No one cares if you like black people.

—He respects the music.

—That doesn't make them like you any better. It's theirs. They'd rather you left it to them. Even if you did something, I don't know, really selfless. Black lives matter or whatever. They still wouldn't like you.

Then it is night. Leonie navigates the car slowly down a twinkling strip of lights, semis high-beaming us as we dawdle in the slow lane. She passes the usual fast-food restaurants, doubling back after a couple of miles to crawl the other side of the highway. Finally we find a low-roofed bar sitting like an island in a darkened lot, a place with a beer sign in the window and scarred wooden booths that hide the world in a comforting way. We flip over laminated cards and give our order to a weary middle-aged waitress. When the food comes, neither of us are hungry for the baskets heaped with chicken and okra and dessert-sweet slaw.

Leonie rubs her hands over her face, trying to wake herself up.

—I don't know what I'm doing here. I can't even remember why I said yes. I think I want to go home.

—Really? What about Carter?

—What about him? You told me this crazy story and it made sense. It made sense at the time. Now I don't know. If you need to stay down here I'll drop you somewhere, an airport or a hotel. But I'm driving back tomorrow. At a certain point it's just self-care to turn back when something isn't really working out, right?

—You're just going to give up? Just like that?

—Don't take that tone with me, Seth. He's my brother, not yours. I was feeling like shit, and you told me all this stuff about debt, how we had to go and face up to the past. It seemed wrong that I could just walk around all day, getting coffee, doing stuff, without thinking of him. I liked that you had a plan. But now we're here, it doesn't make sense. My whole creative life literally depends on me being contemporary. This whole scene, this dead musician, this record. It isn't what I should be focused on.

She carries on, talking mostly to herself. She's been taking pictures of Carter, she says. More shots of the two of them together in the ICU. She ought to do something with them. They might become a show.

My silence must convey to her that I'm hurt, because she reaches forward and squeezes my hand.

—It's not that I don't think this is real. I do. But maybe it's more real for you. It's something you had to do for him, not me.

We drive back down the strip, looking for a motel. A string of No Vacancy signs. The lights come to an end. The night closes around us. Leonie squints blearily into the darkness, then suddenly she gasps and hits the brakes. I'm thrown forward in my seat, my face almost hitting the windshield.

—My God. Did you see that?

—What? I didn't see anything.

—There was something in front of us, something in the road.

—What?

—I don't know. A cat maybe. A big black cat.

—I didn't see anything.

—Fuck. That was so scary.

—You want me to drive?

—Yeah. Yes, you drive. Please. I'm too tired.

We push through the humid night past the epic lights of a chemical plant, a magic castle glowing over the trees. We are far from any city, crossing a river that we see only as a darkness through the steel truss of the bridge. Leonie reclines the passenger seat and closes her eyes. I have the sense that I am no longer in charge of my life. I know that none of what I am doing can touch me, not at my core. My memory is a mystical conspiracy of connections. Everything has already happened. I am merely a man, sitting in a chair, listening to a recording made long ago. The needle is traveling in a predetermined track. Eventually, sooner or later, it will hit the run-out groove at the end.

THE PATROLMAN STOPPED US as we were leaving Clarksdale, pulling out of a turning behind us and sounding his siren. We stopped and waited for him to complete a leisurely inspection of our taillights. Then he leaned into the window and inspected us. I saw broad shoulders, a square face mostly obscured by sunglasses and a broad-brimmed hat. I told myself to be cool.

—License and registration.

I handed over my documents. Chester was staring straight ahead, looking, to my mind, not cool. Looking weird and strung-out and suspicious.

—What's your business in this county?

—We're buying records, sir.

—Records.

—Old records. Race records.

Ten seconds in and I'd blown it. The patrolman held up my New York State driver's license like something he'd fished out of a gutter.

—Ask you a question, son. You a believer in equal rights?

Chester leaned across me.

—Absolutely not, officer. I am a private researcher, a musicologist. This is my assistant.

—Musicologist? That New York for musician?

—No, I collect music. Old Negro folk music. I am associated with the New York Public Library.

He took out his wallet and handed the man a card. To my horror, it was just a library card, the kind you'd use to take out a book. I had one in my own wallet. As the cop examined it, I fixed my eyes on the steering wheel.

—"Professor C. Bly." That you?

—Yes.

And you down here collecting nigger music

—That is correct.

—OK Professor, I'll tell you something for free. This is a peaceful county.

—I quite understand, officer. Let me assure you, I'm a proud American.

—Well that's good to hear, but I warn you, don't go on anyone's land, and don't go talking to their boys less you clear it first.

—As I said. Proud American. I stand with the white man, one hundred percent.

I stared over at Chester. The patrolman stared at him too. A pause. He straightened up and slapped the roof of the car.

—Y'all can be on your way. But stay out of neighborhoods like this. It ain't safe.

He handed back our documents. Chester pocketed his library card with an air of satisfaction.

—Drive on, he said.

I don't think Chester meant a word of it. No one could have loved that music so much and harbored a speck of racial prejudice. All the same I felt ashamed. It seemed wrong to have said what he said. For a moment I wished I really had driven along those bumpy roads to register people to vote, to tell them they ought to be free. Then Chester said something about a barrelhouse pianist I was interested in, name of Cow Cow Davenport, and the feeling slipped away.

▼

WRONG SIDE OF THE TRACKS. Overgrown tracks, a branch of the railroad that was abandoned years ago, but the geography persists, the line of convention. The river is invisible behind the steep slope of the levee, but you can sense it muttering and shrugging on the far side, looking for a way to spill over and spread itself out across the land. We ought to be on the road, finding somewhere to stay the night. Instead we're in a juke, no more than a shack with crates of Schlitz beer and Double Cola behind the bar. We have brought a dead hush to the place, not busy at this early hour.

They have electricity, a bright bare bulb dangling from the ceiling. According to Chester, electricity has been their undoing. Gleaming in the corner is what in these parts they call a Seabird, a Seeburg jukebox, decorated with Cadillac fins and crammed with little plastic 45's, a monster machine that seems to have landed here from the future. The Seabird is Chester's enemy. It has "killed music." We are the only white people to have walked in here since the last time it was raided by the police and now he's giving the assembly a lecture about the evil of the Seabird.

—"Select-o-matic." What is that? Why do you people even have this thing in here? Goddamn Sam Cooke.

—Come on, Chester.

—You are being corrupted, you know that? Do you know what you are throwing away?

—Chester. Let's go.

—Forget this plastic trash. Pick up a fife! A fiddle! Blow over a damn jug!

The barman, who is perhaps also the owner, nervously smokes a cigarette. The other patrons, two or three old men, are staring at Chester, without staring at him. Everyone in here knows that trick. In this place, in all the places where we knock on doors, they know it. I always have the sensation of being stared at, but I never meet anyone's eye.

▼

AS WE MADE OUR CALLS, I found out that Chester was chasing information as well as records. Leads, details of the biographies of certain musicians. If someone had no records, but was willing to talk, he would run down a list. You heard of a guitar picker, singer, fellow used to play piano at a barrelhouse off of Sixty-one? Live round here? Played at dances or picnics? Went to the Mount Zion church? The names would change, depending on where we were. Kid Bailey. Joe Reynolds. Willie Brown. Charley Taylor. Calvary, First Baptist, Lamb of God. Up by the river around Friars Point, he started asking about Charlie Shaw.

It was the first time I ever heard the name.

Twilight. A few more calls, Chester said. Just one or two. We were driving on an old rural road. We passed a cabin and stopped to talk to a man outside working on a truck. When we asked him about records he said he had none. Chester ran his list of names. *Garfield Akers, Robert Johnson, Charlie Shaw.*

—Charlie Shaw, you say?

—Played guitar.

—From around here?

—Would have been about thirty years ago.

—Go on up the road. Ask Miss Alberta, maybe she help you.

He gave us directions, told us to look out for a white porch and a roof that was all cedar shakes, no tin. The light was failing as we found the cabin, which was set back from the road under a huge cottonwood. I switched off the engine and suddenly the night was full of information, the susurrus of insects closing over me in a great wave. On the porch burned a kerosene lamp. A little boy, maybe six or seven years old, scraped a bottleneck along a piece of wire nailed to one of the uprights. Up and down, a melancholy twang like a Jew's harp.

—Evening, son. My name's Bly. Is your mother home?

The boy just stared at us and carried on playing. Then I saw there was someone else on the porch, an ancient woman in a rocking chair. She was made of shadows. I can't tell you how I knew, because I do not understand, but shadows were woven into the flowers on her cotton dress, the scoop of her eye sockets, her toothless jaw. I saw her and I lost the power of speech. Chester did not seem to see what I saw, or hear what I heard. That terrible insect war cry, that scraping.

—Good evening, ma'am. My name is Bly. We're buying up old gramophone records. I'll pay you a dime apiece for any we take.

—Ain't got nothing for sale.

Her voice was like rustling paper, fugitive, near to silence. Chester put a foot up on the porch and smiled.

—You sure you don't have anything just hidden away?

—Not interested.

—All right then. I won't take up more of your valuable time. Just one last question, please indulge me. Man down the road said you might know something about Charlie Shaw.

Her silence lasted forever.

—Charlie.

Chester seemed unsure of her meaning. He leaned in.

—Charlie Shaw, a guitar player, from somewhere round here. I heard he came from along the river, between Rosedale and Friars Point.

Above his head, insects battered themselves to death against the glass chimney of the kerosene lamp.

—Boy was a rounder. Always traveling here and there.

Insect static. The crackle and hiss.

—You knew Charlie Shaw?

—Have mercy. He never came back from Jackson.

—Ma'am, I'm interested in all the blues players from round here. It sounds to me like you knew Charlie Shaw. Did you ever hear him play?

—Of course I heard him play.

—Where?

—Right here, on this porch. He was my only brother.

Chester's face in the firelight, transfixed. Chester's avaricious eyes.

Maybe I dropped off, just for a moment, or maybe I kept dropping off. My memory is full of holes. From here on there is no logic. The scenes are out of order. I don't know how we got inside, whether she invited us or Chester just wedged his foot in the door. I don't know what words were used. Chester was talking all the time, spinning stories, doing his pastor act. In my memory it's a series of still frames. I'm at the car, then I'm on the porch, then I'm inside sitting on a stool, watching the dust dance in the lamplight. The small room is full of darkness. It is dense with darkness, stuffed with it like cotton wool. I scuff my feet on the rough boards and listen to the old woman talk about her brother Charlie, who went to Jackson and never came back. Chester has no interest in Jackson. He has a little leather-bound notebook. He is scribbling with a pencil, asking questions. What about his repertoire? What songs did he know? Who taught him to play? Miss Alberta remembers a man called Tommy or Copperhead, who used to come around. Man who worked the river. Charlie used to sit with him.

—Do you remember what songs he taught Charlie? Any in particular you can remember?

—Some. I suppose you want to hear him.

—Hear him?

Oh yes, Chester wants to hear him. The sequence is hard to untangle. We go inside. I'm sitting on a stool, watching the dust dance in the lamplight. The small room is dense with darkness. I am on the porch, under the screaming insects. I am out by the car.

I go inside.

▼

ANOTHER NIGHT. In another motel, indistinguishable from the last, we lie on a bed looking at our phones. The TV in the room seems like an old model. Rounded tube, wooden housing, a rabbit-ear antenna sitting on top. It is showing a musical. Men in blackface makeup are singing on a riverboat. In spats and tail coats they twirl around. By the bed is a slot which takes quarters. You put in a coin and the mattress vibrates.

You put in a coin now. Long ago, you put in a coin. We shared a joint in the bathroom, blowing the smoke into the air vent.

—So in the morning, you're turning back.

—Maybe. I don't know. Is that what I did before? I don't know what's waiting for me in the city. I walk around and there's always some guy with one hand on his junk yelling at me like he literally owns the sidewalk I am walking on and because I won't talk to him I'm a bitch and a whore. These guys watching me. And it's not just guys. I mean, they could be young or old, male, female. But they're all the same. They—none of them—shit, it's not easy to talk about this. What I'm saying is it's never white people.

She exhaled deeply.

—I'm not a racist, Seth. I swear I'm not.

—Of course not. Racists aren't like—I mean, I know you're cool. You know you're cool.

For a while she talked about healing, a medical NGO she'd volunteered with in Africa. The people were so poor. The little children sang a song to her outside their tin-roofed school. The truth, she said, was that no one knew how to fix anything. People had all kinds of theories but in the end that's all they were.

—But it's as if they're in communication. The, uh, non-whites. I know how that sounds. I don't mean that. It's hard to explain. It's like they all have the same information about me. Like they've formed some kind of opinion and I can't do anything to change their minds.

—You feel judged.

—Right. And I resent that. It's grotesque, actually. They don't know me. They don't know what I've been through. I don't want to feel like this, Seth. Six months ago I was alive. I can't even remember what that was like, to be honest with you. Every day I feel less and less connected.

—What are we going to do?

—About what?

—All of it. Us.

She looked around sadly.

—You're too timid to even ask me why we're renting a double room in a shitty place like this, but you're all like "us" as if me and you are a thing?

She went outside for a cigarette, closing the door to show that I was not invited to follow. I sat on the edge of the bed, my knees grazing the bulky air conditioner under the window. I felt shriveled, shrunken into myself.

She came back in and sat down on the bed.

—I can't sleep in places like this unless someone's in the room. That's all. You seemed pretty harmless so I thought it was OK. But you turned out to be a very tense person. You are not relaxing to be around.

She came back in. She sat down beside me. She had always been coming back in, sitting down, again and again, forever coming back in and sitting down. She spoke to me and it was as if she spoke in my voice. She said she knew what I wanted. She said she'd seen how I looked at her. I don't want you, she said, but it's the quickest way to end it. Sometimes you're with a guy and you know you're the only door he'll leave through.

—Do you understand, Seth?

I squinted at the TV screen, pretending I hadn't heard.

—Take what you want.

She sat down on the bed beside me, again and again, and she leaned over and kissed me and we began to kiss deeper and suddenly everything happened always and forever and I was hearing Leonie Wallace gasp, licking Leonie Wallace's nipples, the areolae of Leonie Wallace's nipples, which turned out to be wide and brown, and I was brushing my face against a down of hair, smelling Leonie Wallace's smell, my cheeks slick against Leonie Wallace's wet thighs, seeing Leonie Wallace looking up, looking me straight in the eye as she sucked me. Choose a picture on your hard drive. Jerk off to Leonie Wallace, jerk off to me and Leonie Wallace.

We were doing it with Carter, of course. He was in there with us, in us. Inside our movements, in the angles between our bodies. Afterwards Leonie took a shower, locking herself in the bathroom for over half an hour. When she came out, she was dressed in sweat pants and a flannel shirt. She fussed with her luggage, then got in to bed, slipped on an eye-mask and switched off her bedside light. During all this routine, she never once looked at me. I was left there, naked in the reek of her, my body bathed in the major glow of the TV and the minor glow of my phone, a rhombus of light on the bed illuminating a snail trail of semen that ran down my thigh. I was thinking, did that happen? That may not have happened.

MISS ALBERTA'S SHACK EXPANDS. Its tiny confines are a great shadowed concourse that I am watching her cross. She moves continuously but makes no headway, shuffling her old bones in place like a deck of cards. It is infinite, this moment, Miss Alberta always receding into the darkness, into the shadows. The slow scrape of her shoe on the boards.

In her hand, as she turns, is a record. And I know I am slipping into darkness, but I am powerless to stop it. Oh God, says Chester, and there is something repulsively sexual in his tone. Oh God, he says, it's true.

I want to get further away, but I can't move. I am falling down into starless desolation and I cannot lift myself up off the stool.

—He went to Jackson. Mr. Speir made him an appointment.

—He recorded. I knew it! I knew it!

—At the Saint James Hotel in Jackson.

—Do you remember the year? Oh God, you actually have the record. Can I see it?

—It's not for sale.

She does not hand the record to Chester, though he is beseeching her with every cell of his body. The man is a gut-string, taut, vibrating with need.

—Please can I see it?

—Maybe I'll play it for you.

—Could you just turn it so I can take a look at the label?

—Haven't used this thing in an age.

She is blowing great puffs of dust off an old Victrola, the kind with an external horn and a crank handle. Chester looks worried.

—Maybe you ought not to play it on that. Those discs are very easily damaged.

She cranks the handle and drops the needle. A hard crackle rises up out of the horn. Chester is rigid, mute with panic. I know what he is thinking because I am thinking it too: Metal needles. Blunt needles that can strip a fragile record, a rare and valuable record. Then I cannot bother any more about what he is thinking, because Charlie Shaw's voice swoops down, and it is ancient and bloody and violent and it is coming for me, hunting for me as I sink lower and lower, into the darkness.

> *Believe I buy a graveyard of my own*
> *Believe I buy me a graveyard of my own*
> *Put my enemies all down in the ground*

Charlie Shaw's voice is looking for me, for what I have kept hidden, the guiltiest of my secrets. His voice is filled with such terrible pain that I can hardly bear it.

> *Put me under a man they call Captain Jack*
> *Put me under a man they call Captain Jack*
> *Wrote his name all down my back*

I should not be obliged to hear this voice. I need it to stop. It is not right. I haven't done anything wrong. The voice wants payment, but how would I even begin to afford the price?

It ends. At last it ends.

—How much do you want for it, Chester asks, before the needle has even run into the gutter. His greed is naked. He is totally powerless to hide it. Again Miss Alberta says it is not for sale.

—Why not. I'll give you a good deal. Here, how about a dollar?

—A dollar.

The little boy watches us.

—That's right. Cash money. A shiny silver dollar right here.

—A dollar for my brother's memory.

—I'll give you ten for it. Ten dollars, Miss Alberta. That's a good price. More than fair.

—I said it's not for sale.

—Twenty, then. You can't argue with twenty dollars. You should trust me. I'll take good care of your brother's legacy. I'm a connoisseur. I'm a very respectful man. If you like I can give you an undertaking, all drawn up and legal. You understand what I'm telling you? I will write you out an official undertaking. A paper, Miss Alberta, if you just let me have the record. I'll make sure a lot of people get to hear him. That's what you want, isn't it? For people to hear poor old Charlie?

—You like the record?

—Of course I do.

—And what about you?

She turns to me. I can't see her eyes. I want no part of this. Mutely, I nod.

—Then why am I only hearing about money? Twenty dollars says one. The other can't manage a word. I played you my brother's record and you ain't got a word?

No no no, says Chester. He's stuttering. A misunderstanding. No one could be more excited about Charlie Shaw. One of the great question marks. The gap, the missing link. So many questions.

—Questions? No, I don't believe so. I don't believe you have any questions at all.

Chester laughs his big fake preacher's laugh. I want to tell him to stop with the molasses. He is pouring it into a great red maw.

Ha ha ha ha

ha ha

ha

Chester does not know where he is. Around us the night is screaming messages and he isn't listening. I can't raise my eyes from the floor, because each time I look at Miss Alberta, she becomes more terrifying. Her substance is absence. She is made of it, made of loss. I am slipping into darkness. It is enveloping me like a shroud.

—I'd like you to go.

Only now does it dawn on Chester that she is angry, that it is possible he might leave without the record in his hand.

—No you wouldn't, Miss Alberta. Think of your brother. I'm only thinking of poor Charlie.

—Poor Charlie?

—That's right. Poor Charlie. Now, do you just have the one platter? Or is there more than one?

I find my voice, croak at him.

—Chester, come on. Leave her alone. We're not wanted here.

—Keep out of it.

His face, snarling at me. *There are some about which I will brook no argument.* I look at him and nothing I see makes me any less afraid. He is prepared to do whatever it takes to get that record. He would bite out her throat.

—Now, he says. Now. Now I don't have the money with me, but I can give you a hundred dollars. One hundred dollars, Miss Alberta. Maybe even more, if there are others. Did Charlie just record the two sides? The two songs?

—He went to Jackson, never came back.

—That's right. Poor Charlie.

—He went to make the record.

—In Jackson. While you're thinking about it, why don't you play me the other side? And if you'd just let me look at the label? I could maybe tell you some things about it. Wouldn't that be nice?

—I just want you to leave. Go. Get out of my house.

—Miss Alberta.

And then I have more holes, more gaps. I am sitting on a stool, watching Chester, who is looming over the old woman, raising his voice. I am sitting in the shadows. I sit on a stool. I stand out on the porch, I sit on the swing. I am in the driver's seat of the car, waiting outside the Saint James Hotel. Turning the key in the ignition. He never came back. Turning the key, outside the Saint James Hotel. And Chester is shouting damn you old woman. Are you going to take that record to your grave?

▼

I SLEPT. AND WHEN I WOKE in the morning my suspicion was a tangible thing, a taste in my mouth. It had never happened. The whole episode had been an illusion. Leonie was moving round the room, cleaning her teeth, doing her makeup, and I was no more a sexual presence to her than the men on the television, the newscasters and pitchmen and interviewees from the world of entertainment. The disappointment was crushing. I hadn't slept with her. She'd rented a single room. She was rich but she'd rented one room and I had spent the night in there with her, in the bed next to her bed, and nothing had happened because I was harmless, not enough of a man. And yet I had those memories. Her sounds, her intake of breath by my ear. I had the memories but I could not trust them. That morning she seemed entirely unchanged by what had happened between us. Her indifference was immense. There was none of what there should be between lovers. No complicity, no shared secret.

As we walked to the car my suspicion grew, parasites of doubt clenching and unclenching themselves in my gut, looking for an orifice through which they could escape into the world. I assumed that we were heading home to New York, as she had said, but at the entrance to the parking lot she turned to me and asked which way.

—Aren't we going back?

—We're so close. We're close, right?

—Yes.

—So we might as well go on. Which way?

—Take a left.

We drove out of the lot, through the summer sunshine. We drove down a steep hill, down, down, down into the dark until we came to the river, a road that ran beside the levee, a threatening elevation that formed an artificial horizon off to our right. All the weight was on that side, the unseen bulk of the Mississippi. We passed the turnoff for an archaeological site, Choctaw Indian burial mounds, a group of low grassy hills. Trailers and cabins were scattered haphazardly across the land, housing like litter. By the side of the road, convicts in green striped uniforms were picking up trash, under the eye of a guard sitting in the cab of a *Walxr* corporate transporter.

We knocked on a few doors, met country people who did not want to be bothered. It wasn't long before someone showed us a gun. A white woman came to the door with it, a rifle. What did we want? We got smartly back in the car, reversed off the property. Hand-painted religious signs were nailed to a boundary fence. GOD HATES A LYING TONGUE PROV 6:17 SAME SEX MARRIAGE HELL HATH ENLARGED HERSELF ISAIAH 5:14 FOR WITHOUT ARE SORCERERS AND WHOREMONGERS AND MURDERERS. We left that door alone. Sorcerers, whoremongers and murderers, we slunk on by.

My phone was telling me we were close. JumpJim's directions had taken us all the way from New York but he couldn't be certain about the exact location of the cabin. The car bumped over the rutted track. I was vibrating at all the resonant frequencies of the system, my actions amplified into the past, into the future. Each time we saw a house I went to the door and said the name. Charlie Shaw, Charlie Shaw. They shook their heads but I could feel him getting closer. And I knew he could hear us coming too.

—A cabin with wooden shingles, under a tree.

—I don't recall anything like that.

Charlie Shaw?

—No one of that name.

We drove down the road, we drive down the road, we have always and forever been driving down the same dirt road. We drive inside our bubble and I look at my phone and the little red pin is on top of the checkered flag. *You have arrived at your destination.* I see a giant cottonwood tree. I know nothing about trees but this is what I say to myself. *A giant cottonwood tree.* As if I have said it before. I see a trailer park of rickety single-wides up on cinder blocks. Washing strung on lines, children's toys in the yards. We sit in the car, squinting at the trailers.

—We're here.

—This is it? I don't remember it.

—This is the place.

—You looking for someone?

A kid on a bike. Maybe ten years old, his hair pulled back from his face in severe cornrows.

—Yeah. You live here?

—Nice car, lady.

Thanks, says Leonie.

—You know a Charlie Shaw?

—No.

—Or anyone by that name. Shaw. Alberta Shaw maybe.

—No sir. There's us and Sharlene and Mrs. Jackson and then you best not walk any further.

—Was there a shack here, ever?

—A what?

—A timber shack, with shingles.

—There's only us here, is what I'm telling you.

He cycles off. I feel like I am coming down off something, crashing. The predawn light of some psychological day has revealed me to myself: exhausted, out of juice. We get out of the car and walk around by the side of the road. A woman appears at the door of her trailer and watches us. Leonie does some quad stretches, lights a cigarette.

—Now we can go back. We made our pilgrimage for Carter but now it's time to go back.

At that moment I believe she is right, but the present is out of reach and once again I understand that we have done all of it before and I am like a skin stretched over a hollow drum, all my will and striving just surface tension. We have always been here but it has taught us nothing. We still don't know what we have forgotten, what it is we owe. My phone shows a blank screen. We have always been standing there, Leonie pulling at one ankle, then the other, me looking at my phone, and the car that is coming down the road has always been coming, always coming down the long dirt road. We hear it before we see it, we feel the bass in our guts. Ultra-low frequencies, nausea-inducing. Waves physically displacing human tissue. The emitter is some kind of old muscle car, a Mustang or a GTO, murdered out in matte black paint. Black wheels, black trim. Over the weaponized bassline runs a vocal, chopped and screwed.

Believe I buy a graveyard of my own

The driver kills the ignition, and with it the sound. For a moment we stand in silence, Leonie and I, relieved of the awful sonic pressure, returning the machine's inhuman gaze. Then the door opens and out steps a young black man, who swaggers towards us. He wears a crisp white XXL tee shirt and jeans. Short dreadlocks poke out beneath an angled cap. As he gets closer I see his light-skinned face, delicate and mournful. Tattoos snake down both forearms, onto the backs of his hands. He shows me his left wrist. Numbers 8 11 18 23. *Musician. To dream you hear one play foretells grief and sadness . . .*

Do we feel lucky?

Even standing still before us, he is relentlessly in motion, rolling his shoulders, hands plucking at his jeans, his shirt, the brim of his cap. As if he is neurotically performing liveliness or perhaps merely aliveness, the continued absence of death. When he speaks, his voice is a surprise, a barely audible rasp.

—Yo. Who asking about Charlie Shaw?

He becomes theatrically still, even his stillness a form of motion. He scrutinizes us, stroking his chin with a thumb and forefinger. The passenger side window of the car rolls down. Someone else is watching us too.

—We're not police, says Leonie.

—Why would you feel the need to say that?

I tell him Charlie Shaw's sister lived on this spot. Lived here. A long time ago.

—What's the name?

—Charlie Shaw.

—I know plenty of shorties, Charles.

Inside the car, the passenger laughs. He hangs an arm out of the door, an arm like a twist of black wire, ending in a gold-ringed hand holding a Big Gulp cup of purple soda. I am cowed by these men, conscious of my meager white body.

—What this guy do?

—He was a musician.

—No Charles, what he do? What you want him for?

—He didn't do anything.

—So how come you need to talk to him, Charles?

—Something happened. A friend of mine owes him. Owes him money.

—And if I know this Charlie Shaw?

—We just need to speak to him. We—my friend really wants to make it right.

—Is this him, asks Leonie. Did you do something to my brother?

—Leonie, I say. This isn't the guy.

—Step off. I don't know you or your brother. Your friend wants to make it right? Well that's OK then. Sure I know the guy. Charlie. He live just up the way.

—Really?

—Really? Fuck outta here.

The man in the car laughs again, spilling a little of his drink. A red cap is pulled low over his head. The driver bares his teeth and takes a step towards me, but for all his bluster I know he will not hurt me because we've been here before. I know I'm only talking to the messenger. The real power lies with the man in the car.

—I said get the fuck out of here, Charles. You ain't deaf.

—No. I'm not deaf.

—So why you ain't moving? Get in your fucking car and turn the fuck around.

—I didn't mean.

That arm, black fuse wire. We didn't mean.

—Turn the fuck around.

—Just chill out, says Leonie.

—Oh, and fuck you too bitch. You think Imma talk to you about who I know and don't know? Fuck all y'all.

—Let's go, Seth. Let's just go.

Charlie Shaw is in the car and I need to speak to him. I need him to break his silence, to come out from behind the veil and say what it is he wants. If he doesn't explain, I'm scared that this will go on and the next person it touches will be me. I am a good person. I have done nothing wrong. Carter was the one. The young man is stepping towards me, holding out his arms wide, the palms of his hands open, herding us into our car. He makes me feel insubstantial. It is not logical to feel this way. I am alive, I think as I fumble with the car door. The ghost is him.

All I can do is roll down the window and shout as we reverse away.

—You're the one! You're him! We're so sorry! We didn't mean any disrespect!

The passenger turns the music on high, drowning me in bass and that terrible, pitched-down drugged-out vocal.

> *Put me under a man called Captain Jack*
> *Wrote his name all down my back*

The driver walks backwards, lifting up his shirt. He indicates a gaping wound in his side.

—Right through my motherfucking lung.

I slam the accelerator and we fishtail backwards along the track. We are still alive, I repeat, over and over. My mantra. We are still alive.

▼

WE ARE CROSSING THE STATE LINE, leaving Mississippi. We are driving home. It's morning and I'm eating eggs and drinking coffee at the counter. The cook is scraping burned food off the grill and the waitress is taking orders. It is dark. I am asleep in bed. It is dark and I am asleep in yet another motel room with thin walls and I hear the key in the ignition and I am on the porch turning the key in the ignition and the little boy is watching me. I'm trying to get Chester to leave. The boy scrapes the bottleneck along the wire and sings.

> *Pharaoh*
> *Pharaoh*
> *Pharaoh army sure got drownded*
> *Pharaoh*

Chester has gone somewhere. I'm asleep in yet another motel room, asleep in old sheets that smell of lavender detergent. I want to go home. I am eating eggs at the whites-only counter and the vibration of trucks on the highway rattles the windows and the sheets smell of lavender and there is the sound of a key in a car ignition, outside in the darkness at the Saint James Hotel, a gearbox grinding as someone tries to find first.

And the next morning I am eating eggs and drinking coffee and Chester is beside me, unshaven, eating eggs. I butter a slice of toast.

—Did you go somewhere last night?

—Where? I went out for a smoke, if that's what you mean. Where else would I go?

▼

CHESTER SEEMED TO FILL UP THE CAR. I was sick of him, the look of him, fidgeting and mopping his brow. He called frequent bathroom breaks. He said he must have eaten something. I suppose at some point he ran out of heroin, and I ran out of any desire to be around him. A sharp ammoniac scent rose up from his clothes, curling into my nostrils. Somewhere around DC I began to feel nauseous, as if my very guts were rejecting his presence. I was never more happy to pass the turnoff for Newark and see the Manhattan skyline on the other side of the river. It was frustrating, having to wait in the fug of gasoline fumes, edging the old station wagon forward foot by foot to enter the Holland Tunnel. We sat on Canal for almost an hour, crawling towards Brooklyn. Finally I dropped him at his hostel and was free.

I abandoned the car in the first spot I saw in the Village, not really caring if it would still be there the next day. Carrying my suitcase and a package containing thirteen rare 78 records, I staggered home, pushed open the front door and climbed the six flights to my stifling little room. When I got in, I opened the windows, switched on the fan, and bolted the door. Manhattan in August had never felt so good. I tried to do the things you do when you get home, the things you do to make yourself feel "at home." I showered. I lit the burner and made a cup of coffee. I sat and drank the coffee, listening to the whirring sound of the electrical converter in the closet, the soundtrack of every cheap apartment in the city.

I did not feel at home.

I went out again, drifting down to the Washington Square fountain. As usual it was a nut house, art school girls in leotards and long skirts and Mexican peasant blouses, bearded guitarists sporting the plaid and denim of the working man. I got a hollow laugh out of a guy in overalls, doing a phony rendition of "Reynardine," accompanying himself on a lute. The asshole college bongo players were out too. It was unbearable.

Back at the apartment, I opened the package. I carefully cleaned my acquisitions, sleeved them in uniform brown paper, wrote out cards for them and filed them with the rest of my collection. The real thing, not the circus down by the fountain. The real thing, in my possession.

But I didn't play my records. I filed them and looked at them, lined up on the shelf in their brown paper sleeves. I was pleased with the way they looked, but I didn't play them. Instead I did other things. I went to work. I drove around, looking for new hubcaps for my aunt's car. I dropped off the car with my aunt and took a train back to the city. I hung around on Fifth Avenue, looking in shop windows. I went to work. I drank an egg cream. I rode the subway. I went to work. But I didn't play those records. I didn't play any records at all.

Without understanding how it had happened, I found myself locked out of the world. The perimeter was everywhere and nowhere, but it excluded me as surely as a wire fence. The city seemed hazy and insubstantial. I moved through the newsroom, across Washington Square, without really touching anyone or anything, braced for the moment when I'd try to take a sheet of copy or lift a cup and it would pass straight through my hand. When I got dressed in the morning, my image in the mirror seemed like a film overlaid on the moldy fixtures of the bathroom, thin, nearly transparent, not the substantial body of a living man. At the *Tribune,* I avoided Chester. I only saw him in the distance, through the haze of smoke. He looked raggedy and tired. Before, he'd always looked sharp at work. I kept my head down and tried to do my job. I didn't talk about my vacation. I didn't talk much at all.

It was too hot to spend time at home. There I sat around in my underwear, a wet towel draped round my shoulders. I felt guilty every time I ran down the stairs, out onto the street. Guilty for leaving my record collection. It was too hot for shellac records, which turn to the consistency of pizza dough when you leave them in the sun. They needed to be stored somewhere cooler, or they could get horribly warped. Instead of rescuing them, I draped a batik cloth over the shelves and left the apartment. Out of sight, out of mind.

I hung around a bookstore on 8th Street, pretending I had enough money to buy. I kept ending up back in Washington Square. The folksingers there were terrible frauds, but at least they were alive. They were young people singing in the sunshine. And there were some passable musicians. A burly man with a booming voice and a decent fingerpicking guitar style, a little curly-haired guy who played an autoharp. Usually you could wander around, hang at the edges of different cliques—the bluegrass mafia, young communists singing about unions, Zionists singing about irrigation. There were a couple of Flamenco guitar players, a Senegalese who plucked a kind of lute-harp thing called a kora. That dude always drew a crowd. Whenever he was there, I listened to him, this living man plucking living strings.

I needed more life all the time. I craved it. It wasn't that I didn't make an effort. I asked one of the secretaries at the *Tribune* to go to a movie with me. We saw *The Defiant Ones* and made out in the subway on the way home. I began to think I might be finished with 78's. Maybe all that had run its course.

Then I got a card from Chester, slipped into my pigeonhole at work, an invitation to one of his listening parties. I read his meticulous handwriting and swore to myself I would not go. I would not travel out to his spartan room and sit on a hard chair as he played music he had grubbed up out of the past.

A long subway ride. The train clattering across the river. The train going underground, running express. Stations flitting past, rectangles of light, there and then gone. Insects battering themselves on the kerosene lamp.

I did not want to go. I did not want to go and listen in that stifling little room.

THE CHESTER WHO OPENS THE DOOR does not look well. Gaunt and sallow, he barely speaks to me. I hand him a fifth of some godawful sweet wine and take my seat among the others, the sweat running down my body, soaking my shirt. The usual crowd is there. Morton, coughing. Fat old Pinkus, lecturing Tom Grady about some instrument, the origin, he is saying, of all blues guitar.

—What is?

—The diddley-bow. Just a simple length of wire.

—Jesus, Morton. Put a hand in front of it. You sound like you got TB.

—Don't joke about such things.

The men bicker in the distance. The insects are murdering themselves overhead and I'm leaning on the porch in the heavy night, listening to the little boy scraping, singing

> *Pharaoh army sure got drownded*
> *Pharaoh*

Voices far in the distance, at the very edge of perception. I'm outside in the summer heat. I'm in a tiny stifling room. I'm at the fountain, watching a pretty redhead dancing to a drum played by a young black man in a fez. The cops don't like it, the lewd dancing.

They move everybody on. No bongos without a permit, Sammy Davis. Chester is playing something I have not heard before, Vocalion 1704, Jelly Jaw Short, "Snake Doctor Blues":

> *I'm the snake doctor man: everybody trying to find out*
> *my name*

He is playing Patton, very worn.

> *They got me in shackles wearing my ball and chain*
> *And they got me ready for that Parchman train*

I am on the train, going underground. The kids at the fountain are arguing with the cops. If you sing, dig, it's just an extension of speech. You can't tell us not to sing. This is Nazi Germany.

—You ain't in Nazi Germany, you're in denial.

Rotten old cop yuk-yukking at his own joke, doubling down.

—And that's where you can make your protest. In de Nile.

The kids at the drained fountain. Chester, haunted. He has a conspicuous mustard stain on his shirt. Ordinarily that kind of thing would be intolerable to him. He plays some Texan gospel singer asking *what are they doing in heaven today* and coughs into his sleeve. Then he takes a record out of the box and I see it's on a nothing label called Key & Gate. A label that only lasted a couple of years, it put out novelty records, minstrel acts and third-rate dance bands. All trash, every side. Nothing a collector would care to own.

—This, Chester says, is the only copy.

And it rises up to meet me.

> *Believe I buy a graveyard of my own*
> *Believe I buy me a graveyard of my own*
> *Put my enemies all down in the ground*
>
> *Put me under a man they call Captain Jack*
> *Put me under a man they call Captain Jack*
> *He wrote his name all down my back*

Went to the Captain with my hat in my hand
Went to the Captain with my hat in my hand
Said Captain have mercy on a long time man

Well he look at me and he spit on the ground
He look at me and he spit on the ground
Says I'll have mercy when I drive you down

Don't get mad at me woman if I kicks in my sleep
Don't get mad at me woman if I kicks in my sleep
I may dream things cause your heart to weep

It ends. Around the room there is silence, a palpable relief.

—What was that?

—Exquisite. Do I detect Piedmont in the guitar picking?

Chester looks smug.

—Yes, I'm guessing Georgia?

Voices in the distance. He can't meet my eye.

—How did you get it?

A long subway ride. The train clattering across the river. Sitting on a hard chair and listening. The train going underground again, running express. Rectangles of light. Insects battering themselves on the kerosene lamp.

He puts the needle down on Okeh 8885 "Honey Babe Let the Deal Go Down" by the Mississippi Sheiks, ending the conversation. The collectors applaud.

—Good call, Chester.

—Oh yes. I like the flip, too. "She Ain't No Good." Real swing to that one.

—Shut up and listen, Pinkus.

What has Chester done?

I'm a stranger to you and you a stranger to me

I did not want to go. I bolted the door. I lay down in bed. The train ran express. As soon as he lifts the needle I make my accusation. My voice is loud, in the small room.

—So you have Miss Alberta's copy.

—It's the only copy.

—And you paid for it.

You don't happen to know where this Sheiks was recorded? Pinkus tapping a pencil stub against a little notebook. Jackson or Atlanta? Who's Miss Alberta, asked Tom.

—You paid for it, right, Chester?

—I only ask you to be quiet. To do these records the courtesy of not talking through them.

I put my paper cup of wine down on the table.

—I think I'll leave.

Chester sets his jaw, looks furiously at the floorboards. The others are openmouthed, gawkers at the theater of human emotions. They feel no more empathy than fish. As I open the door he shouts after me.

—Don't you want to hear what's on the other side? Well, don't you?

The train clattering across the river. Underground, running express. Stations flit past, rectangles of light. Insects batter themselves on the kerosene lamp. I bolt the door. I lie down in bed. The train runs express. Passing stations, commuters shadowed against white tile. Chester's eyes glitter in the lamplight. His bared teeth. He would have bitten out her throat. I climb up the station stairs and walk along the street to the Saint James Hotel. The sheets smell of lavender. I bolt the door. I lie down. I am afraid.

▼

I WAS GOING BACKWARDS. I was driving, exhausted. The traffic ran behind my eyes, headlights and taillights, smears of white and red. I must not slip, I told myself. I must not. I reached down to the radio and music flooded the car. I could not hear the music. I could not relax. I am always on the road, I said to myself, so why am I going backwards?

I could not remember. I could not remember if we had done what I thought we had done. The heavy fob clinked against the door as she put the key in the lock. We were always in the same place, this motel made of particleboard and sadness. Rooms rented by the month. The front desk protected by a thick scuffed sheet of Plexiglas.

The door rattled when our neighbors walked by.

She was from long ago. I saw her in the yellow light of long ago. In the yellow light I watched her unpack, concentrated, burrowing down, throwing shoes and underwear on the floor. She took out her Ziploc bags of supplements. You could hear next door moving about in their room, then an EDM beat began to punch its way through the wall. Neither of us could speak. We knew we were both thinking about the same thing, about the gaping wound in the young man's side. The bloody rise and fall of what? Not his heart. Some other organ.

From the second-floor walkway, you could see the oil-stained parking lot. A line of fast-food neon over a chain link fence. Some guy was kicking the hell out of the vending machine.

motherfuckeryoufuckeryoumotherfucker

The clerk hovered nervously. Stop with that. You break it I'm gonna call the cops.

Hello my name is. I had the pleasure of cleaning your room. A handwritten *God Bless* and a smiley. Leonie's head, moving back and forth at my hips, the hollow of her cheek, the eye drugged or lazy, fixed on me, daring me to challenge her, daring me not to come.

—Not my machine, I tell you not my problem! Call number on side and talk to them.

—Seth.

motherfuckeryoufuckeryoumotherfucker

—Seth. Calm down. Stop doing that. Get a grip on yourself.

I told her I'd go out for food. Let her go, I thought. She'll never find another man like you.

—Get a bottle too?

—What kind?

—Anything. Tequila? Get tequila and a big bottle of Sprite. The ice machine works, right?

I was too tired to drive to the liquor store. I couldn't trust myself at the wheel of a car. So I was walking, and I had always been walking, I have always been walking, I am walking and my mind is clear, my consciousness sharp, in the present moment, in the bubble, and I even dare to think of the future. A starless night, nobody on the street. I have wandered off the strip into a landscape of dead theaters, one on every block. Roxys and Ritzes with their blank marquees. Do not trespass signs. *For sale serious only save the BS.* The other stores all boarded up. I can't see anywhere that might sell liquor. I can't see anywhere open at all. There is a diner on a corner, blazing with light, a beacon of plate glass and chrome in the darkness.

I take a booth and order a steak, looking out at the desolate street, the red sign of the Saint James Hotel visible over the roofline.

My steak, when it comes, is thick and bloody. I cut into it with relish. I realize I have been very hungry. The sign over the counter. *Whites Only.*

At one point I had been carrying records. I look down to check. No records. Instead, by the side of the bench is a battered black guitar case. How long have I been carrying a guitar?

I am sitting in the booth. I am walking along the highway, as trucks roar by. Let her go, I think. You have to let her go. I am paying my check, scattering coins over the table. I am in the darkness, the highway in the distance, picking my way through parking lots, over the barrier from one to the next. I am leaving the restaurant, stepping over the dividers, carrying a bag from a liquor store. Behind me, taking the same path, is a man walking a large dog, a pit bull or a mastiff. I look over my shoulder every so often. The man and his dog keep their distance, neither gaining nor slowing. I walk more quickly. The man with the dog is behind me, making his way between the parked cars.

The motel sign up ahead. A red neon arrow. *Rooms.* At first I take the blue lights for decoration, some feature the manager switches on at night. Then I see there are police cars. Uniformed officers everywhere, on the walkway, milling around in reception. I walk through the parking lot and they see me and as one organism, one blue body, they turn and draw guns and there is the sound of running feet in the lot around me and someone yells drop it.

—Drop it! Now!

Three, four guns. Panic, repeating it, shouting. Slowly I put down the guitar, I put down the box of records, I put down the plastic bag with the tequila and the plastic bag with the Sprite and the paper bag of takeout on the ground. I straighten up and raise my hands.

The door to our room is open. Cops all milling round, craning their necks to take a look.

—Down! On the floor!

My hands are forced behind my back. There is a knee on my neck. I can't breathe, I say.

—Shut up.

—Leonie? Leonie!

—Shut up. You're calling out to her? You vicious little bastard. You sick fuck.

The open doorway. The shadows beyond it. All the uniforms down now. Down on me. Knees and elbows and heavy out-of-shape breathing and someone grinding his knuckles into my temple, digging on some nerve. I begin to scream. All the uniforms down on me.

▼

AFTER I LEFT HIS APARTMENT, Chester Bly vanished from my life. The next day he was missing from his desk in the newsroom. By the following week, someone else was sitting there, accumulating messy piles of paper in a way Chester would never have tolerated. One of the other messengers said he got fired. No one seemed to know what for.

Soon afterwards I quit my own job at the *Trib* and become a clerk at the 8th Street Bookstore. The owner said I was hanging around so much I might as well get paid for it. I went to readings, hovered on the edges of conversations about art and politics. I told myself I was done with record collecting, and whatever evil hung around Chester Bly had spared me as it passed overhead. My only unsevered connection was the shelf of 78's lurking behind the batik cloth, untouched and unlistened to.

I kept meaning to cancel my magazine subscriptions, but the issues kept coming. I couldn't bring myself to throw out the pile of unread *Down Beats* and *Jazz Reviews* without at least looking at them, so one day, instead of throwing them into the trash chute, I found myself crouching down in the hallway outside my apartment, flipping pages, skimming headlines and reader's polls. In one I found a small ad.

WANTED:
BL. ON K&G
ANY WITH S.J.H. MASTER #'S

K&G. Key & Gate. The advertiser was searching for blues on Key & Gate, any record made in a particular session. The address at the bottom was Chester's. On that label, the letter prefixes usu ally told you where something was recorded, but I couldn't think of a town or city with the initials S.J.H. The magazine was only a couple of months old. I looked through others. The same ad had appeared in every issue of every major collecting magazine for at least five years. Long before I drove Chester to Mississippi, he'd known that Charlie Shaw did a session for Key & Gate. Even now, it sounded as if he wasn't sure that any more material was out there. He quoted no titles, no catalog numbers, just the master number of the session. Chester had no proof anything had been released, or even recorded, except the two sides he had. But he was hungry. If something was out there, he was determined to have it in his hands.

I threw out the magazines, every one. The stink of Chester's record-lust rose up off the pages and I could not get far enough away from its taint.

Time passed and slowly my unease began to ebb. I did normal things, ate and drank and went to movies, ignoring the faint air of unreality that had settled over the world around me. One cold and rainy fall day, I was heading down MacDougal. I had my head down and my collar up, my hands jammed into my pockets as I hur-ried from the bookstore to the diner where I usually ate my lunch. When Chester stepped into my path, my mind was on the blue plate special and for a moment I didn't recognize him. He looked haggard, drained. He was wearing a filthy gray suit, the legs of the pants spattered with mud. His long wet hair was plastered down over his face.

—Damn it, he said. You stole it and by God I will have it back! His chest was quivering under his grubby shirt. He wasn't wearing shoes, and his feet were black with city grime.

—Chester. You look like hell.

—Enough with the soft soap. As if you care about me or anyone else but your own damn self!

I realized that he must have been waiting for me, standing there shoeless in the weather. I wondered why he hadn't come into the shop. He kept pulling a sordid handkerchief from his pocket and dabbing foppishly at his face. I raised my hands. I wanted to placate him. He looked agitated, capable of violence.

—I don't understand. Chester. Has something happened to you?

—Don't play the innocent. You had the gall, the goddamn effrontery to chastise me for my—well, my act of preservation, because that's what it was. And now, I don't even know what to say. How the hell did you do it? That's certainly one question.

—I still don't know what you're talking about.

—I invested in some heavy-duty door furniture, top of the line. Never trusted that super further than I could throw the wop bastard.

—Chester, are you OK?

—Chains. A dead bolt. You are a goddamn snake, you know that? A polecat. I don't have a clue how you got into my room but it's gone. And you do know what I'm talking about, mister high and mighty. Your hypocrisy stinks to heaven. So what if the old woman didn't give it to me? She was too dumb to know what she had, surely see that. Unless I took matters into my own hands, Charlie Shaw's legacy would have been dust in the wind. That makes me the rightful keeper of that record. I am acting on behalf of posterity.

—I don't have it, Chester. I didn't take any record.

—It's mine. I want you to give it back. They're like children to me, every one.

—I said I don't have it.

—You're a liar. A goddamn dirty liar.

His handkerchief bunched in one hand, he began rooting around in a pocket with the other. I thought he might pull a knife.

—No need for this, Chester.

—My collection has an integrity, you little bastard. It is a single document, a unified design. What you have done is an act of vandalism. Did you pick my lock? Is that how you did it? At least have the grace to tell me.

—I didn't pick your lock.

—Well, did you break in? Just tell me, for the love of God.

—I didn't break in.

There was no knife, just another handkerchief, which he bunched up with the first. By this time, the rain was coming down hard. I was shivering. I could feel water seeping under my collar. Chester looked pathetic, disordered. I didn't have his record. All I wanted was to get away.

—I have to go.

—You goddamn thief!

As I took a pace backwards, he grabbed the sleeve of my coat and began shouting for a policeman.

—Get off me!

I pulled away and began to walk off down the street. He came after me, still shouting police stop thief. No one wanted to know, passers-by rushing to get under cover, unwilling even to look at us. I turned back, water streaming off the brim of my hat, and saw him limping far behind, unable to put his weight down on one foot. I left him standing on the curb, supporting himself against a street sign, impotently shaking his fist.

I spent weeks looking over my shoulder as I went to and from the bookstore, always expecting Chester to be lurking in a doorway, ready to wreak his revenge. But he never appeared. I saw in the New Year at a party of laughing West Village bohemians who danced to the Modern Jazz Quartet and threw confetti at people down on Bleecker Street. As I looked out of the window at the happy roiling crowd of drunks below, I believed—once again—that I was done with Chester and Charlie Shaw and the whole rotten apparatus of the past.

Then a letter arrived. It was a sort of mimeographed circular that must have gone out to all Chester's wide circle of collectors. Though it was not a personal message, it made me almost physically sick. The flyer announced that he intended to sell his record collection. I thought I'd misread, it seemed so unlikely. His entire collection. He wanted to sell as a single lot and would entertain offers in the region of ten thousand dollars. I crumpled it up and threw it away, pretending to myself that I wasn't scared. The price was ridiculous, no collector had that kind of money. But what could have brought him to sell? Anyone else, perhaps. People do fall on hard times, but Chester Bly would have plucked out a kidney or an eye before he broke up his collection, let alone got rid of the whole thing. What in the world did he have but those disks? I thought about my own records, possibly already unplayable, deliquescing behind the batik cloth like a guilty conscience.

One evening Tom Grady came bursting into the shop. I was furtively reading a science-fiction novel under the counter and dreaming of Los Angeles, a city where I would not have to trudge through slush and horizontal sleet to get home. Tom, the youngest and most socially integrated of Chester's disciples, was a bulky Irishman with a fund of surplus energy that should have been directed into digging canals or writing stream-of-consciousness novels instead of working in a photographic lab or whatever low-commitment day job it was he held. He was wrapped in a heavy woolen coat that seemed to exhale steam as he entered the shop, throwing off moisture like a large dog. Since my exit from the collecting scene I'd nodded to him a couple of times in the White Horse, but we'd never spoken beyond a few pleasantries. I'd let him know that I was no longer interested in old records, and since there was little else he cared about, we had no reason to detain each other further.

—Did you hear about Chester, he said at once. No preamble, straight up to the counter, quick enough to startle me.

—No.

—Dead. Burned to death. He had some kind of accident with a space heater.

—You're kidding.

—No I am very much not kidding.

—How did you hear?

—Pinkus called me. He went by the building. He's over there most days. He thinks Chester is going to give him his collection.

—Sell it to him?

—No, give. Pinkus says Chester had some kind of change of heart about being a collector. He just wants it—wanted it—off his hands. Pinkus doesn't think he's sold them already, though apparently Chester was very unclear. Pinkus thinks they were probably in there with him. All of them.

The records.

—Keep up man. Yes, the records. He can't be sure, though. He says he can't be a hundred percent. But I expect it's all burned to hell.

—Why can't he be sure? Either the records were in the room or they weren't.

—Chester never even lets the poor bastard in. He makes him talk through the closed door.

—Seriously?

—Chester's kind of let himself go.

—But the room was gutted by the fire? Everything's gone?

—I don't know.

I had to serve a woman, who bought Schopenhauer and the Tibetan Book of the Dead. I wrote the names down in the ledger alongside the prices and stamped a receipt. Grady paced about behind her, pretending to look at a dictionary. As soon as she left, we took up our conversation.

—I saw him a while back in the Village. He didn't look good. Have you been going to his parties?

—Jesus, no. That pretty much ended when you left. My God, that night. What happened? You slammed the door and Chester ranted on and on about your ingratitude and then kicked us out. All over a Mississippi Sheiks side.

—It wasn't the Sheiks.

—So what was it? He played a Patton that evening, didn't he? One I hadn't heard. And he finally told me the name on that finger-picking record.

—Bayless Rose. Anyway, you stopped going.

—Well, I never got another invite. Maybe Pinkus did. I don't think so. It sounded like Chester stopped having anyone over at all. The last time I saw him he turned up at that bar on Sullivan yelling about how you'd stolen a record from him.

—He told you about that?

—About what? It wasn't anything. Pinkus says he found it again a week or two later.

—He found it?

—Then he decided he'd lost it again. Told Pinkus he couldn't stop it slipping away. Odd thing is, he wouldn't say what it was. I mean, how are you supposed to talk about a stolen record with a fellow who won't even tell you its name?

I realized I was sweating. I felt as if I might be running a fever. Grady lit his pipe and shrugged.

—Crazy as hell, Chester. He always had that in him, you know? I thought so, at least. But those records. Jesus, just that Bayless Rose record on its own! To think that's all gone!

—You didn't want to buy his collection?

—Sure, I *wanted* to.

He rubbed fingers and thumb together.

—There's a lot of things I want.

There was a great unspoken urgency to him. The thing he could not talk about because it was indecent, because proper form would be to dwell further on the personal qualities of the deceased.

—Look, you don't have to approve, but it's an important collection. There are things that will be lost forever.

—If it's a fire, they're already gone. Just the heat in the room.

—But if they're not.

—Well, what's stopping you? Why don't you go and check?

—Christ, you have to make me say it. I don't want to go on my own, OK? Pinkus says they found his feet. Just his feet, nothing else, in those awful old leather slippers he wore. The rest of him was completely incinerated. That's a terrible thing to happen to anyone.

—You want me to go out to Brooklyn on a night like this?

—Come on. I'm begging. You're the nearest thing to a sane person in the whole gang. I didn't know who else to ask.

—You understand I'm not collecting anymore. I told you that. I'm not involved.

—You sold your records?

—No.

—So you still have your records.

—I don't listen to them.

—If you still have your records, you're still in.

Train going express. Both hunched in our coats on the El platform, hands crammed in pockets. The wind slicing at us like a mugger, inverting Grady's puny umbrella.

—Chester went to see Pinkus at the bank.

—Pinkus works in a bank?

—Some savings and loan in midtown. Chester turned up there, stinking all to hell, Pinkus said it smelled like he shit his pants, pardon my French. Told Pinkus he needed to come over to his room right away and take all the records. Pinkus was worried about the customers. He could have lost his job, someone in a state like that running around in the office. He just wanted him gone, but Chester wouldn't leave until he promised that he'd come and take the records, as soon as possible, that very night. Pinkus didn't think he was serious.

—Did he go?

—Of course he went. Pinkus can't stand Chester, you know that. He puts up with him because he's obsessed by the music. But he went all the way out to Williamsburg and Chester wouldn't let him in, just talked to him through the door.

—Well of course. He'd never just give them away.

—Here's the weird part. He told Pinkus he couldn't give him the records because it was too dangerous. He couldn't have it on his conscience. That's what he said. Word for word. Pinkus tried to persuade him, but nothing doing. He's been going back every day hoping Chester will change his mind.

—Did you tell Pinkus you were planning to do this?

—No. I thought—put it this way. If we find anything, he'll be on to us soon enough.

He gave me a straight look.

—Fifty-fifty, OK? Split right down the middle.

—Grady.

—Just say it.

I could have replied, I don't want anything. I could have told him

I was just there out of curiosity, or any number of other things. But I didn't. I shook on the deal.

—Fifty-fifty.

I was still in.

Chester's building looked doubly sinister in the darkness and rain, a great brick slab set on a corner, with a soot-blackened stone porch and an empty lot on either side. Five bucks to the super got us into Chester's room. I could smell the stink of smoke as we climbed the stairs. The guy unlocked the door for us but didn't want to go in. Some kind of accident while cooking, he said. Hell of a mess.

As soon as I stepped inside, my eyes began to water. The room was soot-blackened, but weirdly undisturbed except for a rough circle, about three feet in diameter, scorched into the floor. One of Chester's two chairs was intact. The metal skeleton of the other lay on its side in the scorched patch. There was no space heater, or anything else I could see that might have set him on fire like that. The mattress was gone from the bed frame, and there was nothing stored underneath it. No boxes. No records. Grady looked stricken.

—Poor bastard. What a way to go. I mean, Jesus, the feet. Imagine his two feet, just sitting there.

He flashed another five at the super, who was standing in the doorway, a handkerchief over his mouth.

—Were there any records here?

The super looked wistfully at the money and shook his head. He hadn't carried out any records. Some books, a few cups and plates. I flashed on Chester sitting in that chair. Sitting and listening, or just sitting and waiting in the silence. Was that how it was? Chester, rigid in his chair, knowing he couldn't escape, waiting for the heat to erupt in his core. Suddenly it was all I could do not to run for the door. I fought it for a few seconds, then gave in. The records weren't there. Nothing could keep me in that room a second longer.

I could hear the sound of boots, clattering on the stairs. My own boots. Chester had gotten rid of his collection, but it hadn't been enough to save him. I still had mine. I was still in. Panic completely overtook me and I fled along the street. I didn't know where I was going. It was a primitive urge, fight or flight, unmodulated by civilization or decency. Grady caught up with me as I reached the El. I was shouting, hyperventilating. Somehow he managed to calm me down. He said the best thing would be to go to a bar and get drunk. All the way back into Manhattan, he babbled on at me. A couple of drinks. Steady the nerves. How he wished Bly had answered the letter he wrote. Grady had his hopes set on the success of a certain little scheme. He thought maybe Chester would consider selling his Broonzys separately or perhaps even the Robert Johnsons. He thought, with a little notice, he could have raised enough money to take a few, at least. But it wasn't to be. We ought to look on the bright side. They weren't in the room so they weren't damaged. That meant he got rid of them before it happened. So they were still out there. All we had to do was find who had them. Someone would know. We just had to keep an ear to the ground . . .

I left him on a street corner, still talking. In my apartment I bolted the door and lay down on the bed, knowing that I would not sleep that night. The next morning I sold my records to a guy at the Washington Square fountain. I just walked them down there in a crate and sat for an hour or so with a cardboard sign saying *Blues* until a buyer turned up. He was a rich kid who wanted to start collecting. I told him a few of them might be warped but he didn't mind. He knew nothing, less than nothing. Though he handed me enough money to pay a couple months rent, he didn't really understand what he'd bought, the burden he'd taken on. I didn't try to explain.

▼

THE OPEN DOOR TO OUR MOTEL ROOM. The ambulance pulling into a parking bay as I am thrown in the back of a patrol car. The hand on the top of my head, pushing me down through the door. Me yelling, smacking my forehead against the window and the partition that separates me from the front seat. Screaming her name again and again until both rear doors fly open and fat deputies pile into the space on either side of me, leading with batons and elbows and fists. They drag me out onto the concrete. You're resisting, they shout, for the benefit of some dash or chest cam. I am not resisting. I am just screaming. I am screaming out my grief and loss in the blackness framed by the doorway. I am screaming at the crowd of jostling cops.

Through the kicks and punches, I dimly realize they are setting a scene, erecting a legal framework within which I can be killed.

—Stop going for our guns!

It will be quick, a justifiable homicide. Brave officers acting in self-defense. I flinch from the next thing, the bullet. When it comes, I am going to go through that doorway into the dark. I will push my way to the front of the crowd.

Excuse me. Excuse me.

But instead of shooting me, they just hit me some more with their nightsticks and then bounce my head off a concrete parking divider.

After that they drive me downtown.

Leonie, oh Leonie. I remember the car in motion, an intermittent orange flare against my eyelids. I remember getting to the precinct, half-supported by two uniforms into an office where they took my prints and wiped my cuts and bruises with a greasy cloth fished out of some sink. They cleaned me up that much for my mug shot, after it was taken I waited as the arresting officers were seen by a doctor, who took more pictures, documenting their not immediately obvious bruises and contusions. I was told there would be assault charges, resisting arrest. I sat there, hunched on the bench. The entire night shift stopped what it was doing to give me the hard stare.

It was a relief to be put in an interview room, a solid door shut behind me. Cuffed to a table, I waited and stared at the peeling green paint on the walls, the scuff marks at the foot of the door, suggesting that it was frequently kicked open or shut. Slowly the room began to contract, to compress itself around me. I could feel the pressure on my eardrums. Against my will, I began to tune in to what was there, just at the limit of perception. I tried not to hear it, the static sorting itself, separating out into syllables. No conversation held in that room had ever stopped happening. The interrogations just carried on.

Why did you. Where is. Don't give me that. Captain, have mercy.

She was dead. It was the only possibility. They would only behave like this towards me if she were dead.

Murder.

I'd left to get a bottle. A bottle of tequila and a bottle of Sprite. I'd left her alive, watching television.

> Don't get mad at me woman if I kicks in my sleep
> I may dream things cause your heart to weep.

I had left her alive.

Through the crowd, through the door, into the darkness. What was in the room? Leonie was in the room. All of them, staring at her, so cold, so fair.

Murder.

What was it they wanted so very much to see?

A detective came in, carrying a phone directory and a cup of coffee. Lacking a free hand, he kicked the door shut with his heel. He was a bulky man in his forties or fifties, with a broad blunt face and thinning sandy hair. He registered nothing much as he looked at me. A man eyeing his inbox. He put the coffee and the fat book down on the table, scraped a chair across the floor and flopped down on it, wearily loosening a button on his suit jacket. He smiled to show a mouthful of widely separated teeth, then the smile faltered, to be replaced by a look of consternation.

—I forgot my notebook and pen. I need my notebook and pen, right?

He waited for a response. The pause lengthened. He raised his eyebrows and nodded encouragingly.

—I guess, I said.

—Right. Because you're going to make it easy and write out what happened. College guy like you, am I right?

A telephone directory.

—But you haven't told me anything. What happened to Leonie?

—Aw, shucks. Really? Don't be like that.

—Like what?

—All what happened boss what happened. Trust me, things will go quicker if you write it out.

When did I last see a telephone directory?

—I need to know what's happened to Leonie. Is she OK? Is she in the hospital? Please, what's going on?

—So you don't know what's going on?

—I keep telling you.

—That's all you want to say to me? That you don't know what's going on?

—That's right.

—Are you fucking kidding me?

He put his coffee cup down, eased himself out of his chair and picked up the telephone directory. He swung it a couple of times in one hand, and decided to use a double-handed grip to hit me, bouncing it off the side of my head so hard that I jerked sideways, upending my chair and crashing to the floor. My arm, still cuffed to the desk, was jerked violently in its socket. My shaken brain hazily registered him crouching down behind me. Then he pulled a hood over my head.

I know the things you are supposed to say, the things you're supposed to do. You're supposed to ask for a lawyer. I didn't say or do those things. I didn't ask for a lawyer. I was hyperventilating into burlap that stank of vomit and something I'd never smelled before but recognized on an animal level: the smell of other people's fear. All I could hear in my left ear, where he'd hit me, was a blast of static. The smell. The fear smell. The pit of my stomach was knotted tight, but everything else in my body was loose, not under my control. I needed to piss and I tried hard to hold it in, but somehow I couldn't and urine began to leak out into my shorts. I pleaded with the detective to uncuff me so I could go to the bathroom, whimpering promises into the hood. I kept on and on, but there was no response. Gradually I accepted that I must be alone, and at some point he had left the room.

In one ear nothing but the roaring, in the other office sounds, somewhere nearby. Phones ringing, someone laughing. I knelt there, my forehead on the cool wet tile. When they came back, a long time later, I did not hear their footsteps.

I was crouching down by the desk in my urine-soaked pants, fishing for the chair with my uncuffed hand, when the hood was suddenly taken off. Blinking in the light, I found that the chair was lying on its side, just out of my reach. The sandy-haired detective was accompanied by another man, taller, thinner, with small features clustered at the center of a round flat face like a dirty white plate. They folded their arms and looked at me, approvingly.

—Now we're making progress.

—I don't know about that. Take a look at him. Looks like the stubborn type.

—Be careful what you wish for, son. You want to be a rebel, here's where you end up.

—You're in our house now.

—Where the fun ain't got no end.

They uncuffed me and lifted me to my feet.

—Don't you dare get piss on me, boy.

The sandy-haired detective examined his pants. The other one propped the chair back up on its legs and shoved it against mine. Sit down, he said. I sat down.

—Now stand up.

I stood up.

—Sit down.

I sat down.

—Now stand up. Sit down!

—Stand up!

—Sit down! Stand up!

—Sit down!

I half-crouched, braced in position, hesitating between sitting and standing. The thin detective swept my legs out from under me and I fell sprawling on the floor, hitting my head against the side of the desk as I went down. It was the surprise as much as the pain. It robbed me of my power to act. As I tried to collect myself, they hooded me again, shoved me down on the chair and began to shout. What filth I was. They knew what I'd done. They knew because they'd seen with their own eyes. What I'd done to that girl. I wasn't human. I did not deserve the name. I was refuse, offal.

So cold, so sweet, so fair.

Was she dead? Leonie couldn't be dead. I begged them to tell me what had happened.

—Because you don't know?

—Stand up.

I tried to stand up. I could hear one of them moving round to my side of the desk. I flinched. No one touched me.

▼

I AM SITTING AT THE DESK. THE HOOD IS OFF. My eye has swollen up. There is a roaring in my left ear. The detective opens a folder and starts placing photos on the desk like a tarot reader laying down cards. Black-and-white eight-by-tens of a woman, a female corpse. Lying on her back, the arms flung out. The skirt is lifted up over her face. Her old-fashioned underwear has been pulled down around the thighs. A second photo. The skirt down. Just her torso. Black everywhere. Black on the bedsheets, filling the great hole, the cavern of her chest. A third picture. Two feet, one bare, dirty or bloody, on the other a vintage shoe with a strap and a rounded toe. None of these are her clothes.

—What is all this, I ask.

—I got to show you her face? You need me to show you a picture of what you did to her fucking face?

This is not. They aren't her photos. This is not her. This is not Leonie.

—These are old pictures. This all happened a long time ago.

—Can't you cut the crap for a single minute?

He flips another photo onto the desk. We have always been here, sitting at the desk. We had always been here. He showed me another photo. Until then, I had not known what obscenity was. Not really.

That was what they had been looking at. All the cops clustered round the door, jabbing each other with their elbows to catch a glimpse, getting hard inside their uniform pants. All gathering round to take their turn with the real.

They told me it was time to confess, and when I would not, they cuffed my hands behind my back and walked me to the corner of the room, where they hooded me and ordered me to turn and face the wall. One of them hit me with something heavy, a sap or a nightstick. As I stumbled, they pushed me down on the floor. My mouth began to fill with blood. It felt as if I had bitten through my tongue. I coughed and spat into the filthy hood. They switched out the light and left the room.

It could not have been Leonie. Those were not pictures of her. Her face was still beautiful, to me, but the hair, the clothes, the wallpaper in the background, all of it was wrong. Rose pattern wallpaper. The motel's walls had been plain magnolia. She was dead in an old room with rose pattern wallpaper. The clothes were not the same. It was impossible. Leonie, dead in another room, years before she was born.

They left me alone for a long time. They had forgotten whatever string or tie they used to secure the hood and I was able to worm it partway off my head. I lay and looked at the world on its side. Table legs jutting from the wall. A tin mug, coffee spilling up towards the door in the ceiling. The cop had been carrying a paper cup, with a plastic lid. This was an enameled tin mug. A chipped white tin mug with a blue rim. I was lying on a floor covered in white hex tiles. At another time the room had a concrete floor, sealed with some kind of rubbery paint. All the voices whispered in the darkness, all the confessions that had ever been made there.

A tiled floor. The shoes came down from the ceiling and walked around me. Two pairs of wingtip oxfords, highly polished, prodding me with their toes. Argyle socks, wide cuffs on suit pants.

—Make them shine, boy.

The leather toecap, knocking against my mouth and nose.

—Lay off, Gene. You'll just get blood on them.

They walked around me. They turned out the light. They turned it on again. They asked questions, suggested various things that I must have thought, things I must have done. I stood up, I sat down. They sat and smoked, told me how bored they were. One of them put out his cigarette on my hand.

I screamed.

—Jack, he can't handle it no more. Look at him.

—See, we know you're a good boy. Deep down.

—But you're the type thinks he's a sport. Hanging round outside the general store.

—Drinking liquor, throwing dice.

—Just sign the paper.

—If you don't know how to read, we'll read it to you.

Propped up at the table, the light in my eyes.

—I thought you were one of the good ones. Not like them city niggers.

—They think they're so slick.

—Please.

—See that, Jack, he can't handle it no more. Wants to go back to his momma.

I told them I didn't do it, but my tongue was swollen in my mouth.

—What you say, nigger?

Please not that word. I did not hear that. I am not that.

I looked down at my hands. I have always been looking down at my hands, but as in a dream when you find yourself unable to read text or tell the time, they are vague. Though I see them, though I know they're there, I can't concentrate on them to extract the single piece of information I need.

—There's been a mistake, I say.

I pull up my shirt. The same thing. I can't tell. I look at my stomach but I can't tell what color it is. I can't tell what color I am.

I may dream things cause your heart to weep

—You sick little bastard.

Hood on. And they dragged me downstairs, down into the red

maw, into the entrails, and I tried to keep my head up off the concrete steps but I couldn't and it was slammed again and again, each concussion doubling the roar, the red raging in my ears. I had disappeared. No one knew where I was. No one knew and no one would come to get me.

A clip attached to my fingers, another up under my hood, its metal teeth biting down on my ear. The sound of a handle being cranked, then the electricity, sending my muscles into spasm. I screamed until I was just a mouth. Electricity, the past of the future, primitive and brutal. Screaming, sucking. The clips were pulled off. A high white sound. A high whine.

—Why did you do it?

Hands tugging at my pants, tugging down my filthy underwear.

—Now look at you.

Oh death spare me over.

After a while I lost consciousness.

Then I was back at the desk, cuffed to its leg. A wooden desk, pitted and scratched, my face very close to its surface. A wheedling voice in my ear saying boy let me give you a helping hand. You can talk to me. I know how it is.

I felt so grateful.

—You know what pain is now, am I right?

—Yes.

—You want to be cool? Outside of society? Be careful less you get what you wish for.

—But it wasn't me. I never wanted this. Carter was the one. The one who wanted to be cool.

—I don't even know what you're whining about, boy. Let me tell you how it was. You wanted to have one of those sweet little girls. You wanted to break yourself off a little something something.

—Please don't talk about her.

—But she wasn't interested. She told you no. But you went ahead and took some anyway. Those rich fancypants white girls. They got it all. Their parties and tennis lessons. But you deserve something in this life too, am I right?

I can't see his face.

—Don't talk about her.

—What you say?

Cranking the handle. The whirring electrical sound. No hands no arms no fingers no feet no cock no guts no teeth or eyes or ears or hair. Just a screaming voice, just panic. Juddering behind the desk. The smell of charred skin, my rigid body a vibrating membrane. No mouth, no tongue, no teeth, no belly, no anus, just a tympanum, amplifying the pain and passing it on.

Back at the desk. The polish pitted and scratched, my head yanked back.

—We'll try again. You wanted her. You wanted to fuck her so bad. But she's way out of your league, right?

—Yes.

—Yes what?

—Yes sir.

—Yes sir what?

—Yes sir she's out of my league.

—That's right. Say it one more time for the Captain.

—She's out of my league.

—Yet you wanted to fuck her all the same.

—Yes.

—Yes what, you little punk?

—Yes sir, Captain, I wanted to fuck her all the same.

—You piece of shit. They are going to turn you out on the farm, you know that? You are going to take it from everybody. Say to me, I wanted some.

—I wanted some.

—Say, I wanted to stick it in her. I wanted to do that rich white girl in her every hole.

—I wanted.

—That's right. And it's what you did.

—I wanted to stick it in her.

—And?

—And she wouldn't let me.

—Now we're getting somewhere.

—So you're in the room with this fancy piece of heiress pussy and what do you do?

—I stick it in her.

—That's right.

—I fuck her.

—That's right, boy. You fucked her. Oh, you did. You fucked her good.

FOR A LONG TIME I WAS ALONE IN THE DARK. I am alone in the dark. I have always been here, now, all those years ago, alone in the dark. But around me the darkness was shifting, is shifting, subtly altering its disposition. I can feel a Formica surface, slick against my sweating cheek. I open my eyes a sliver and see a pair of gleaming white tennis shoes shuffling over the floor. Men are gathered outside in the corridor, muttering. Someone's ringtone: a little snatch of a country rock song. The door opens and I squeeze my eyes tight, anticipating pain, but a meaty hand claps me on the back and I open my eyes to find them all around me, the detectives, in attitudes of tiredness and dejection, wiping their faces with handkerchiefs, free hands jammed in their pockets.

—That you, son?

On the table in front of me is a fax. A mug shot on a curling piece of paper. A pair of eyes is just about discernible in the black dot-matrix field of the face. It's absurd. It would be impossible to recognize any human being from an image which is no more than a shape, a smudge. My mind is forming unwanted associations. My mind was forming associations, long ago. I was thinking, you communicate with other law enforcement agencies by fax? What year is this?

Blank. Say something.

—No sir.

—Looks like you.

Freeze.

Ha ha ha ha!

Ha ha ha ha!

Ha ha ha ha!

Ha ha ha ha!

How they all fell about. Good old boys. I looked down at my hands, turned them over. My skin was white. I touched my ear, my white fingers came away wet. Clear fluid was coming from my ear.

Cop's finger jabbing at the mug shot.

—Looks like that's the guy. The perpetrator. Nasty-looking son of a bitch. They found him close to the scene with, shall we say, certain *items* of hers. Got a record, too. Real ghetto type.

—He killed Leonie.

—That's right. You're free to go. I'm sorry that we had to keep you overnight.

Blank. Say something. Still blank.

—But Leonie is dead.

—Unfortunately so. But try to see it in a positive light. At least it weren't you what done it. We won't need to detain you any further.

—Detain me?

My hands, my fingertips.

—Look at the boy. Never seen anyone so reluctant.

—Go on, get out of here!

Ha ha ha ha!

Ha ha ha ha!

Ha ha ha ha!

—Knock it off, Bob.

Clear fluid, coming from my ear. A long low roaring and a higher tone, an insect whine.

—Look, I'm sorry we had to get rough on you.

—About. About this man.

Not a man. A black shape with two eyes.

—How do you know he killed her?

—He had her things.

—What's his name?

—Honest answer, it don't matter. Put it out of your mind.

—Is it Charlie Shaw?

—Like I said, it's nothing for you to worry about. Just leave all that to us.

—Charlie Shaw. Are you telling me to my face that Charlie Shaw killed Leonie?

—Look at you, all self-righteous and spoiling for a fight. You have every reason to feel sore, I suppose. Best I can tell you, crime like this, passions run high. You got to cut the department some slack. A lot of feelings around this sort of thing. Guy in the picture, he's a knucklehead. Long list of priors. And now, thanks to you, he's off the street. So it's a win. You got to think of it the right way.

—You arrested Charlie Shaw. You have him in custody.

—Looks like you didn't do it, kid. Just sign the paperwork and we'll have you on your way.

—Where is he? What facility?

—I don't have that information, but if you call the number, the switchboard or whatever, they'll set you right. That's it, your name on the line there.

It was some kind of waiver. I didn't read it. I expect it said that I was never there and none of what happened happened and in any case no one would believe me if I told. My hand held a pen. The lead detective slipped the signed paper into a folder.

—I'm sorry for your loss. She was a good-looking girl.

I sat in my chair, unable to move. Though I didn't dare look up at him, I could feel the change in the detective's bland blunt face, the weight of his frown.

—Move along, son. It's time.

O Death spare me over.

Another detective leaned over me. I did not look up. A forearm on the table, skin the color of brick. A hand gripping the handle of a mug that said Number One Dad. I still could not move. I thought it must be a trick. Any moment, when they saw that I had let down my guard, the mood would shift and the pain would start up again. I struggled to keep my composure, always on the verge of moaning or flinching in terrorized anticipation. I stared down at my hands, their raw pink knuckles, the blue veins, terrified that I would see them begin to change, all my security slipping away.

—My advice, the man murmured into my ear. Go to church. Drop some money in the collection plate and leave your questions with it. Go live your life.

Move along. As if it were all settled. Time for me to move along, when nothing was settled at all.

I stood up unsteadily from the table and walked through the crowd of men. Each pace was an effort. I expected to be tripped, taken down. I did not believe for a second that my reprieve would last.

▼

MOVE ALONG.

Excuse me, excuse me.

It is daytime and I'm standing on the sidewalk outside some police precinct. What city? A dun-colored block. Office buildings and a parking lot with a chain link fence. Tall weeds grow up through the sidewalk. After the catastrophe. I don't seem to have anything with me, no phone, no wallet, no box of records. I'm not wearing shoes. I am not sure why I am here. Something happened, something in the past. I am in pain. My whole body feels pulpy, disarranged.

A lawyer is waiting on the sidewalk. A man dressed as a lawyer, in the costume of a lawyer. Sharp suit and tie pin and rapacious cuffs. He approaches, grinning like a long lost friend. It is as if he has been superimposed on the blasted streetscape, a man moving through another context (a meeting room, a restaurant) that would allow for such apparent ease and expansiveness.

—The media are all at the other precinct. We asked the Police Department to tell them they were holding you over there.

He's carrying two large cups of coffee. All I'm seeing, really, is the coffee.

—Sugar's already in that one.

Reaching out my arm is painful. I only have hearing in one ear. There is a whisper in the other, a flutter of static. Media, I ask.

What media? To hear when he speaks, I have to hold my head at a certain angle.

—Look, can I drive you somewhere? They're probably already on their way over. The PD only stalled them as a favor to us. Out of respect for our privacy.

He can't be much older than me. Handsome, alpha, well-adjusted. A perfectly symmetrical face in a frame of accurately cut dark hair. When I look away it is hard to retain the details of his face in my mind. All I am left with is a sense of attractiveness, plausibility, an invitation to trust without any of the accompanying qualities (reassurance, warmth) which actually inspire trust.

—Our privacy?

—The family. I represent the Wallace family. And yours, of course. Your privacy. The privacy of all those affected by these terrible events. Please, my car's just here.

I nod, mutely. It hurts to breathe. I want to get in a car and go home. I want someone to pick me up and drive me to an orderly suburban house, to sit in a kitchen and eat a sandwich and drink a glass of orange juice. We pull away from the police precinct and the solid sound of the doors locking is so comforting that I begin to cry. The lawyer pretends he has not noticed this. After a while I collect myself. We drive out of town along a straight road lined with junkyards. I ask if he knows where my things are and he says what things.

—My clothes. I left my stuff at the motel. I have no shoes.

—Sure, buddy. Thoughtless of me. Let's get you fixed up.

We pull in at a big box store and the lawyer buys me shoes and underwear, a polo shirt, toiletries, a little rip-stop nylon hold-all to put it all in. I change in the bathroom and wash my face and brush my teeth and plug my ear with toilet paper, muting the roar and the whine. Dressed in my oversized new shirt I feel like a service sector employee. *Hellomynameis.* When I'm finished changing, I watch the lawyer for a few moments from the doorway before I step back out. He is tapping keys on his phone, pacing to and fro just inside the sliding doors, bathing in the chill of the air-conditioning. Everything about him is precise. The knot of his tie, his unblemished skin. Some men thrive under discipline. They express themselves through correctness. All that pent-up energy is probably released by playing some slightly esoteric sport (fencing, pelote) on weekends.

—You look a lot better.

—I just want to go to bed.

—Rough night. I get it. How about some breakfast? I need to talk to you. It'll only take a few minutes.

A big grin. Overdoing it. I realize he is nervous. There is something he wants. We drive a tortuous route out of town, taking turns on small rural roads that run between fields of soy and corn. Finally we pull over at a diner, an old wooden shack with peeling pink paint and a barbecue pit in the yard. Inside it is crowded with solid citizens, the atmosphere a steamy fug. An obese young cashier is wedged behind the register at the door. Beyond him, in some kind of open kitchen, women are frying steaks in iron skillets. As we wait, the lawyer sends more texts, updates to whoever is controlling him. The walls are covered with framed photographs, crowded together in drifts and clusters. Black-and-white eight-by-tens of forgotten singers and actors, groups of men holding fish, giving the thumbs-up. White people together, at work and leisure down the generations.

We squeeze through to our table. The lawyer takes off his jacket, revealing a pair of suspenders embroidered with the crest of some team or society. He orders breakfast. I have to turn slightly to the side to hear him talk. He says my privacy matters. He says the family wants to help me protect myself.

—Did he do it?

—Who?

—The man they arrested. Charlie Shaw.

—Try the tamales.

Above our table are pictures of judges, an astronaut. I eat a little food. I am very hungry, but the inside of my mouth is raw and my tongue is swollen, so it hurts to swallow. The lawyer notices that I am in pain. He adopts an expression of concern.

—What kind of health insurance do you have? I'll give them a call, get them to cover some out-of-pocket expenses.

—I don't want a doctor. I want to see Charlie Shaw. How would I do that?

—Why would you want to? I mean, come on. You're being too hard on yourself. You don't need to take every burden on your shoulders. You know?

—No, I don't. I don't know. How would I find out where he's being held?

He sighed.

—About all that. I understand you must feel very emotional right now. This is an emotional time for you. For all of us, but you especially. My own personal opinion? You should take a step back. The family is grieving for a beloved daughter, as well as their son. Can you imagine what they're going through? The last thing they need right now is intrusion, and the potential media interest is, well, you understand. It's not what anyone wants. So they're worried about you. You don't have the same resources, so you're more vulnerable to—to press intrusion.

—Intrusion.

—Violations of your privacy. At this difficult time.

—Why would I worry about my privacy?

He shows me an email on his phone. "From the personal office of Donald Wallace III." Rich people grow organizations around themselves like hair or fingernails. This personal office, this tentacle of Carter's father, has authorized a monthly transfer into my account. Enough money, I quickly calculate, to cover rent and living expenses.

—Forget about him, the killer. Go away and rebuild your life. Don't get involved in any of this. In return you can look forward to a little stability. You're freelance, right?

I nod. I feel very tired.

—So you'll appreciate some regular income. I mean, I know how it is.

—Oh yeah?

—Well, not personally. I have a couple friends, entrepreneurs, you know.

I am not sure what relevance his friends have to me. I nod again.

—Great. The conditions are straightforward. When I say forget about this, that's exactly what you do. No matter what you see or hear or read in the paper, you keep quiet. You don't speak to the media. If anyone from the media tries to contact you, you do not engage in conversation. You put the phone down and call me straightaway. You don't attend the funeral. You don't try to contact any member of the family, except through me. If you have any business to transact with the family, you can do so through me. It is strongly suggested that you do not base yourself anywhere in New York State or the State of Mississippi, but I will need to have your location, phone and mailing address and so forth so I can get in touch. We just want to help you to put this behind you, which I'm sure is what you want to do anyway. Start afresh.

—Did you say don't attend Leonie's funeral?

—That's right.

—So Leonie's dead.

—Yes. Are you feeling OK?

—And they don't want me at her funeral?

—It's going to be private. Immediate family only, is what I understand.

—Tell me what happened to her.

—I'm sorry, but I don't know all the details.

—They don't want to talk to me? Who is they? Cornelius or the parents? I was with her, you know? They need to understand that. We were together.

—I'm sure I didn't mean to imply anything.

—But that's what I'm saying.

—The family takes the view that, although they bear you no ill will, it is best to maintain some distance from you at this time.

—This is all Cornelius. That motherfucker. And not contacting any member of the family would include Carter?

—From what I am given to understand, Carter is no longer capable of making decisions for himself. His father holds power of attorney. He is authorized to act on Carter's behalf. The Wallace Family wish you to respect their privacy in their time of grief, just as they are respecting yours.

—Fucking Cornelius.

—Sure, man. I hear you. But this is coming from Mr. Wallace senior. I have some documents for you to sign. Basically what I just told you, plus language that confirms that the payments are in no way an admission of fault or liability for anything that may have happened to you.

—For how long would I get these payments?

—Indefinitely, as long as you comply with the terms of the agreement.

He unzips an expensive-looking leather portfolio, and takes out some papers.

—Also, with the understanding that this invalidates any existing contract between you and Carter Wallace.

—What existing contract? You mean our music? There wasn't any contract as such.

—I see.

—That's my—that's our music. I own half. That's how we do. Fifty-fifty. Straight down the middle.

—But you have no written contract specifying those terms?

—No. We never needed a contract. He was my friend.

I begin to hear myself, like every rube in every movie. I hear myself becoming a cautionary tale.

—Carter's lawyers handled everything with the labels.

He nods.

—That would be our firm.

I realize I am being fucked. The Wallaces are fucking me. It has, says the lawyer, been interesting to hear me clarify. I have confirmed his understanding of the situation. He talks about subsequent to this and further to that, and then into my lap he drops "the younger Mister Wallace's incapacity" and the news that "his copyrights" have "been assigned to a 501c3."

—Since it looks, sadly, as if Mr. Wallace has entered a persistent vegetative state, the family has decided to create the Carter Wallace Foundation, to work on releasing his music and honoring his creative legacy by providing scholarships to deserving young student musicians from a minority background. By accepting this payment, you assign to the foundation whatever rights you hold in your joint endeavors.

—Carter's dead.

—Technically, no.

—But this foundation would own the music we made together.

—Correct.

—As a sort of monument to Carter.

—Yes.

—All rights.

—In perpetuity. I understand that Carter Wallace was primarily responsible for the creative content of your musical productions, and you acted in a technical capacity.

—You piece of shit.

—I beg your pardon?

—I made that music. I made the sounds that made that music. I made the machines that made the fucking sounds. That is my fucking music.

He is not fazed. He does not flinch or even alter his expression.

—The Foundation's mission is to ensure that Carter Wallace's unique creativity is recognized and honored. However, we foresaw that you might view yourself as a collaborator, and so I've been authorized to offer you a one-time payment of seventy-five thousand dollars, nonnegotiable, on condition that you sign today.

My ear hurts. I tilt my head to see if it feels any better.

—I'm not signing.

—It really is nonnegotiable. And the offer won't be repeated if you do not sign today.

—I said I'm not fucking signing.

I'm raising my voice, but the people at the other tables take no notice. No one even turns around. The lawyer sips his iced tea. I often suspect that I make no impression on others. Gestures that ought to have an impact seem to fade before they reach their audience, before they bridge the gap between me and the world of the living. This lawyer can take my music away, the music I made with Carter, the evidence that despite what people say, we were partners, that Carter respected me and I understood him better than anyone, and when I shout out in protest the man doesn't even feel the need to acknowledge my anger. He just lets me wind down my spring and adjusts his tie and carries on.

—You should really take this seriously. It is a one-time-only offer. Not wishing to be blunt, but you don't have any resources to fight a copyright case. And of course, if you did decide to go that way, the discretionary monthly payment would be withdrawn.

That is the price. My music is not my music. I have never even been friends with Carter. I am to make myself vanish from the Wallace family's gilded life. The lawyer speaks, his words moving in and out of audibility as I shake my head in disbelief.

—We were like brothers.

—Honestly. Look at your circumstances. This is the best deal you're going to get.

I am so tired. At least I now have a figure. A dollar amount. I have always wondered what my friendship with Carter was worth.

—Cornelius must really hate me.

—I couldn't speak to that.

—He locked me out of my studio. He took everything, equipment I built from scratch. And now he gets the music too? Unreal.

—I assure you, the Foundation is very respectful of your friend's musical legacy. We've already been in touch with several of the artists he worked with. There are some great ideas. A box set. A tribute concert. Look, I can probably get you another twenty-five K to buy yourself some new gear, set up another studio, maybe in LA.

—You don't know what you're saying.

—I'm saying you need to sign this paper and move on. It's the only sensible play.

—You don't understand. The data. Just the sample libraries. Thousands of hours of my life are in those libraries. None of that is replaceable.

—I see.

—Do you? Do you see? There are boxes I built myself from schematics.

—Call it an extra thirty, to acknowledge your time and effort. The Foundation is very keen to draw a line under this. They don't want any gray areas. I'll have to make a call to confirm, but that should be fine.

—And will Leonie get a foundation?

—Beg your pardon?

—Do they each get a foundation, or just Carter? What charities will Leonie's foundation support?

—The family may opt to expand the mission of the existing nonprofit.

—I won't take a cent of your money.

I am tired. In pain. He knows that. He knows I only have so much fight in me, so he leads me round in circles, ducking and weaving, coating everything in legal language. I raise my voice. He increases his offer. Sometimes he gets up from the table and glances nervously out of the window. I think he is looking out for news crews. Eventually my knees buckle and I find myself on the canvas, documents in front of me, a heavy pen in my hand. I scratch my name on the paper. Once he has my signature, the lawyer goes back to issuing threats.

—If you break any of these conditions, the payments will cease. Any suggestion that you have tried to contact the family and the payments will cease. Any conversation or communication with a journalist. A journalist comes to us, says he has a source, we have reason to believe that source is you, the payments will cease.

He puts the documents in his portfolio.

—I'm supposed to take you to the bus station and buy you a ticket to wherever you want to go.

—The bus station.

—The family was quite specific about that. Not the airport. You are expected to be discreet.

—Where will I go?

—That's entirely up to you, within the scope of our agreement. Entirely your call. Just phone me when you're set up.

The fluid has stopped seeping out of my ear. I take out the toilet paper plug.

I WAS POLITE WHEN I BOUGHT TICKETS. I did not engage anyone in conversation. I stayed in motels, or slept in bus terminals. When you know nothing, you have many reasons to keep silent. Language exposes you to other people. It commits you to versions of the world you may not trust. At many times of day and night I would find myself, just for a second, a fragment, a terrifying splinter of time, back in the underground room with the detectives, waiting for agony, hyperventilating inside the hood. It was hard to concentrate. The stink of my abjection seemed to follow me around.

I rode the bus. I got off in small towns. I did not call the Wallace lawyer. I could, I suppose, have gone to an airport. After a few days, no one would have been looking for me. But instead I rode the bus. Somehow an airport seemed risky, inadvisable. To be forced to check each situation, to watch this man's posture, each expression passing across that woman's face. In any transaction, I had to be on my guard. Any encounter with authority.

Plastic seats, coin-op armrest televisions.

Waiting rooms. *White* and *Colored*.

When you are powerless, something can happen to you and afterwards it has not happened. For you, it happened, but somehow they remember it differently, or don't remember it at all. You can tell them, but it slips their minds. When you are powerless, everything you do seems to be in vain. You stow your bag, show your ticket, climb the steps. All the sinners climb aboard. You shuffle down the aisle to your seat and pluck at the little concertinaed curtain that does not block out the sun. Days spent with your forehead pressed against window glass. Nights turning your shoulder, trying to get comfortable, feeling the cold air freezing your neck. Your road seems dark. Your path is not clear. You only feel alive when you pass a source of light, driving through a town, pulling in for a rest stop. Your trace on the window, on all the windows the same horizontal smear. The grease of unhappy foreheads.

I got off in small towns, my pack landing in the dust. The driver pulling out the cases, throwing the cases in the dust. The bus terminals of small towns. Hunched sleepers and vending machines. The driver's peaked cap, pushed up high on his head.

Sweating in the heat, throwing out the cases. I fish in my pocket for a quarter. The TV eats the coin, shows strobing shadows, ghost heads . . . *heiress Leonie Wallace's death at a motel in rural Mississippi, where she was found after what appears to have been an overdose of sleeping pills. Wallace was one of the heirs to a $10 billion global logistics empire. Her shares in Wallace Corp. stock were worth a reported $80 million. In a statement to media, a company spokesman said that they were not able to rule out suicide at this time. Now, friends and family are asking themselves why the beautiful and wealthy artist would feel so bereft of hope for the future.*

I pass through the world, but I leave no trace. Leonie's death is a suicide. I was never her brother's friend. Money says our friendship never happened. Money says that I was never really alive at all. The Wallace family, struck by a double tragedy. The suicide of their daughter, a senseless attack on their son. Dignified in their grief, they appear in long lens pictures taken at the crematorium. I do not see how I can win, not against them. They are too old in the game.

They believe in me, the Wallaces. They believe in me enough to pay me money. Charlie Shaw believes in me too. I know that I am only provisionally, tenuously alive, caught like a bird, a bubble, in whatever reality has been imagined for me. I wonder where it will come from, what direction. How my death will come and fill me up. I look for people following me. I make ATM transactions for variable amounts, at irregular intervals.

Sleeping on plastic seats in bus terminals. Standing in the doorways of dead theaters, consumed by shame. The police kicking the sole of your boot to wake you up.

—Where you headed, sir?

—I hold a valid ticket.

Standing by the dumpster, watching them taser a man outside a 7-Eleven. All the men on the ground outside 7-Elevens. All the spilled Big Gulp cups, all the ice sprayed across the concrete.

I make ATM transactions just before I leave town. Only then.

My inquiries are, of necessity, discreet. By asking questions, I put myself in breach of the family's terms and without their money I will starve. But I don't really have a choice. Move on, they said. Move along. As if everything had been settled. Nothing has been settled. Nothing is over. I take what precautions I can. I call from public pay phones. I scout locations before I use them. Exits, lines of flight. If I sense any anomalies, any wavering in the fabric of the present, I pull out.

—Yes, the inmate's name is Shaw. Charles Shaw. What agency? I'm sorry I don't have that. Well, yes that's why I'm calling you. That would be who? The Metro police? And you're. Oh, I see. Well, can you put me through. Yes. Hello is this. I am seeking information on. What do you mean you can't see him in your system? If I could what? Surely you have that information. I'm an ordinary private citizen. Why would I need to tell you something you already know. Surely you hold that hello hello hello

Secrets are shared at the back of long-distance buses. Whispers and confessions. A young couple furtively masturbate each other under a blanket. A fat woman clutches a prayer card. The back of the bus is a place of lottery tickets and ritual candles, fast luck and money drawing, because all the riders know it would take a miracle for good fortune to settle on these shiny fabric seats. Twenty weeks of lottery numbers for twenty dollars. If that's the best you can do, maybe you even borrow the twenty dollars. You buy the rabbit's foot, the reputed swallow's heart. You sprinkle a little powder, add a root to your bag. You ride and you try to be careful, but however still or silent you make yourself, there is always the risk that someone will turn their eye on you. People are bored on buses. They will break down any wall. *I lost my apartment lost my car lost my dogs I'm in the navy visiting my kids my moms down in Florida see that on my arm I got that in my tag name is but my government name*

Sometimes I crack under the pressure of all that language. I find myself moving my lips and before I know it I am trying to explain. The pain in my heart. The things they did. To me, to Carter, to Leonie. The shame. Every time you get suckered into thinking she wants to listen, but it slips off her, just rolls away and gets lost somewhere under the seats. You try to tell her but she loses her appetite for talk. Every time. This is how you learn: none of what happened to you happened.

Gradually I learn to keep a check on myself. On my mouth, on the sounds of my body. The slight fluttering wheeze in my breathing that never will go away, the creak of my joints as I shift position in my seat at night. Such things are tells, to a sensitive listener, someone who may wish you harm. You try not to express, but there is always something. You give yourself away and one morning the jinx is there again, all round your bed, rubbing against your ankles like a cat.

I hire someone to make inquiries on my behalf. A week later I call from a phone by the entrance of a Tulsa park and he lets me know that I shouldn't get my hopes up. All he has is word-of-mouth. There are no documents or photos, nothing that would really hold up. But he believes his information was reliable. A suspect was taken into custody under the name of Charles Shaw. Yes, his contact is sure of the name, definitely Shaw, but there are complications. The suspect was taken to a special unit, a place which did not participate in the usual police booking formalities. I tell him I don't understand. Participate? I thought it was the law. He tells me the place is an exception, a black site. It is exempt from scrutiny. There is no publicly available information about the special unit. There is no website for the special unit, no phone number. There is no public access. Yes, he is working on it. He is trying to find out more.

Got to keep moving. Never look in the restroom mirror. Small towns. Rusted water towers with green vines climbing the legs. Water towers overgrown with vines. Sleeping in the terminals, under the porch of a church. Sleeping in the bushes by a lake. When you are powerless, your belief or disbelief is irrelevant. No one gives a damn about what you believe. But if some reality believes in you, then you must live it. You can't say no thank you. You can't say I don't want this. If horror believes in you, there's nothing to be done.

Black sites. I know all about black sites. A pay phone on the dock at a marina in Pensacola. Evening. Standing in a narrow cone of light. I have bad news, he says. Or good news, depending. Your man was definitely being held at the special unit. No, no paperwork. Nothing like that. Everything happened very fast. Thing is he's dead. Yes, that's right. The day of his arrival he was found unresponsive in an interview room. They only had him for a few hours. Yes, they did. Natural causes. No, I only have what I was told. Where is he now? You mean you want me to find out what happened to the body?

Motels and bus stations. Small towns. Rooms rented by the week, by the month. I live like a spy in a wartime city, a state of constant managed terror. Where is Charlie Shaw? I close the blinds, so eyes on the walkway can't see the order in which I pack my bag. Try to stop your body sending or receiving. Try to stop all signal traffic. And now remember that you have to eat and maintain yourself in certain other basic ways. It is not straightforward. It puts you under pressure. I climb the steps, take my seat, press my forehead against the smeared window glass. I listen to the top forty through headphones, the same songs over and over again. Bobbysoxer records. "Sentimental Journey." "Don't Fence Me In." There are always audible ghosts, remnants of compression. If you make a file of all the parts that are lost, you can hear them quite distinctly. I was making eight-hour round-trips to use an ATM.

The crowd at the door. Slipping down into the dark, running down the dry hill, pushing through the jostling crowd at the door, stepping over the threshold, the crowd of uniforms competing, climbing over each other just to take a look.

Excuse me, excuse me.

A pay phone on the outside wall of a convenience store in Midland, Texas. A high wind blowing dusty topsoil into my face. No record of an inquest, says the man. But he's dead and buried. I can give you a plot number, a location. Yes, absolutely. I have that. You can go and see for yourself.

Until I see you. Until we come face-to-face. See you for myself. Until I see you. I cannot let it lie. If I don't find out what he wants I will have to step through the door, into the dark. I will have to see her lying there, stretched out, so cold and fair. Late one night, I walk out into a potter's field with a spade and a flashlight and a grid reference. I find what I think is the place and begin to dig, but I can't be sure I have it right. I am full of doubt. The ground is hard and stony. It does not look as if it has been recently disturbed. The spade feels like rubber as I try to push it in. I dig and sooner than I expected I am exhausted and my palms feel raw, already blistered at the base of the fingers where the handle of the spade has been rubbing. I lie down on the pile of earth and rest and the sky begins to lighten to a proto-gray and in that gray light I come to the realization that I will never be able to dig my way to Charlie Shaw. What do I expect to find? A body? A living man down there in the coffin? A man singing and playing a guitar, with whom I can negotiate, a man I can beg for mercy? Is that what I am digging for? To beg back my life?

STANDING AT A PAY PHONE outside a yard lined with identical storage units, somewhere outside Baton Rouge. A chemical tang in the air. Naphtha vapor, refinery smog. My clothes are covered in mud. Trash whips around my feet as the trucks go by.

I punch numbers. Nothing has changed. I am out of ideas. It is impossible to catch up with Charlie Shaw and now I am falling fast. It is impossible to live without leaving a trace. Hit the resonant frequencies of those long-distance waiting rooms and you understand soon enough. The thick dark muttering. The residue. Every complaint and every argument, every day of every year, happening simultaneously. A roaring in the consciousness.

There is no reply from my man. I put down the phone and feel a sort of flickering, an unsteadiness about my surroundings. I look down. At my feet, beside a crushed plastic cup and a burrito wrapper, is a sheet of yellowing paper, an old flyer.

KEY & GATE ARTISTS PLAY AND SING FOR YOU.
ASK TO HEAR THEM!

The greatest stars perform for you only on Key & Gate.

"A smile on the face and a song in the heart!"

<u>25000 Series latest releases</u>

25800—*Down On The Old Camp Ground* and *Father, Prepare Me*,
The New Cotton Blossom Minstrels

25801—*My Old Pal Rastus* and *Beans, Beans, Beans*, "Uncle"
Vernon Sylvester and his guitar

25802—*I Don't Know Where To Go* and *Goodbye Honey Goodbye*,
Esther Shaver piano Acc. Will Robinson

25803—*The Stars and Bars* and *Yessir I'm Going South*, The
Savannah Club Orchestra

25804—*Mysterious Coon* and *Run Rabbit Run*, Emmett Charles

25805—*Dry Bones* and *My Old Dog Bow Wow*, The Westmoreland
Institute for the Blind Quartette

25806—*Graveyard Blues* and *The Laughing Song*, Wolfmouth
Shaw

I look around. There is no one on the street, no place for anyone to hide. I scour the trash in the gutter, but see nothing out
of the ordinary. I can feel the hair on my arms begin to stand up.
My whole body is charged, expectant. "Graveyard Blues" and
"The Laughing Song." Now I know what is on the other side of
the record. But what is "The Laughing Song"? I can only guess. At
one time there was a fashion, a whole genre, music hall songsters
emitting staccato bursts in time to upbeat rhythms. The laughing
fad was all over before the First World War. It seems an unlikely
choice of material for Charlie Shaw, or Wolfmouth Shaw, if that
was his nickname or stage name, but then a raw country bluesman
makes no sense on a list populated with bad-sounding vaudeville
acts singing songs that went out of style before the turn of the cen-
tury. None of it makes sense. Wolfmouth. The wolf's mouth. What
kind of person would have such a name?

At the bottom of the page is the label's contact information.
Write to us to find out more! An address on 28th Street in New York
City. I look around again. There is no one on the street. No sign of
life at all. The giant semis grind past as I shoulder my bag and walk
down the road towards the bus station.

▼

I WOKE UP AS WE CROSSED THE BRIDGE into Manhattan. Midtown lay under a fog, which moved and shifted uncertainly between the buildings. The bus riders coughed and stretched, preparing to face the city which had already closed around them. I didn't recognize anything, not the rain-slicked stone buildings, not the crowd of men and women in their gray hats and coats. The bus reached the Capitol Greyhound Terminal, and I took a trolley downtown. I could remember certain places, though I was not sure when I had been to them. My memory was faulty, more broken every day.

I found a room, I kept a low profile. I knew better than to approach Key & Gate by any straight route. The phone number in the catalog did not work when I tried it. Too few digits. I understood that I would have to chance upon the path, that simply going to the address would not work. I spent my days walking far uptown. Mott Haven, Hunts Point. Empty blocks, drifts of rubble, a patchwork of gang territories. Boys in cut sleeve jackets made way for me to pass. Black Spades, Ministers, Seven Immortals. No one wanted the evil eye on them. X's were marked on structures judged unsafe to enter, burned-out tenements that looked like rows of crying women, blind-eyed window sockets smudged arson black. Here and there I could see signs of life. A washing line. A little girl trying to ride a tricycle over a sidewalk that had degenerated into a mountain range of broken slabs.

One day I took the subway downtown, watching my fellow riders slump in their seats, the tangled magic marker tags over their
heads ramifying like a shared map of thought. There was so much
I could not call to mind. Was I being followed? I expected so. Someone, some agent, had put the flyer into my hands. Someone wanted
me there. I tried to sense my pursuer. Who had come after me as I
changed cars? Who had been behind me on the stairs? I rode downtown to the tip of the island and the sand and rubble of the landfill.
A gaunt man was selling paletas in the shadow of the twin towers. I
bought one and wandered through the abandoned waterside of the
city, dawdling in the middle lanes of the empty West Side Highway,
past the piers. Coal barges plied the river. A kingdom of rotting
wood and rats.

Day after day, I walked the blocks or rode the subway. Though
the weather was cold and windy, I came to feel as if I were burning
up, that some source of radiation, lodged in my chest, was threatening to incinerate me, just like Chester Bly. I drank gallons of water,
carried around a big plastic jug. Because I was afraid, I tried to rush
things. I went to the address on 28th Street given on the Key & Gate
flyer. When I passed a young woman taking pictures on her phone,
I knew it was hopeless. On the wrong side of a gulf of years I found
a condo building, the ground floor occupied by Kailash Perfumes,
a misspelled inkjet sign taped to the door reminding the customer
that "We Sell Only Orignal." The men knew nothing. They'd had
the lease for a while, I would have to ask the boss. They did not run
a retail business so minimum purchase would be ten units.

And so I tried to take my mind off my fear. I walked the blocks, I
guzzled water. I went to listen to the musicians playing in Washington Square. Sometimes, when I went uptown, the elevated railway
was a park. At other times, I made my way beneath the thunder of
trains passing overhead. Once, there was nothing but a bridle path
through farmland. I walked until the heels of my shoes had worn
down. Then one afternoon I found myself there and all at once I
had always been there, standing in the doorway of a Chinese laundry, looking at a row of buildings whose façades were caked with a
hundred years of soot. Painted signs advertised services: Booking,

handbills, printing, scenery and costumes. From open windows came the sound of people banging at pianos, three or four pianos playing different dance tunes all at once.

I pushed open a door and climbed a winding staircase with a rickety rail, squeezing past men carrying horns and violin cases, folders of sheet music. I climbed past the Solomon DeVere Agency, the Rabbit Foot Company. I climbed until I was short of breath and the light faded and I had the familiar sensation of going down as I climbed, into the bowels of the earth. There, on the frosted glass of a door, gold letters announced the offices of *Key & Gate Recording Laboratories*. I knocked and someone on the other side made a sound. It was not the sound of a voice, exactly. More like an object dropping with a thud onto a heavy carpet. I turned the handle and opened the door.

Stepping through into the dark. Excuse me, excuse me.

Behind a cluttered desk sat an exophthalmic young woman with dyed black hair. Her bug eyes were ringed with shadow and she was conducting a telephone conversation in a language I could not identify. Behind her, a half-glass door was closed on what was presumably her boss's office. As I stood there, waiting for the woman to finish her conversation, shadows flitted across the glass, as if there were people inside, two or three or more. If they were conducting a meeting, it was completely silent. In fact, as I realized with a chill, the whole office was acoustically dead. We were in an old building, a box of quivery joists and planks. Outside was a busy street. It was not possible. Wearily the secretary cupped the receiver and suggested I take a seat. Her voice fell without leaving a trace. My panic rising, I tried to leave but nothing came of it, my will did not translate into action, and instead of escaping out onto the street I found myself moving some old copies of *Variety* and sinking into an armchair.

The chair was snug and dark and deep. I felt like a sleepy child, a feeling accentuated by the unusual height of its arms, which rose almost to my shoulders. So I rested my hands on my knees. In my nose was the scent of rose water, under my feet a thick Persian carpet into which my broken shoes were sinking like mud. On the walls of the dark cluttered room I saw posters and handbills, so many. All the memories of all the theaters, all the stages. A starlet looked out of a frame made of the text *Oh But How She Could Play A Ukelele!* Another was dancing *That Egyptian Glide.* As the secretary chatted, in a low murmur suggestive of a conversation with a lover, they strummed and shimmied. I sank on down until the arms of the chair were above my head and the room seemed far and I began to grow suspicious of my sudden sense of ease. Dimly I remembered that I had no reason to feel easy. On the contrary. My panic rising again, I struggled back to the surface and stood and moved a stack of papers from another chair. The secretary watched me without emotion as I sat down. It was a hard upright chair, a chair in which I thought I would not be so quick to lose myself. However, another unpleasant sensation soon arose. I began to feel that something was behind me, which was not possible, because the back of the chair was against a wall. This feeling grew until it became a definite presence. Though I looked round more than once, I could see nothing out of the ordinary on the patch of wall behind my head, or the back of the chair itself. Then perhaps my eyes or mind became accustomed to the light, because the next time I turned, looming over me was a poster in a gilt frame, the kind made to hang outside a theater. It depicted a winking black face, a wide grin flowering between white gloved hands:

Here comes Wolfmouth! Famous Figure of Fun!

A red maw, a tongue like a receding highway, white teeth framing an enormous darkness. The eye was full of malice. The eye was turned on me.

—I'm sorry, sir.

Involuntarily, I had already risen to my feet. I could barely hear the secretary's small dead voice.

—Mr. Khatchadourian is not available at this time.

I muttered an apology—something about having made a mistake, not wanting to waste anyone's time—and backed out towards the door. If, a few moments before, the poster had depicted Wolfmouth, now it seemed merely to contain him. He was hanging inside it, lolling, floating, one leg lazily swinging backwards and forwards like a pendulum. For now he was a jolly minstrel, taking his rest. At any second, he might spring into lethal action.

From behind the door of the inner office came the crackle of a gramophone. I heard two voices, comedians doing a routine.

—Sam you sure am look like you got the miseries.

—The miseries? Why there's another name for what I got.

I realized the terrible error I'd made, all the errors. The enormity of my mistakes overwhelmed me. Nothing would ever make up for them. I turned and fled down the stairs.

I could hear him behind me, Wolfmouth singing out, brimming with good humor. He followed me down onto the street, loping behind with an easy stride as I quickened my pace up Fifth Avenue and through the Garment District, trying to melt into the crowd. I dodged in and out of office lobbies, through revolving doors. How hard I tried to shake him, under the flag-flying midtown façades. He followed me along the great hollow blocks and the tight bustling blocks. He followed me over a bridge and along the cobbled streets squeezed under its great pillars, where the sidewalks were checkered with shadow.

I couldn't always see him, but he was never far, somewhere just round the corner, scuffing and shuffling his patent leather shoes, laughing his great rich hearty laugh. A mouth like a trap. A mouth you could drive a carriage through. A fearful gap. He followed me back into the city, through the saltmarshes into the warren of Little Germany, the tenements by the garment factories. He nipped nimbly through the crowd of dirty bodies migrating through the Lower East Side, heading to the bathhouses for their morning ablutions.

Excuse me, excuse me. Into the dark.

Day after day. Always on the move. My boot heels quite worn away. Wolfmouth only left me alone when I came home at night. Even then he followed me through the hallways, tap dancing up the stairs. He followed me, he follows me. Step scuff smack step, step scuff smack step. Echoing in the stairwell at the end of another long day.

—The kooks, there are more of them all the time.

—That's right, Mrs. Waxman.

Carrying my groceries past her door. The stink of her cats.

I hole up, lock the door, fix the chain. Step scuff smack step, shuffling in the hallway. Then, at last, silence. I am not sure if he goes away. Chain checked, door double-locked, I sit down at the kitchen table and write a letter. *Some time ago I asked you to send me your wants and still I have received no list from you. I have offered to sell the whole collection, which as you know is a significant one. I urgently need money. Without it I am unable to complete my plans.* When darkness falls there are voices in the hallway. Other voices. I never open my door to look. Things happen in the hallway, fearful nameless things. The knife blades work like pistons, making dead men in the hallway. In the mornings I find stains, smears on the tile, covered up in newspaper.

When there is water, I fill up containers from the tub. Buckets, bottles, bowls, placed around the apartment. The burning coal in my chest sometimes drives me up to the roof, to loiter by the tank, ready to dive in. Up on the roof there are pigeon lofts and a silt of stolen purses, half-rotten, rat-eaten. Down below boys pass a bottle, rulers of the handball court. TITO + SWISS + ANGEL + L'IL MAN + JESTER + TONY + RICO = DIRTY DOZENS. I can hear them argue. Puta this, puta that. I can hear Wolfmouth laughing down in the handball court, dancing the Broadway Shuffle in the street. That big belly laugh floating upwards in the stairwell, through the hallway, oozing in under my locked door.

I can't ever shake him. He follows me through deserted streets, hiding in doorways when I turn round. I see him in the distance, sauntering down the ghost blocks in a long coat, swishing past inscrutable wreckage. Outcroppings of masonry, anonymous piles of brick. I see him sitting on the fire escape. Sitting on the stoop. Sitting on an orange crate outside the Fiery Cross Ministries, bumping his back against the side of a parked car. Leaning on a lamppost at a windswept intersection. Rolling bones against the curb in a clean white tee shirt and shiny shoes.

I wait in the alley for the knife, the bat, the lead pipe. My breath exits in a little plume. His footfalls echo in the stairwells as I climb. My breath, like ectoplasm. Even in the cold of the night, my chest is burning. The coal in my chest. The cold. I have to keep writing letters. There are obstacles in my path. Everything I do seems to be in vain. *This is a betrayal. I understood us to have a good business relationship. I expect a reply, I urgently expect one, a postcard at the very least, a simple acknowledgment that you have received my offer and are considering it. I have exigencies. The records must be sold. This price is absurdly low anyway. I offer it to you because I consider you a genuine collector. I believe my terms are more than reasonable. I have burdens to bear. If I don't hear from you by the date above, I won't be able to wait. You are delaying. Why would you introduce these difficulties? I absolutely cannot have any more delays.*

All I want is to be able to reason with him. I just need to find out what it is I've done. It's not fair to blame me for things that took place long before I was even born. That is what I want to say to him: *I am not the one to blame.* But I don't know to whom I should address my complaints. Sometimes he is one person, sometimes many. He goes running, wilding through Central Park. A wolf pack, circling round, tongues lolling. I have rights, I want to say. I want to say, what about *my* rights?

I think my only hope is to outrun him. My only hope was to outrun him. To outrun him, but I was always slipping into the past. Is to was. The black mouth gaping, the wolf pack behind, and though I ran as hard as I could, it made no difference. I found myself slipping ever further into the dark. I opted to go North. Ultima Thule. The whitest place. I figured he would have no power there. I took the subway to the Port Authority Bus Terminal. I had always been on the subway, heading to the Port Authority Bus Terminal. At the gate I waited nervously, taking slugs of water from a gallon jug, feeling the eye on me. Wolfmouth was the beggar in the wheelchair, rattling a can. He was every one of the young men, hanging around, trying to sell things. A watch, a transistor radio. I turned away when they came near. The eye was on me.

All aboard the bus. Pleasure is the headlight, the devil is the driver. The smeared window glass. The bus pulled away. Outside it had begun to snow. By the time we reached the expressway, it was impossible to see. The city had faded into blessed forgetfulness.

—Ain't no secret to geeks.

The voice like sandpaper, a shock. JumpJim's claw of a hand on my back. He was wild and ragged now, wearing sweat pants and some kind of faded patchwork coat over a tee shirt advertising a community fish fry. He eased himself into the seat beside me.

—Thing about geeks. Any man will bite the head off of a chicken if he's hungry enough or has enough taste for booze. The key is getting him to *understand* he's a geek. You catch my drift?

I shook my head. JumpJim sighed.

—I'm sorry for you, son, really I am, but you ain't the sharpest tool in the box. So where is it you think you're headed now?

—Maine. Further on, probably.

—This bus ain't going to Maine.

—Yes it is.

He turned and poked a finger into the ribs of a middle-aged woman hunched into her seat on the opposite side of the aisle.

—Where's this bus going?

—You don't know?

—I know. The kid doesn't know.

—You want me to tell him where the bus is going?

—Give the broad a frickin medal.

—There's no call to be rude.

—Just tell him.

—Why doesn't he look on his ticket?

—Jesus, woman. North or south? Is the damn bus going north or south?

She turned her shoulder to us and pulled up the hood of her jacket, refusing further conversation. JumpJim gave the finger, doubled fisted, to her back. I told him I had to use the bathroom, and reluctantly he let me pass. At the back of the bus, I locked myself in the coffin-like toilet, bracing myself as the road vibrated underneath. I tried not to panic. When I came back out, I sat down in another row. For a few minutes he left me alone. Then he made his way back to where I was sitting.

—Sulking?

—I'd just rather be on my own.

—Oh you would, would you? Well, that's all right. We'll come soon enough to the parting of the ways. Besides, you need some time to practice your act.

He did a kind of gnashing mime, which I supposed was biting the head off a chicken.

—I don't know what you're even talking about.

He sat down beside me, nudging me over with his hip.

—What's your problem? I'm giving you the window. Look, you're going to do what Charlie wants, sooner or later. Why not just get it over with? Bite and spit.

—You think it's that easy? What does he want? I don't know what he wants. If he'd tell me, then maybe I could sort this out.

—You want to reason with him.

—Exactly.

—Man to man. On a level.

—Right.

—You are fucking soft in the head. You think he wants to negotiate with someone like you? Look at yourself. What have you got to offer?

—I don't know. I don't know what he wants. I just want him to understand that, whatever happened to him, I'm not to blame. He shouldn't be picking on me.

—Picking on you? Ha! You should get a tattoo of that one. My advice: accept it. You're the horse and he's the rider. You're going to do what he tells you, in the end. Seems bad, probably, but beggars can't be choosers and your old uncle Jim is going to give you a way of looking on the bright side. There's a great breakfast place down where you're going. Hear that? Start your day off right. Steak and eggs, tamales, they got a hot sauce'll take the roof of your mouth clean off. All these fine old pictures on the walls. Convivial scenes from days gone by.

—Breakfast.

—Catch up, boy. Don't fret, I'll give you directions.

He reclined his seat and then twisted round and tried to force it back further, onto the legs of the person in the row behind. When banging and straining didn't produce results, he petulantly folded his arms and went to sleep.

We traveled for some hours. I leaned my forehead against the window and watched the road, the signs, the place names passing by, and I saw that he had been telling the truth. We were heading south, we had always been heading south. I wondered how I had got on the wrong bus, the very last bus I wanted. Perhaps there would be a rest stop where I could get off again. Could I escape without waking him? If only I could still turn around.

As I explored the mechanics of climbing over him into the aisle, JumpJim had a coughing fit, which woke him up. He spat into a wad of tissue paper and peeled off his patchwork coat, releasing a pungent unwashed odor into the already stale air of the bus.

—Damn bug in my throat. How about you share a little of that water?

I clutched my jug to my chest. He excavated something from his nose and flicked it at the sleeping woman, his enemy on the other side of the aisle.

—OK I'm awake now. Back in the game. You're kind of a prick, you know? So, a question. Do you have any idea what the word miscegenation means?

—Sure.

—Sure, he says. You ever hear of Eddie Lang? No? I always forget it wasn't you, it was your friend. Eddie Lang was a guitarist. Born Salvatore Massaro, in Philly. Played with Paul Whiteman's band. Clue's in the name.

He paused. When I didn't show any reaction to his joke he shrugged and carried on.

—No one more sophisticated than Eddie Lang. He played with Bix on "Singin' the Blues" for pity's sakes. Smooth player, total pro, forget about it. Now, you ever hear of Blind Willie Dunn's Gin Bottle Four? Probably not. But you couldn't get a more downhome name. That's got to be some gnarly old bluesman and his pals, am I right? That's Lang with Lonnie Johnson. King of the fucking slickers. And who else is in the band? King Oliver and Hoagy Carmichael. Lonnie Johnson and King Oliver, Storyville Negro royalty, with Hoagy Carmichael from Bloomington, Indiana, and Italian Eddie Lang. So tell me, was that a black thing or a white thing? No, that was *music*.

—Why are you telling me this?

—Because you need to hear it, you little prick. You got the picture yet? It's a business. The record company needed to give it a certain spin. Salvatore Massaro had to be Blind Willie Dunn because that's the only way the product would sell. You and your buddy, mixing it up, trying to plug into the real like it's some kind of amplifier. You're the worst of them. Looking for that uncut hit. That pure. Fucking vampires! Why can't you accept there ain't no pure. There ain't no real. It's just people.

—Charlie Shaw is real.

—Now this comes out of his mouth. It's a Greek fucking tragedy up in here. Yeah, I know. Big bad Charlie Shaw, coming at you out of the heart of darkness. Sold his soul to the devil, most probably, to learn to play guitar. So here's where I get to break it to you that he's also twenty-four-carat vaudeville.

—We didn't make him up. He exists. He's stalking me. He's threatening my life.

—Sorry, does baby need to go to his safe space now?

—He's messing with me. He's going to kill me, if the thing in my chest doesn't get me first.

—What thing?

—I have a burning. A thing in my chest. Like your friend.

—My what?

—Like Chester Bly. I know what happened to him. The same thing is happening to me. I'm in danger.

—Like Chester? Sure, like Chester. Well, I don't think Charlie's going to let you fry before he's finished with you. That'd be a rookie move. But you need to know something about Charlie. He's Wolfmouth Shaw, the Wolfmouth who toured with the medicine shows. Sure, he knew a lot of black people. That's how he got it down so well. The voice, the guitar picking, the dance steps.

—What are you saying?

—You know what I'm saying.

—It's not true.

—It is so. White as me and you.

—That cannot be true.

He imitated my voice, making it into a vile constipated whine.

That cannot be true, that cannot be true. Fucking folk collectors, all the same. Let me tell you the trouble with you people. You hate the real music, the music that was actually happening, because you're so hung up on what you like to call the *authentic*. A man plays a lick he learned from a record, you throw him out because he ain't *authentic* enough for you. I arrive in your studio with a spear and a damn bone through my nose, you'd get down on your knees and pray to Jesus because there I was and I hadn't been *influenced*.

—He can't be a white man.

He paused, scratching at some eczematic patch buried in his chin stubble.

—Well, I admit I'm not a hundred percent. Never easy to tell what's going on when they're in the makeup.

He began to splutter with laughter. The laughter turned into a coughing fit, and he made another lunge for my water jug. I twisted round to keep it out of his reach. He recovered himself and looked at me sullenly.

—Fine, just my little joke. So he's black. Where does that leave you? Charlie Shaw is a professional entertainer, is all I'm saying. Not some fucking mud man, crawling out of the primal ooze. And he ought to get paid.

—For what?

—What does anyone want to get paid for? For the work they've done.

—You act like you know everything, but you're full of shit. You don't know what he wants any more than I do. You don't even know what's on the other side of the record he made.

—About that.

—Yeah, who's the bigshot collector, now? The one with all the information. You were desperate to know what was on the other side. You were begging me to tell you. Well, now I'll tell you. It's called "The Laughing Song."

I thought he'd be impressed, or at least interested, but he just made a face and started fishing around in his pockets. Finally he uncrumpled a piece of paper, a photocopy of some kind of form or index card, filled in by hand in a scratchy ink pen. Dates, song titles, timings. On a line headed "location" were the letters SJH.

—What you have here is the log for a recording session that took place at the Saint James Hotel in Jackson, Mississippi, in November of 1929. Look at the lineup. Slim Duckett and Pig Norwood. Emmett Charles. He was a minstrel too, by the way, worked with Daddy Stovepipe. And you see there, Charlie Shaw.

—His name's scratched out.

—That's right. And what does that tell you?

—I don't know.

—That he didn't make the session, dumbass. He was down to be recorded but for whatever reason, it didn't happen.

—Well, he must have been recorded another time.

—There was no other time. That's it. That's the only time Key & Gate ever recorded in Jackson. All their other sessions were in New York. I've seen those session sheets. All of them. Every last one. I have a contact, a collector friend. I've seen every name, every date. This is the only time Charlie Shaw comes up anywhere.

—So the crossing out must be a mistake. He made the session. I've heard the record, for God's sake.

—The record you told me you and your friend cooked up.

—I don't know. I don't know why we thought that. It seemed obvious at the time. I don't know. I think he must have made the record. How else could I have heard it?

—Charlie Shaw went to Jackson but he never came back. He vanished. They scratched his name out of the session log and no one ever saw or heard of him again. Charlie Shaw never recorded.

—So what was it we put out?

—There's a question. I got to warn you, when you eat at that breakfast place, go easy on the hot sauce.

I don't remember anything after that. Night had long fallen. The lights in the bus were dimmed. I was exhausted. Headlights streamed past. Everything was a jumble. Eventually I slept. I was woken by the driver calling out a stop. The seat beside me was empty. It was the parting of the ways. JumpJim had gone.

▼

NEXT STOP. JACKSON. Jackson, Mississippi, where this bus termi-
nates. Jackson, the air like syrup. The driver throwing down the
cases, sweating under his cap. A big laugh echoing through the bus
station waiting room. Shuffle step, shuffle step. I couldn't spot him,
though I tried. However many sudden turns I made.

A downtown of brown concrete and squat modern blocks, eighties money frozen in smoked glass and olive stone cladding. Chemical freight, tank after tank, moving slow and heavy along tracks
running over the roadway. I walked until I saw the Saint James
Hotel, a stern brick building looming over the boarded-up shop
fronts of Farish Street. Mounted on a scaffold on the roof, the single word HOTEL, illuminated at night. I was not ready to go there.
Around it lay an obliterated grid, ruins and grassy intersections,
weeds growing chest-high in vacant lots. One solitary store was
open, selling hats and belts. The clerk didn't think for a minute
I would buy anything. In the distance was the new city. Parking
lots, a couple of office buildings, a high-rise perimeter about a mile
away. I climbed through glassless windows, found sleeping bags,
plastic soda bottles of urine. I saw tags and throwups, many names
and signs. Propped up against a wall was a board with a carefully
painted picture of a pianist, the remnant of some community mural
or children's project, a smiling jazz man tagged by $eeWeed and

$Murda on either side of his head. I had a camera. I do not know how I came to be carrying it. While I was taking a picture, my back to the street, I heard something behind me and turned to catch a glimpse of a man walking a large black dog. I had no distinct impression of him, but at the same time I knew who he was. Dark skin, a flash of a white tee shirt. He had been following me as I walked back to the motel where Leonie died. He had followed me at other times, in other places. Papa Charlie, guardian of the crossroads, where the two worlds meet. Excuse me, excuse me, as I step across the threshold . . .

When I went outside, the street was empty.

I took pictures in the old Palace Auditorium, a treacherous shell of rotting boards and missing joists. I photographed the Alamo cinema. I went back out onto the street, and wandered past vacant lots until I saw a lone building with glass in the windows, occupying one corner of an intersection. A sign in the front window said *Closed,* next to a sticker: *Got soul?* I was framing the little building amidst the emptiness, composing my shot.

—I saw you.

I had no idea where she came from.

—I saw you! Poking your nose in.

She was in her sixties, perhaps. A head wrap in red, black and green, heavy wooden earrings, her arms fiercely folded.

—Who told you you could take photographs?

I said something about the historic blues neighborhood. She rolled her eyes and turned away.

—Is this your business, ma'am?

—What if it is?

—Is it a music store?

—It is a community bookstore. And it's closed. And it's not for you.

—I'm just interested in local history. This was called the Black Mecca, did you know that?

—Local history. Have mercy. Only two reasons people like you come down here. The blues or taking pictures of ruins. We're fascinating to you, long as we're safely dead.

—Look, I had nothing to do with whatever happened to your neighborhood. I'm not the one to blame.

—You for real? Get the hell out of here. People live here.

—I just have some questions.

—I am not obliged to be your goddamn cultural tour guide.

I walked away hurriedly.

—That's right. Go on. Hipster asshole!

I flinched. Not that she was telling the truth. I'd seen her eyes. Her empty eyes. No one lived there. She didn't live there, among the ruins. She was no more alive than I was. And so I walked away from Farish Street, out of town, until the city streets became dusty rural roads running between cotton fields. Sometimes I carried a box of records. Sometimes I carried a guitar. Finally I came to the old wooden shack with the peeling pink paint and the barbecue pit in the yard and the line of expensive cars parked out front.

The smoking skillets of the women in the kitchen, the greasy bills changing hands. I was shown to a corner table covered in a red-checkered vinyl cloth. I ordered steak and eggs. Plotting was taking place all around me. Machinations. Allocation of funds. Though the surroundings were humble, even crude, I saw gold watches, handmade shoes scuffing the bare board floor. When my food came, I spooned on the hot sauce and examined the photos on the wall. Convivial scenes, said JumpJim, and so they were. Smiling fellows in aprons holding out cuts of meat, groups in sports and military uniforms. Then I found myself examining the faces of three old men, sitting, it appeared, in that very corner, sometime in the nineteen forties or fifties. Three men in their shirtsleeves, with wide silk ties and prosperous bellies and frosty glass tankards of beer. The caption: *"Big" Jim Wallace, Judge Wilbur Wallace and Jack Wallace: still rolling along.*

I knew those faces, versions of those faces. I'd seen many of those faces on the family pool house wall. I forgot about food and got up from the table to look around. Leaning over other diners, I began to cause annoyance and consternation. I was eventually made to leave, thrown out physically by a burly cook, but not before I had seen a photograph of Judge Wilbur as the winner of a 1932 fishing competition and another, dated 1929 but otherwise uncaptioned, tucked away on the wall near the bathroom. It was taken high on a ridge. A river was visible down below. Three white men stood in postures of ease and authority, one with folded arms, a second with his hands in his pockets, the third cradling a shotgun. Behind them, scattered through the frame, were black workers, carrying spades and picks or paused in the action of wheeling barrows along a duckboard path. They were dressed in convict's stripes.

Captain Jim, Captain Jack and Judge Wilbur, up on the levee. Starting the family firm.

Sprawled in the dirt outside the shack, I could feel the earth rising up, the cold wet earth of the levee. These were Carter's people. This was the earth they came out of. I remembered something Leonie had said, about grandpa somebody or other moving the family up to DC, so the firm could bid for Federal Government contracts. Already big by then, Wallace Construction became a money machine. Then, years later, the DC children took the next step and moved to New York, to convert all that capital into culture. An invisible thread connected Carter and Leonie to Charlie Shaw. I thought of the buildings I had lived in, the expensive things I had handled and consumed. Whose work had paid for them? I peered at the faces, the black men with their picks and shovels, but they were too small, too blurred to recognize. I could not see if he was one of them.

I walked back into town. Whenever I heard the sound of engines or saw headlights in the distance, I climbed into the ditch and hid. As I reached the suburbs, the light began to fail. I walked the blocks until I saw the red HOTEL sign. As I grew closer, I kept it in view, or perhaps it kept me in view. The sign seemed to follow me as I walked the blocks. Sometimes I carried a box of records, sometimes I carried a guitar. I went to sleep under a carport, picking up my sleeping bag when the flashing blue lights came around. Later I walked to Farish Street and found a spot in an abandoned building. I lay, curled up on a broken-down cardboard box, listening to Wolfmouth prowling in the alley outside. Step shuffle switch, step shuffle switch. Wolfmouth, Papa Charlie, Charlie Shaw, crossing the threshold, walking out of the picture frame. For much of that day, he had left me alone. Now he seemed closer than ever. As the thought formed in my mind, the spray-painted walls around me were lit by a flickering light and I sat up in a state of terror to watch him slowly come cakewalking in, a lantern in one hand and a silver-tipped cane in the other. He bowed with a courtly flourish. I could not move. His teeth were like tombstones, his great mouth ready to swallow me up. He swung his cane, pointed it at me.

—Sam, you sure am look like you got the miseries.

There was another name for what I'd got. On the floor beside me was a cracked sliver of mirror. Wolfmouth put the lantern down and handed me a champagne cork, which he produced from his pocket like a magician with the card I'd just been thinking of. I started to burn it on the flame. I had always been burning it on the flame, turning it round so it seared on all sides, just as I'd done many times before. Wolfmouth held up the lantern so I could see as I smeared my face. When I was finished, he examined my work, first one cheek and then the other, careful not to dirty his white kid gloves. He laughed his great hearty laugh and stretched like an athlete limbering up for a race. Then he stuffed his hands into my mouth, pulling my jaws wide open, then wider still, until I was in excruciating pain. I tried to scream but I could not, and he stretched my jaws until they cracked, the top and bottom hanging a whole hands-width apart. He peered inside like a dentist or a plumber examining a pipe, then stretched some more. Even that wasn't enough for him. He pulled ever wider until he was able to fit, first one patent-leather pump, then a knee, then a second shoe and a second knee into my mouth, and finally it was the work of a moment to climb inside entirely and disappear down my gullet like an eel down a chute. My jaws snapped back in place. Now I was the horse and he was the rider.

Somewhere near the river. Frogs croak from a swamp at the edge of the field where we're set up. Kerosene torches spit and gutter at the four corners of the stage.

Spat spit. Spitting, guttering. I am sitting by the tent, as I always do, and as always a crowd of white children is watching as I put on the greasepaint and the cork. I make my eyes wide, my mouth wider. I show my pearly white teeth. I make them squeal and run.

The comedian comes on, to tell the story about the loyal old slave who got lost in the war.

—Lord I am Found Again! I done brought you a whole mess o'new niggers, Marse George! Some folks tell me dey is free, but I know dey b'long ter Marse George.

Putting on the burnt cork. Age of seventeen years, singing "He's In The Jailhouse Now" before the pitch doctor comes on to sell his Congo salve. The learned professor has consented to share with you a secret discovered at peril of his life! Purifies the blood and cleanses the stool!

I left after a season. I could not hear myself anymore. I could not see myself in the mirror.

▼

LET ME BE CLEAR. I PLAY TWO KINDS OF MUSIC. God's and the other kind. That is to say I play both sides. Sunday picnics and work camps. All the different kinds of camp. Logging camps, levee camps, places where they'll kill a man and step over his body to get to the barrelhead. Ruled by the knife and the whip and the gun. Turpentine in Louisiana and coal in Alabama. Cane on the Brazos River in Texas. It's all the same, the whole country one big camp. They are making dead men in camps all over this land. No one bats an eye.

Since I was a child I could always play, always find the thread of what I was feeling and follow it up and down the strings. I grew up playing rags and jigs and whatnot for Mister Billy, as he sat in a rocker on his porch and slapped his fat thigh in time. When you play music you don't always have to work. I teamed up with a pianist in Memphis and we made money then. But I worked too. I picked on Mister Billy's farm. I cut willow and drove a team. I did all those things at one time or another. There were years I stayed in one place. The Choctaw mounds by the river, the glitter of the water sliding by. Time slowed down. But I was a rounder, born to roam. I had a little girl in Greenville, another in Natchez. I found it easy to say goodbye, easier not to say goodbye at all. I rode buses and trains. On Farish Street I built a reputation as a slick young sheik, in any game you care to name, a winner. When I smiled, everyone smiled back because I was so damn pretty. Farish Street, the Black Mecca, the shining beacon of the race. My shiny shoes. I never stayed at the Saint James Hotel. I never shut one of those heavy wooden doors behind me, the doors with the brass numbers, never shut the door and lay down and went to sleep on clean white cotton sheets that smelled of lavender. There were black-owned boardinghouses around Farish Street. The musicians all stayed in those, when we came in to town.

Sometimes I played on street corners. I played outside a general store. I played outside a Chinese laundry.

> *Oh what a beautiful city*
> *Oh what a beautiful city*
> *Twelve gates to the city, hallelujah*

There was a café. There was a furniture store. A tailor. A Frosty Freeze ice cream. People in from all over, farmers in their overalls, gawping at the windows. There was a music store. Speir, the man's name was. H.C. Speir. A white man. It was a long dark narrow store. Four listening booths, two white, two colored. Racks and boxes of records behind the counter. In the front window, he'd fixed a black rubber snake to a phonograph turntable, so that when the handle was cranked, the snake jumped and juggled, rearing up like it was about to strike. Everybody loved the black snake. Kids, everyone. Speir knew how to draw people. Every day someone was out in front of his place with a guitar or a fiddle, trying to catch his eye. If he liked your music, he could get you twenty-five dollars to do a recording session. That was a generally known fact.

I played for Mr. Speir and he told me I was good and to come back in a month when he would give me an answer. In that time I rode clear to Birmingham and back, playing every night. The people loved me. They put money in my pocket and hollered for more. You're in luck, Speir said, when I turned up at his door. You won't have to go nowhere. They gone come to you. He showed me a telegram. HAVE SHAW AND PARTNER IF HE HAS ONE REPORT DIRECT TO SJH TEN AM TUE 6 AUGUST I CAN'T BE THERE COHN AND

ENGLAND WILL HANDLE. Ten dollars, he said. Not twenty-five, but enough. And all the dreams of what might happen after that. The train car with my name on the side. The silk suits.

I did have a partner at one time. Went by Guitar Jimmy. Boy had talent. I never seen him learn a song, it was like he already knew. Any kind. Polka, Irish, you name it. He just had to put the hat down and they'd drop the money right in. Guitar Jimmy or Jimmy Clean. You could walk all day in the summer heat and he looked like he just stepped out of a limousine. Together we were free. No man to tell us where or when or how. You could finish playing at two and he'd wake you at three saying I heard a train, let's get on it. And we would. We were under nobody's command. One time we were staying at a boardinghouse in Evansville, burned down in the night with our guitars inside. Burned right to the ground. We started up Sixty-one, walking. He had a harmonica, started blowing it with me singing. People stopped their cars to give us dollar bills. By the time we reached Clarksdale we had enough to buy ourselves new guitars. That's just how it was with me and Jimmy. But he liked pussy and that was his undoing. Some woman, her man found him, shot him with a forty-four right in the side. Right through his lung. I see him in the kingdom. I hope to see Jimmy there.

I know exactly to the moment when my own luck ran out. There was a woman over the river in Arkansas. When she call, you better come. She fix you so you come. That woman call me and told me to sing for her. She was powerful. She could have a man rolling on the floor, walking like a hog. I sang to her about money and good fortune and the suit of clothes a woman in Memphis promised me if only I would stay with her just one more night. Her husband's suit of clothes. The granny woman was tickled by that one, so she made me a conjure hand, but I lost it and after that I couldn't get along. I lost the hand she made for me, just left that little root bag on the sink in a bus station bathroom. I don't know why. I was riding away before I knew. After that, everything I did seemed to be in vain.

So by the time the recording session came around, I was a worried young rounder with a troublesome mind. I could not sleep and I could not eat. I knew all my power had been in that hand. I knew

I ought not to go to Jackson, but all the same I waited for the Yellow Dog to take me there, sitting outside the Moorhead depot playing my guitar. Something must have stopped my ears, because I never even heard the train coming. No way I wouldn't have heard it, unloading its cargo and taking on more. No way I wouldn't have heard that whistle blow, but it happened. I ran and watched it pull away down the track, and right then I could feel it, the jinx, slipping round my ankles like a cat. I thought I was doing OK when I got a ride most of the way on a truck, but those boys were making a delivery at a farm and I had to walk the last four or five miles into town. That way took me through a white neighborhood, where it was not safe to be on the street after sundown. Though the light was failing, I didn't feel afraid. I had cash money and a letter from the Key & Gate Recording Laboratories in New York City, inviting me to Jackson's famous Saint James Hotel to make a disk of my music. I was a young man, young enough to believe in the power of my charm. Then the policeman drew up beside me in his big Ford car.

There was a lot of dust on the roads. I was tired from walking. My clothes were dirty. Sweat on my brow. Maybe I seemed like a vagrant to him. I told him everything, about the money, the letter. Boy, he said. You look like a ghost.

If you ever go to Jackson, better walk straight. You better not stumble and you better not fall.

—Where you going, Sam?

—Farish Street, sir.

—Farish Street? That's a long way from here. You sure are in the wrong part of town.

He told me to get in the car. And I did. After that came nothing good.

A dark night in a jail cell and no sleep. They took away my guitar. I never saw that guitar again. In the morning I was shackled to a long chain with five other men and taken to the courthouse. The very day I was supposed to be recording. Judge Wilbur Wallace presiding, under the cool breeze of an electric fan. Anderson, Solomon; Boyle, James; Hardy, Charles; Hill, Isaac; Jackson, Thomas;

Mitchell, Edwin; Shaw, Charles. They called my name and found me guilty of vagrancy, fined me a hundred dollars.

—You got a hundred dollars, boy?

—No sir.

—Declared unable to pay and so remitted to J.J.W. Wallace Construction for one year in lieu.

Ten of us they sentenced that morning, everyone the same. Judge Wilbur, on behalf of the thrifty state of Mississippi, set us all to work for his brothers on the levee. Then he broke for lunch.

And just like that, I was thrown into silence and darkness. Never to have my voice recorded. Never to be remembered, never known for who I was or how I could play. Instead of going to the Saint James Hotel to take my first step into history I was driven in a wagon to a camp on the river up near Rosedale, almost within sight of Mister Billy's farm. They took me there and put me to work.

▼

CAPTAIN JACK AND CAPTAIN JIM were the riding bosses. Walking boss was a man called Ferguson, work you from can to can't. First light till you drop, rolling your wheeler and dumping the earth, all in the Mississippi summer heat. Only word Captain Jack ever spoke to me was I don't like your look. You better watch out, he said. My eye's on you. The Wallace brothers had camps all up and down the river by then, building the levee back up after the great flood. Everybody knew them. There were songs about the Wallaces. They were on their way up. Boys, Big Jim would say, when he came around. You ought to be proud. You working for the US Government now.

I once watched Jack Wallace go wild on a man. Just got down off his horse and beat him with a pick handle until he stopped twitching. We laid the body down in the levee and we rolled our wheelers and covered him up with earth.

All day from can to can't. Up at first light, knowing there's nothing until sundown but heat and mud. Knowing I ought to have been sliding down Farish Street in my sharp suit, followed by female eyes. I never knew how many of us Jack Wallace put down in the levee. They say he once shot a mercy man for telling him not to work some broke-shouldered mule. He didn't like to hear the word no.

Not all of us were convicts. Some were even getting pay, just enough money in the pocket to gamble and visit the whores who pitched their tents down below. Sally and Suzie calling who wants me, waving at the river, waving at men on boats. The stink of that camp. The fever in that camp. A kitchen tent, a mess, a commissary, a hog pen, a barrelhouse, a corral of mules and tents for the men. They chained twenty of us bad ones together when we slept. Others could come and go. You tied up and someone wants to cut you or fuck your ass, not a damn thing you can do. The knife blades working, making another dead man while I squeeze my eyes tight, hoping they don't come for me.

Captain Jack rolling down to the water trough to tell his little joke.

—Nigger dies get another, mule dies I got to *buy* another.

That was his joke. My heart was full of hate for Jack Wallace. I polished my hate-filled heart like a precious stone.

I did not deserve this.

> *Went to the Captain with my hat in my hand*
> *Went to the Captain with my hat in my hand*
> *Said Captain have mercy on a long time man*
>
> *Well he look at me and he spit on the ground*
> *He look at me and he spit on the ground*
> *Says I'll have mercy when I drive you down*

I had a mouth, they said. No one liked a coon with a mouth. I worked. I rolled. I dumped the earth. And I knew that if one afternoon I fell in the heat, Captain Jack would set to until I died or got up again. Every day that awful morning bell. You wake up and for a moment you forget where you are. Only for a moment. And always the fines for falling behind, talking back. Everything you do they add days or dollars. And you got no dollars so they add days. That's how they do. That's how they drive you down.

BECAUSE NO ONE REMEMBERS ME and no one living will ever hear my music, because I am down in the levee where it is cold and dark. How did it take me? What difference does it make? Typhoid. Heat stroke. An accident, my body broken or cut or crushed. Captain Jack, looking down on me, telling me to get back to work. Captain Jack with the whip and the gun.

I'm tired, I say. Me and some of the others. We're tired. We want to sit down and rest.

—Plenty of rest where I'll send you.

We are all down on the ground, lying or sitting. Captain Jack waves off the water boy, who is trying to give us a drink, and walks up behind the man next to me and takes out his forty-four. Don't even hesitate, just blows the side of his head off. It sprays all over me, brains and blood. The world is quiet. My lips move but there is no sound. Just a high whine in my ear. Oh, please don't do me like you do poor Shine. Don't do me.

The end is the same, however it comes. They lay me down and cover me in the cold dark earth. Lay me down in the mud with hate in my heart. I ought to have made that session, ought to have walked through the door of the Saint James Hotel. Instead I'm twenty-seven years old and rotting in the levee with hate in my heart. Starless desolation in my heart. I was never paid for the whip and the gun, never paid for the work I done. Hate in my heart that can never die because no one will ever hear my music and no one even remembers my name. But I turn out to be stronger than death. The record I never got to make is out there, at least sometimes, for those that have ears to hear. I put it there. I kept pushing it out. And now I have found a horse to ride. This boy. This weak boy. I have found a way back up into the world.

So I look through his eyes, early one morning, and we wake up on the levee and stare down at a great gray mass of moving water. I am up on the levee, thinks the boy. I am in a bus. I am waiting for a bus, my clothes inexplicably covered in mud. I walk and ride and walk again. In slow stages I make my way back to the city. Far away I can see the sign, the red illuminated sign saying HOTEL. When I get there, I walk up the front steps like Saint James himself. I do not go round to the kitchen entrance. I have a right to be there. I am keeping an important appointment with the gentlemen from the Key & Gate Recording Laboratories. The lobby is bustling. Middle-aged men walk to and fro with conference passes on lanyards. On either side of the entrance doors stand a pair of banners, the vertical kind that come with a lightweight metal stand. *The 33rd Annual Congress of the American Federation of Incarceration Service Providers.* Girls in conference tee shirts are handing out flyers.

—Just over there is the registration table where you can pick up your packet.

—I have a letter. Mr. Speir sent me.

That hard face getting out of the elevator, its expression set and bland. Cornelius Wallace, as I live and breathe. A circle of men surround him as he walks through the lobby, shaking hands, stopping once to have his picture taken with a man in a police uniform. I call out to him.

—Cornelius? Corny?

He looks in my direction, frowns, then turns away.

—Yeah, that's right. Pretend you don't see me. I know you see me. I know you, Corny Wallace. I know you can see me.

People are staring. Men with conference passes on lanyards.

—I know about your family. About how you made your money.

Security people converge on me. Do I hold a delegate's pass? No? They think it would be best if I leave. No, it is not a public event. They don't care about my letter. I am in the lobby. I am out on the street. I am walking up the front steps of the Saint James Hotel, carrying my guitar. The doorman, dark as I am, won't let me any further. He looks at me like I'm crazy for even wanting to try. I have to go through the alley, past the trash cans, into the stink. My clothes are fine. The alley does not touch me. It is an old guitar, the varnish worn away on the back, the neck repaired more than once. The doorman makes me turn down the alley and this is how I make my way into the Saint James Hotel. Through the kitchen and up the back stairs. The room the record company has hired is at the end of a corridor where guests won't walk past. Discreet. They've put a row of wooden chairs outside. Two other Negroes are already waiting, a man and a woman. He has a banjo, on her lap is a tambourine. We nod at each other. No one wants to risk a conversation. This is not our place. A word wrong here and there could be consequences. The door is half-open, and I see two white men sitting in front of an electrical box, wearing headphones. One smiles at me in a welcoming way. The other comes out and shakes my hand, calling me Mister Shaw. I look around to check no one else has heard. They are from New York City. They don't know how to behave. He hands me a printed sheet of paper.

Walxr (part of the Wallace Magnolia Group) is a leading provider of detention, correctional and community reentry services with 58 facilities, approximately 25,500 beds, and 8,000 employees around the globe. Walxr operates in the United States, Canada, Israel, the United Kingdom, Australia and Afghanistan. Our goal is to assist our clients in serving those assigned to their care through provision of high-quality cost-effective solutions, including design, construction and financing of state and federal prisons, detention centers and community reentry facilities as well as the provision of community supervision services, using advanced networked monitoring technologies.

There are two rooms together, a kind of suite. One is the control room where Mister Zachary and Mister Joel sit. Wires go under the connecting door to a microphone on a stand. You sit in the far corner of the room and face the microphone. You sit facing into the corner like a naughty schoolboy. They say it's better for the sound. It's like singing for yourself, without caring if anyone's listening. They're friendly in a way that makes me nervous, a way that could rub other people up wrong. Mister Shaw. You don't call a Negro mister. They say it gives us ideas.

I sing the first number. Right away, they tell me they liked it and I should do it again. This time they will be recording.

I sit facing in to the wall. I finish one song and take a sip of water. I try to read their expressions. What they like and what they don't. What song shall I sing next? Which kind of song?

—No more of those church numbers, Charlie. What else you got?

—I got the other kind. I know a lot of songs.

And I sing into the microphone, not too close, bet they thought they'd have to show me how. Just because I never had the chance before, doesn't mean I don't know. And the sound goes down the wire to the recording box and the vibrating needle writes it on their wax disk. The two white men in headphones, listening and nodding and smiling at me. A white envelope with a ten dollar bill. And they take the wax disk away and shut it carefully in a case and drive it off somewhere and press a record on marbled shellac and the record sells and later I have to go to Mr. Speir's to have my portrait made and I wear a good suit with wide lapels and well-shined shoes and I hold a brand-new rosewood guitar. It is the portrait I will use when I become a name, a household word, when they advertise my records in the newspaper and the rich invite me to dine and I take a steamship to France to sing for the crown heads.

Mister Zachary and Mister Joel glance at their watches.

—Looks like he ain't coming.

—On a drunk, probably. Speir said he was the type. OK, scratch him. Who else we got out there?

And just like that, I am gone. Never to be remembered. Never to be spoken of again. My voice, the way I bend a string, the way I can play a bassline with my thumb, filling in a melody with my other fingers so that it sounds like two or even three players at once. No one has my style, my particular style. And just like that it is gone, vanished into the past.

I go back to the boardinghouse. The red sign blazes over the roof line. In my stifling little room that does not smell of lavender I change clothes and make my way back along Farish Street and down a side alley by the Saint James Hotel. I go down the alley, with the dented trash cans and the rotten smell. This is the way they make me come in. I enter through the kitchen, past the chefs shouting orders and slamming trays into ovens, the waiters pinning tickets to a board. And no one notices me, because in my white shirt and black pants I look like one of them. A valued team member. A faceless face. So no one questions me in the kitchen. No one pays attention when I pick up a steak knife and step through the swing doors into the service corridor.

In the lobby a cocktail party is taking place. The lights are low. Middle-aged corrections officers network with service providers in the romantic light. There is Cornelius Wallace, shaking more hands, then taking a phone call, breaking away from the party and heading to the elevator. I get in beside him. He sees my uniform. That is all he sees. Someone like him never really sees someone like me. He gets out on a high floor and I wait for a moment, until the elevator doors start to shut, then I follow him along the corridor. I stay a few paces behind. If he knows I am there, he pays no attention. Cornelius, fiddling with a keycard, pushing it into the lock. As he opens the door, I come up behind him and shove him inside.

Something breaks. My knife seeks Corny's back, finds only air. Blade cutting through smoke. I am elsewhere, in some other time and place. My eyes take a moment to adjust. Through the haze I see a well-furnished suite, a green baize card table laid out with an ashtray and a tray of fresh glasses, as if later on there is going to be a game. A man is sitting in an armchair, next to a standing lamp. He wears old-fashioned lace-up boots under his seersucker suit.

—We're stag here, so we can afford to relax a little.

The room is full of cigar smoke. I cannot see his face. Then he moves and the light catches him and I see it is Jack Wallace. There are other people in the shadows. Big Jim Wallace, Carter's father, Don. Wilbur, the judge. All the generations here and now. Cornelius stands at the back, whispering in the ear of another man I don't know. Time is flattened here in the back room. Tight collars are loosened. A discreet button on the pants. Drinks are poured, though not for me. Jack Wallace sighs.

—Look, son. The Judge and I were thinking that there must be a way to work things out. You seem very agitated.

He gestures with his cigar at the knife in my hand. The Judge nods.

—You're right, Jack. He looks upset. What's on your mind, son?

I am dead. I am down in the levee.

—Probably not anymore. Flood control system's been upgraded several times since then.

One or two of them laugh at that. What happened to me did not happen. For me, it happened, but somehow they remember it differently or don't remember it at all. Whatever I tell them, it will always slip their minds. Your family made a fortune, I say, because money is what they understand. They talk to each other. They pour more drinks. When I speak I am not speaking. When I speak, it dies away into silence. Still, I carry on, because dimly I am aware that this is only a screen, and something else is happening behind it, something I am unable to look upon directly. Captain Jack carries on in a bantering tone.

—Seems like you're hung up on the old days, trapped in the past. A lot of things happened back then that—well, let's just say those were different times.

The Judge leans forward, the ice cubes clinking in his glass.

—It's a post-racial America now. The only thing we care about is supervision.

He wags an instructing finger.

—You don't have to work 'em anymore. You don't have to walk the line with a rifle. All you got to do is get them into the system. Don't matter how you do it. Speeding ticket. Public nuisance. Once they're in, your boot is on their neck. Fines, tickets, court fees. And if they can't pay, well. Days or dollars, one or the other. Either way, we get ours and they stay in their rightful place. Same as it ever was. So put down the knife, son. There's no purpose to it. You can't kill something that ain't got no head.

Big Jim Wallace moves his bulk through the veil of cigar smoke towards a phonograph, a substantial upright walnut chest sitting in the corner of the room. I had not noticed it before.

—Enough talking, let's play some music.

He slips a 78 out of a paper sleeve and angles it towards me to show the label.

—This is what you want to hear, right?

I shake my head.

—Sure you do. It's about balance. Fairness. You ought to hear our side of the record.

The needle hits the groove, and into the room rises crackle and hiss. Then all I hear is laughter, hollow, forced, mechanical, accompanied by a jaunty piano. It is the sound of a body undergoing discipline. It is the sound of someone who has been told to jump and is trying to work out how high. Charlie Shaw's laughter, my laughter. It is the most terrifying sound I have ever heard.

ha ha ha ha
ha ha ha ha
ha ha ha ha
ha ha ha ha
ha ha ha ha
ha ha ha ha
ha ha ha ha
ha ha ha ha
ha ha ha ha
ha ha ha ha
ha ha ha ha
ha ha ha ha
ha ha ha ha
ha ha ha ha
ha ha ha ha
ha ha ha ha

ha ha ha ha
ha ha ha ha
ha ha ha ha
ha ha ha ha
ha ha ha ha
ha ha ha ha
ha ha ha ha
ha ha ha ha
ha ha ha ha
ha ha ha ha
ha ha ha ha
ha ha ha ha
ha ha ha ha
ha ha ha ha
ha ha ha ha
ha ha ha ha
ha ha ha ha
ha ha ha ha
ha ha ha ha
ha ha ha ha
ha ha ha ha
ha ha ha ha
ha ha ha ha
ha ha ha ha
ha ha ha ha
ha ha ha ha
ha ha ha ha
ha ha ha ha
ha ha ha ha
ha ha ha ha
ha ha ha ha
ha ha ha ha
ha ha ha ha
ha ha ha ha
ha ha ha ha
ha ha ha ha
ha ha ha ha

ha ha ha ha
ha ha ha ha
ha ha ha ha
ha ha ha ha
ha ha ha ha
ha ha ha ha
ha ha ha ha
ha ha ha ha
ha ha ha ha
ha ha ha ha
ha ha ha ha
ha ha ha ha
ha ha ha ha
ha ha ha ha
ha ha ha ha
ha ha ha ha
ha ha ha ha
ha ha ha ha
ha ha ha ha
ha ha ha ha
ha ha ha ha
ha ha ha ha
ha ha ha ha
ha ha ha ha
ha ha ha ha
ha ha ha ha
ha ha ha ha
ha ha ha ha
ha ha ha ha
ha ha ha ha
ha ha ha ha
ha ha ha ha
ha ha ha ha
ha ha ha ha
ha ha ha ha
ha ha ha ha

ha ha ha ha
ha ha ha ha
ha ha ha ha
ha ha ha ha
ha ha ha ha
ha ha ha ha
ha ha ha ha
ha ha ha ha
ha ha ha ha
ha ha ha ha
ha ha ha ha
ha ha ha ha
ha ha ha ha
ha ha ha ha
ha ha ha ha
ha ha ha ha
ha ha ha ha
ha ha ha ha
ha ha ha ha
ha ha ha ha
ha ha ha ha
ha ha ha ha
ha ha ha ha
ha ha ha ha
ha ha ha ha
ha ha ha ha
ha ha ha ha
ha ha ha ha
ha ha ha ha
ha ha ha ha
ha ha ha ha
ha ha ha ha
ha ha ha ha
ha ha ha ha
ha ha ha ha

▼

HOW I FOUND MYSELF ON THE FRONT STEPS of the Saint James Hotel, covered in blood, is not something I know how to speak about. I was dazed, like a man emerging from an anesthetic. The world was new and I was slick and red in the flashing light, looking out at the horrified faces, at the guns pointed, all on me, all down on me. I wondered how I could have done the things I remembered, the chopping and the carving and the slicing and the sawing and the cutting.

Cornelius going back up to his room. Pushing him inside. Begging me, backing away. My blade working like a piston, making a dead man, dragging his corpse into the bathroom. I changed into one of his shirts, a clean shirt, crisp and white. I put the DO NOT DISTURB sign out on the door handle and went looking for the parents.

Carter was only the gate through which it walked. Carter paid the price. Throwing himself at the darkness, begging to be torn up. I was not to blame. Carter opened the gate through which it walked into me. For the first time my way was clear. I stalked the corridors and the ground was steady under my feet. No stones in my passway, nothing to trip me up, except the drunk by the elevator, angling for conversation. You have any of those little shrimp appetizers at the cocktail party? Where you in from? Want to go get a nightcap at the bar? I told him I had no time to talk.

Another floor, another empty corridor. The repeated pattern in the carpet marching away in either direction. I knocked on the heavy wooden door.

—Room service.

Candy Wallace opening it, wearing a toweling hotel robe. A little crest embroidered on the breast. Don lying on the bed, a pair of reading glasses balanced on his nose. Candy and Don, safe in their white cocoon. Don, did you order food, she asked.

I spared them nothing. My blade, working. I could not hear the screams, the pleading. All the time I was in another room, far away in the past, listening to that dreadful laughter. And then the blue lights came and I was returned to myself, drenched in blood, sitting on the front steps of the hotel, as the police circled wide around me with their guns.

Believe I buy a graveyard of my own
Believe I buy me a graveyard of my own
Put my enemies all down in the ground

Charlie watched me, sitting there. A skinny white boy, covered in blood. All ridden out. If I'd been black they probably would have shot me, just put me down right there and then. Instead they hung a coat round my shoulders as they led me to the car.

WHEN YOU LISTEN TO AN OLD RECORD, there can be no illusion that you are present at a performance. You are listening through a gray drizzle of static, a sound like rain. You can never forget how far away you are. You always hear it, the sound of distance in time. But what is the connection between the listener and the musician? Does it matter that one of you is alive and one is dead? And which is which?

Living things are those which resist entropy. They possess a boundary of some kind, a membrane or a skin; a metabolism; the ability to react to the world. And to make copies. To pass something on. That's all Charlie Shaw wanted, to reach forward, to obey the urge of life. I have made no copies. I am a punctum, an end. A point, not a line. I do not know if I have ever been alive. How would I tell? Where in the living creature does life actually lie? No single part of a cell is alive. And life itself is just an aggregate of non-living processes, chemical reactions cascading, birthing complexity. There is no clear border between life and non-life. Once you realize that, so much else unravels. Death walked into me through Carter, but even before that I'm not sure. My blameless suburban childhood and its small pains: none of it felt real to me. And then I brought death back to those I loved, to Leonie, to Carter. I thought I wanted life, but maybe that's not true. Maybe I never wanted it, was never even capable of wanting it. And now I am here. If this is not hell, it is what comes before it, its antechamber, its downward slope.

The irony, of course, is that in here skin is everything. The color line is absolute. You may not believe in race, but in prison it believes in you. I am supposed to stand with the white man and I have not done that. Here I am the lowest of the low. They have abused me in every possible way.

On your record deck, you played the sound of the middle passage, the blackest sound. You wanted the suffering you didn't have, the authority you thought it would bring. It scared you, but you thought of the swagger it would put in your walk, the admiring glances of your friends. Then came the terror when real darkness first seeped through the walls of your bedroom, the walls designed to keep you safe and dreaming. And finally your rising sense of shame when you admitted to yourself that you were relieved the walls were there. The shame of knowing that you would do nothing, that you would allow it all to carry on.

That is not me. I had darkness enough already. Carter was the one. I never wanted the authority of suffering—I suspected it would have a bitter taste. The needle vibrates, punctures my face just below my left eye. The tattooist's homemade gun is powered by a motor from an old CD player. The ink is made out of soot. Four tears, one each for Carter, Leonie and their parents. I listen to the buzz of the motor and think of what I learned by listening through the crackle and hiss, into the past: they either add dollars or days and if you don't have dollars, all you have to give is days.

ACKNOWLEDGMENTS

I would like to thank the John Simon Guggenheim Foundation, without whose support this book would not have been written. I owe a debt to many writers, scholars and collectors, but the work of Douglas A. Blackmon, Marybeth Hamilton, Michael Taft and Bryan Wagner has been particularly important. I'd also like to thank Herman Bennett, Sasha Frere-Jones, Chris King, Amanda Petrusich, Michael Zilkha and Katie Kitamura, my first and best reader. Above all, I would like to acknowledge the singers, poets and musicians whose artistry flows through the blues tradition, particularly those whose names have been lost.